Pure Luck

Arizona Heat, Book One

Hilary Dartt

Also by Hilary Dartt

Arizona Heat

Sweet Luck

Terrific Luck

Christmas Luck

Love Under the Arizona Sky

All the Stars

The Whole Sky

To the Moon

Mint Creek Ranch

My Favorite Story

My Favorite View

My Favorite Place

Seedling Homestead

A Summer of Wonder

A Dream of Home

A Promise of Forever

The Intervention Series

The Dating Intervention

The Marriage Intervention

The Motherhood Intervention

The Garden Club Series

Jasmine's Pact

Studying Sequoia

Just Holly

Pure Luck

Arizona Heat, Book One

Hilary Dartt

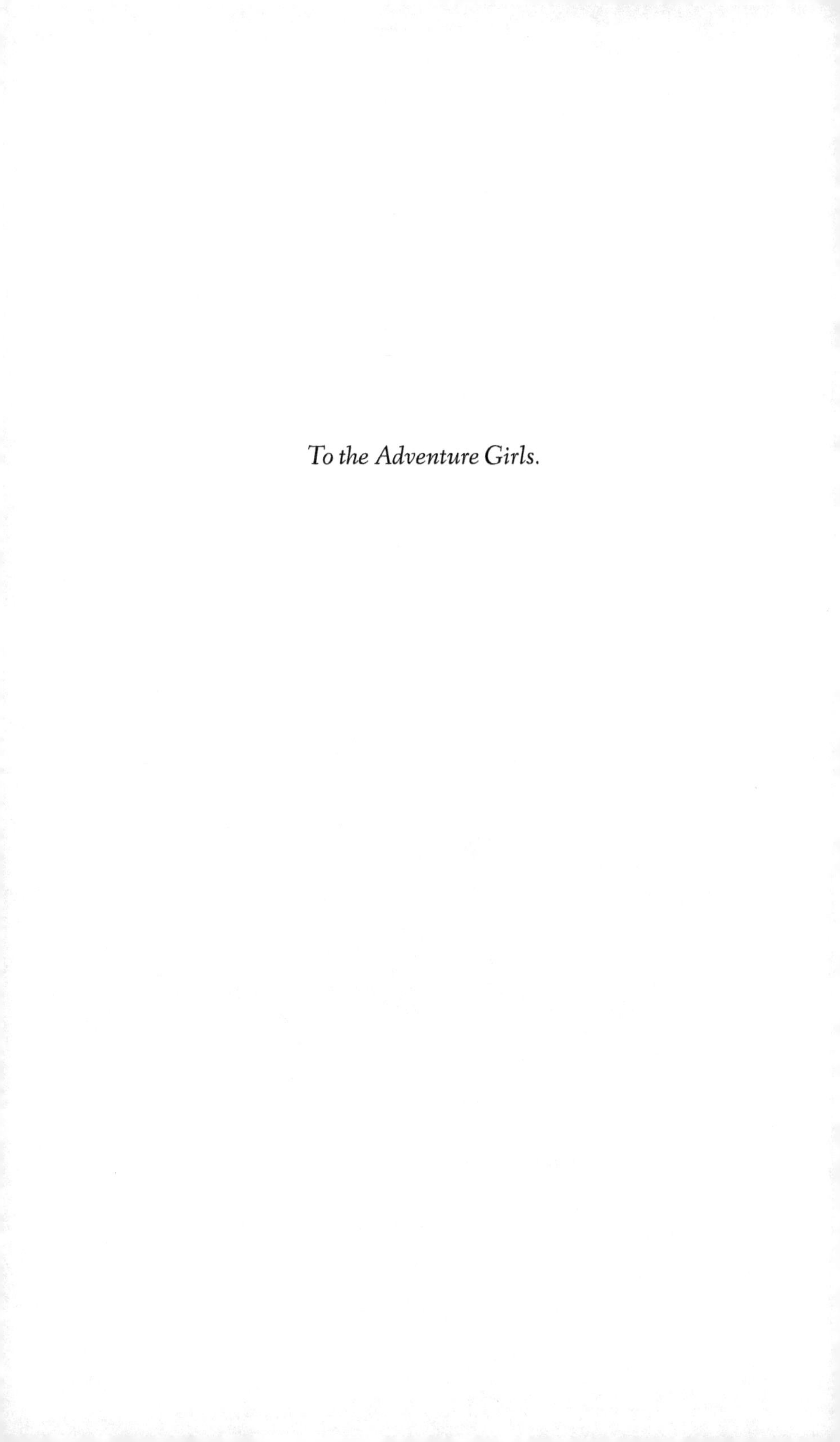

To the Adventure Girls.

Chapter One

June Cartwright wasn't running away. That's what she told herself as, heart hammering against the inside of her ribcage and hands shaking furiously, she rushed out of her office.

"Leaving for the day," she called to her assistant, Maya, doing her best to sound normal. Rational. "Cancel the rest of my appointments for the day."

Still on the move, she caught Maya's movements out of the corner of her eye. Her head snapped up and her arm raised. "Wait! Even the Soros meeting?"

"*Especially* the Soros meeting."

The nasal, scratchy voice of Timothy Alexander followed her. "June! Ms. Cartwright! Wait!"

Without thinking, she increased her speed to a full power walk.

His voice became closer, rising in intensity. "We're not done here! We still have items to discuss! The ice sculptures! The doves! The rainbow!"

"I told you." June's back was to him as she reached for the elevator button. "We *are* done. You're going to have to find somewhere else to house your ice sculptures and build you a skating rink —in July."

By the grace of some invisible force, the elevator dinged immediately and the doors slid open. June stepped in, inhaling the scent of the lubricant on the elevator ropes, appreciating it because it meant an escape from her lunatic client. Only then did she turn around to face Timothy Alexander. His arms pumped and he lifted his short legs dramatically as he rushed toward her. She pressed the button to close the doors.

As they slid closed, he raised his pointer finger, a gesture with which she'd become all too familiar. "You can't just walk out of a meeting!"

Still too far away to stick out an arm and stop her descent from the twenty-fourth floor of the Hotel Cartwright, he fumed, face beet red and mustache twitching as the doors slid shut.

June leaned against the mirrored wall and exhaled. Her parents were going to *kill* her. She'd broken Cardinal Rule Number One of the Cartwright Family Empire (a name they used in jest, but one she suspected her parents were not, in fact, jesting about): The customer is always right.

She couldn't tell them she'd fired a customer and then walked out of the meeting.

"I'll have to come up with a better story," she murmured into the empty space.

As the elevator dropped, June forced her breathing to slow. Only one elevator went all the way to the twenty-fourth floor, and she was on it. Panic set in. What if he ran down the stairs and caught it on a different floor?

No, she told herself. The display above the door showed the elevator had already reached the twentieth floor. There was no way Timothy Alexander, with his stumpy legs and spluttering anger, could catch her.

Still, when she reached the first floor she all but ran for the parking garage. Her phone rang before she even made it through the hotel's revolving doors. Compulsion driving her, she pulled it out of her purse and looked at the screen. *Maya.* Despite the guilt flooding her veins, she shoved the phone back into her purse without answering.

The skirt suit she'd worn today was tight at the knees and

prevented her from walking as fast as she wanted to, especially once she made it outside and into the blinding sunlight. Heat rose from the asphalt in visible waves, and also made her shirt cling to her skin immediately.

The sound of each high-heeled step echoed off the concrete walls of the parking garage. If anyone—namely, Timothy Alexander—was following her, they'd be able to do so by sound. After a quick internal debate, she decided to leave her shoes on. The pavement would undoubtedly burn the soles of her feet. Maybe even melt them right off.

Despite being parked in the shade, her car was sweltering. If she'd been thinking clearly, she would have used the remote start to turn on the air conditioning. But she hadn't been. She slid down into the drivers seat, the smell of leather and Pine Forest air freshener hitting her.

Pine forest. If only.

Sure, she could dream, but she was stuck smack in the middle of her concrete-jungle nightmare in Great Falls, Montana. And she was trapped. Throat tightening, she turned on the car and cranked up the AC.

Her phone rang again.

"Maya. I'm so sorry. I just couldn't—"

"June," Maya interrupted, a tense tone replacing her usual calm, no-nonsense one. "I have Timothy here."

So. He hadn't tried to chase her down to the parking garage. That fact eased some of the tension in her shoulders. But. He'd probably threatened Maya with her job, as if he had the power. June pictured Maya, her dark eyes watching Timothy, her eyebrows knit together in concern.

"Timothy," June said. "Our conversation is over."

She ended the call, then quickly texted Maya's personal phone: *I'm so sorry. I owe you. Please remember to cancel all my appointments. Just tell them I had diarrhea.*

Maya didn't respond right away, and a fresh wave of guilt made her scalp prickle as she imagined her fired client arguing with her loyal, smart, and completely deserted assistant. The guilt wasn't enough to stop her from backing out of her parking spot and leaving the garage with a squeal of her tires.

Timothy Alexander wasn't the first difficult client she'd dealt with as the Event Manager Extraordinaire (another title her parents used in jest-but-not-jest) for Cartwright Hospitality. But he was the straw that broke the camel's back. June floored it through a yellow light. Was it the ice sculptures he insisted on, despite the fact that he insisted on scheduling his wedding during the absolute hottest month of the year? The live doves he wanted to set free right before dinner was served? Or the special light machine that would beam rainbows across the courtyard?

No, it was none of those.

It was the way Timothy Alexander, like so many clients before him, insisted on having absolutely everything his way. He put the term "bridezilla" to shame.

It was the way actual bridezilla Penelope Cummerbund sat down and cried when June said the courtyard could seat only 300 guests ... and then asked if they could just expand the courtyard to fit more.

It was the way a father insisted on a pony, inside the hotel's ballroom, for his daughter's bat mitzvah, despite the rabbi being deathly allergic to horses.

June turned off the main drag and onto the congested highway, where she saw a long line of brake lights up ahead. Sighing, she merged into the lane of traffic and came to a stop. Maybe some music would make her feel better.

Of course, the first song that came on was *Your Last First Kiss*, which she'd promised herself she'd never listen to again after watching a couple dance to it at their wedding, the woman sobbing against the man's shoulder, his tux jacket stained with tears by the time they were done. She'd seen so many red flags during the planning of that wedding, and hadn't been able to say anything. Because she was a professional and the customer was always right. Never mind that the couple divorced within a year. With more force than necessary, she pushed the button to turn off the radio.

Traffic inched forward. June took her foot off the brake pedal and inched forward, too. The air from the air conditioner had started to warm up, and sweat trickled down her back.

Becoming an Event Planner Extraordinaire had been June's dream since she was a little girl planning the most lavish dinner parties and galas for her dolls and stuffed animals (tea parties were *so* archaic). Even back then, she had a mind for detail. Her parents praised her for color coordinating everything from the appetizers to the linens to the party favors. Looking back on all that praise, June wondered if they'd been secretly grooming her to join their company, although at the time, she'd taken their intentions as pure. They'd steered her toward event management as a college major, and she'd walked into the halls with wide eyes and excitement.

Coincidentally (but was it?), right after graduation, their event planner moved away, and they asked June to spend the summer at the hotel, bringing to life the events he'd already planned, and starting on new ones.

"Just temporarily," her mom said, looking at her with the biggest doe eyes.

Summer and wedding season transitioned into fall and the extended wedding season, which transitioned into the holiday-party season and of course, spring wedding season. Before she knew it, five years passed.

"And here I am," June said, her voice barely audible over the whir of the air conditioner. "Still wasting hours of my life each week stuck in traffic."

Yes, her parents encouraged her to live onsite—and the Hotel Cartwright was splendid—but she was a college graduate and craved independence. Buying her own house in a regular neighborhood was just one way she could be on her own (and get out of the concrete jungle at the end of each day).

Her speedometer read ten miles per hour. Not fast enough to cool off the car. The sound of her phone ringing yet again made her jump. This time, it was her mom, not Maya as she'd expected. Her heart sank when she realized Maya hadn't even crossed her mind in the last several minutes. Was she still trapped on the twenty-fourth floor with Timothy Alexander?

As tempted as she was to ignore the call, she couldn't. The Cartwright Family Empire's Cardinal Rule Number Two: Answer your phone. Always.

"Hi, Mom!" June infused her voice with as much cheer as she could muster while simultaneously wondering how long until her mom discovered she'd made a sudden departure from work and canceled all her appointments. "How's Paris?"

"Junebug! Paris is wonderful, darling. So romantic. How are you?"

"Great!"

Someone honked, and her mom said, "Where *are* you? Don't you have meetings all day?"

"Oh! Yes!" June laughed, a tittering she hated. "I'm just walking back up to the office. I left something in the car."

"Okay. Well, listen, honey. I know your dad and I promised this would be a work-free vacation, but—"

"You can't take a day off, can you?" June interrupted, her light tone forced and almost squeaky.

"No, you know I can't. Anyway, I've got a new client for you. We actually met in Paris, can you believe that? Two American couples at a Parisian bistro. Not just that, but two American couples from Billings. Anyway, I mentioned we own the hotel, and you know, one thing led to another, and they want to meet with you when they get back in three weeks. Honey, I looked at their Insta, and these guys are practically celebrities. Look them up on the Insta."

"You're calling it Insta now?"

"Yes, I'm just finally getting caught up on that trend. I've taken some lovely pictures here in Paris. I'm sure you can help me turn them into Insta posts when your dad and I get back. Anyway, if we could land these guys, it could change everything for us. For the whole city. We could put Great Falls on the map."

Coiled rattlesnakes took up residence in June's stomach. "That's great, Mom. Listen, I've got to run. I have another meeting. Go have fun. Enjoy Paris. And take some time off from working, would you?"

They disconnected, and June looked into the rearview mirror to assess how far she'd moved since taking her mom's call. She'd never get home at this rate.

"Even when you do get home," she said, "then what?"

Her parents may not take days off, but June did. She had the next two days to herself. In some inexplicable twist, no one had reserved the Hotel Cartwright's ballroom or courtyard for that weekend.

Recently, she'd found she couldn't even enjoy her days off, because work was always waiting for her. She sighed, yet again, and turned the radio back on. The song she hated was over, and a commercial blasted from her speakers: "Want to get away?"

"Yes, sir!" June responded.

As if on cue, the man in the commercial said, "Enter our giveaway to get away. We're giving away two plane tickets to a destination of your choice within the contiguous U.S."

An idea hit June then, right in the middle of her consciousness. "Why wait for a giveaway?"

Inexplicably, traffic sped up to a brisk twenty-five miles per hour. June gave an excited whoop in response. It was Friday morning and two empty days stretched out ahead of her, their schedules absolutely blank on her calendar. She could do whatever she wanted. Go wherever she wanted. Right now. Only, she had to get home first.

"Where will you go, June?"

The beach? The forest? The desert? No, summer wasn't the time to visit the desert. Her college roommate, Callie, had mentioned just the other day that the temperature in Phoenix was one hundred and fifteen degrees.

Callie.

She lived part-time in Phoenix and part time in the mountain town of Prescott since meeting her fiancé, Hayes, over Christmas. And didn't Callie always say, "Prescott is the high desert, June, not the desert"?

Without wasting a second, June dialed Callie and grinned when her voice came through the car speakers.

"Heyyyy, June!"

"Hey!"

"How are you, my friend?"

"To be honest, I've been better. I need a getaway, and I was thinking of coming to see you this weekend. Are you free?" Second thoughts rushed in. Callie probably wasn't free. She was engaged and likely had plans to do something fun. She had a life. Before June could say all that, Callie's laugh, carefree and musical, filled her ears.

"I'd love to have you, Junie! Like I said the other day, I escape this scorching desert whenever I get the chance. Fly into Phoenix and we'll head up to Prescott for the weekend."

"Oh, I'd love to. Thank you so much. I really need this."

"You're going to give me all the details when you get here. I've got to run now, though. I've got a hearing this afternoon. Love you, girl."

"Love you."

For the first time in ages, excitement bubbled up inside of June's torso, fizzy like champagne and warm like maple syrup. She turned up the volume on the radio and danced along to the music. She was getting away from her dreadful job and out of Great Falls ... at least for a couple of days. She squealed.

Her excitement was short-lived. A ding sounded from the dashboard, and the low-tire indicator illuminated. Dropping the arm she'd raised while dancing, June looked over her shoulder before putting on her blinker. She'd have to pull over. If the tire was low, she could make it to a gas station to fill it. But if it was flat? She couldn't risk driving along on the rim. Of course, pulling over meant navigating across three lanes of bumper-to-bumper traffic and took her about three years.

When she finally made it to the shoulder, she saw the problem right away: her passenger side front tire was completely flat, the head of a screw sticking out through the tire wall. She could cry. She did cry, tears blurring her vision as she opened the trunk and removed her briefcase so she could access the spare tire.

Even if they were city dwellers, June's parents always abided by The Cartwright Family Empire's Cardinal Rule Number Three: Be self-sufficient. Without much fanfare, June jacked up the car, removed the offending tire with its offending screw, and put on the spare.

Twenty minutes later, she was back on the road, crying not because she had a flat tire, but because she couldn't drive her car to the airport on the spare ... which meant she'd have to have her tire repaired before she could leave town.

When she finally arrived at her house, she heard an excited, "Miss June!" from the yard next door.

"Hey, Jake." She waved at her eight-year-old neighbor with more enthusiasm than she felt.

"Want to see my school project?" He bounded up to her, a contraption in his hands.

Despite the stress of the past few hours, June softened. Jake was a cute kid. Pride shone in his eyes, and his smile was wide.

"I do," she said, "but first things first. Did you lose a tooth?"

Project temporarily forgotten, Jake grinned even wider. "I did! And the tooth fairy brought me a dollar. Ricky got *five bucks* for his last tooth, so I don't know what's up with that, but anyway. Check this out."

He set the contraption on the ground, and June followed his lead when he squatted next to it.

"It's a catapult," Jake said, picking up a little rock and nestling it into a cup at the end of a lever. "I made it. It launches stuff. See?"

He pushed down on the lever and released it, and the rock went flying toward June's car. It bounced off the spare tire and landed on the driveway with a little *ping*.

"That's awesome, Jake! I'm impressed you made that."

"Yeah," he said. "Me, too. It's like the weapons knights and stuff would use. Only, tiny. Anyway, why do you have a spare on your car?".

"I got a flat." Her voice came out way whinier than she meant to as she stood up.

"Bummer," he said.

"Yeah. Especially since I was thinking of driving to the airport today. I can't drive all the way there on this spare, which means I need to get the real tire repaired."

"You know they've got a shuttle now," he said.

Of course. Why hadn't she thought of that?

"My dad took it to the airport last week when he went to that fish conference. Mom couldn't drive him because his flight was early and she didn't want it to interfere with her beauty sleep. So he just called up the shuttle and took that. Want me to ask my mom about it?"

Hope rising in her heart again, June ruffled Jake's hair. "No, thanks. I'm sure I can look it up online. I'll go do that right now. Great catapult, by the way."

"Thanks." He bounded across her yard and back to his. "See ya."

"See ya," she called, relief flooding in as she realized maybe her weekend wasn't ruined after all.

Chapter Two

Standing in the second-floor window of his latest restoration project—an early twentieth-century home—Sterling Wilder surveyed the tree-lined street below. If he ever decided to settle somewhere, it would be somewhere like this, with history, charm, and neighbors who stopped to talk on the sidewalk.

As the sun sank lower, a glowing orb lighting the sky on fire, Sterling felt a strange sense of longing—a yearning for something he'd told himself for years he didn't want.

"Boss, can I get you to look at something real quick?"

Riggs Foster, his foreman and best friend, came to stand next to him, rolled-up blueprints in hand.

"Of course. If you stop calling me boss. What's up?"

"I had an idea for this window. The blueprint shows a standard size frame here, but I think we could double that. Maybe even triple it. I mean, this view, right?"

"Right," Sterling said. "I was just thinking, if I had to choose a place to live, it'd be like this."

"You gettin' soft on me, man? Thinking about settling down?"

Giving him a gentle punch on the arm, Sterling said, "Of course not. It is a great view, though. Your idea—can you make it work with the peaked roof?"

"Yeah. I've got it drawn out here." He unrolled the blueprint to show Sterling his penciled-in changes.

"Yep, looks like you've got it dialed in. Good thinking. Let's go with it. I'll put in the window order so you can get home to Sarah and the kids."

"Thanks, man." Riggs rolled up the blueprints and tucked them under his arm.

"How's Cole doing, anyway?"

"Great. I can't believe the difference after his surgery. I don't know if I'll ever stop feeling like I owe you."

"Oh, come on, man," Sterling said, uncomfortable with the gratitude for something that had come so easy to him—he'd paid for the surgery, not actually performed it. "You don't owe me anything. I'm happy to help. You know that."

"Still. If there's ever anything I can do..."

"You're the first person I'll come to."

Riggs wrapped an arm around Sterling's shoulders and squeezed. "Damn straight."

"Now, get out of here. We don't want Sarah to come after us if you get home late."

"Damn straight. All right. See you later, *boss*."

"Shut up, bro. See you later."

Riggs was always the last guy on a site, and when he left the silence felt wide open, a blank canvas on which all of Sterling's thoughts would paint themselves. The setting sun now streamed right through the window, illuminating the place with golden light. Tiny dust specks floated in the air, reminding Sterling of fairy dust as he started his evening walk-through.

The crew had done well that day. Upstairs, they'd finished wiring in the new electric. This house was going to be epic. Sterling was a little jealous of his clients, the owners, who would move in when it was all done. They'd have three bedrooms and an office up here, and the downstairs living quarters featured an open floor plan with a giant kitchen and a spacious living room to accommodate their growing family. Sterling felt another tug at his damned heartstrings. He cursed as he walked downstairs.

He wasn't meant for family. Hadn't he proven that time and time again?

On the lower level, the crew had finished framing in the kitchen island and prepped the space for the new cabinets, which should arrive that week. Sterling's vision—for which he was renowned—sprang to life. The industrial stove, just there, across from the island, was going to be a showstopper. He could see the new owners, the Ramirezes, in here, the parents cooking while the kids sat at the island doing homework or snacking. Or, based on what he'd seen so far, roughhousing in the living room.

Just when he was kicking himself for feeling melancholy about the fact that he could create spaces for happy families but couldn't be part of a happy family, his phone rang.

"Damn."

His brother's name on the screen brought up a rush of images: he and Hayes wrestling on their living room floor as kids, fishing in the river, laughing at the practical jokes they played on their brothers—the best one was when they put frogs down Cash and Travis's pants. Also, the time they'd come to blows as adults, bloodying each other's noses before they were done.

How long had it been since they talked? Sterling swallowed the lump in his throat, told himself he'd imagined it, and answered the phone.

"Hey, man. Long time." Hayes's voice was just as he remembered it: gruff and unfriendly.

"Yeah. How's it been?"

"Well. I wish I'd called to chat, but I didn't."

What now? Their dad had died a few months before, and Sterling thought they'd handled all the details around that. And by they, he actually meant Travis, the youngest of the four Wilder brothers, their dad's favorite, and the one who took care of those types of things.

On a sigh, Sterling said, "What's up?"

"Try to hide your enthusiasm."

Shit. He was already messing up the conversation. "Sorry, man. I just walked up a flight of stairs."

"Can you come home? We need to have a meeting."

Sterling checked himself before he knee-jerked a response about how Hayes expected him to drop everything and go home.

"All right. When?"

"As soon as possible."

He bit back another snappy comment. "I'll head out tonight."

Silence. Sterling turned away from the kitchen and looked out over the living room. "Hayes?"

"Sorry, man. I just didn't expect it to be that easy. We played rock, paper, scissors and I lost, so I had to call you. Wait 'til I tell Cash and Travis."

Several responses came to mind. "Screw you, man." "You guys suck." "Shut the hell up." But he didn't say any of them. "Glad I could make it easy on you. I'll let you know when I get a flight. And don't worry about rock, paper, scissors when it's time to pick me up. I'll get a ride."

He detected a faint trace of humor in Hayes's voice when he said, "All right, man. See you soon."

Before locking up and leaving the house, Sterling grabbed his laptop and ordered the windows Riggs had recommended. He let himself imagine living there, setting his computer on the kitchen island, looking out over the street as he took care of business for the night.

Driving back to his home base—a hotel—he took the route that followed the Missouri River, watching the way the nighttime city lights glittered on the water's surface. He considered calling his charter company to grab the soonest possible flight back to Phoenix, but quickly dismissed the idea. Although he'd agreed to go home for the mystery meeting, he didn't need to rush. He wasn't anxious to see his brothers, or Sweet Springs Ranch, again so soon.

Turning into the hotel driveway, his earlier thoughts about making a home came rushing back. He'd always loved hotels. The lack of clutter, the daily cleaning, and the ease of coming and going (mostly going) appealed to him.

But there was something about the lack of permanence that sometimes got to him. The "Good evening, sir," he received at the front desk was about as personal as things got at hotels; nothing like the warm greeting Riggs probably received from Sarah every night when he got home.

And sure, when he walked down the sterile hallway and went into his room, he found that the hotel cleaning staff left a chocolate on top of the dresser and a washcloth bunny on the bed. Nice touches, but the staff didn't provide them out of love.

The problem was that to receive love from people, you had to give it. Sterling pulled his suitcase out of the hotel closet and laid it on the bed. Giving love meant being vulnerable. And Sterling had learned throughout his life that even when you gave every ounce of love you had, you didn't always receive it back.

Taking his shirts off the hangers, folding them, and putting them in the suitcase, then doing the same with his pants, reminded him of the last time he'd packed to go home ... the last time he'd seen his father.

Just like he did with everything else, Levi Wilder lived his final days with drama. He'd been on hospice for some time (Sterling didn't know how long, exactly). When his hospice nurses declared he had only a handful of days remaining, he insisted all four of his sons assemble at the hospice facility together.

He gave them some speech about how family should always stick together, and all Sterling could do was press his lips together to keep from ruining what was probably a special, poignant moment for his brothers.

Then, Levi, the old bastard, wanted to speak to each son separately. Travis going first was a no-brainer for the rest of them. He was the youngest and had spent the most time with their dad in recent years, and therefore, was probably the closest to Levi.

Sterling waited in the lobby with Hayes and Cash while Travis went in. They declined his offer to share his flask; in fact, they gave him dirty looks, like taking the edge off your father's death with a little bourbon was a bad thing. His dad, at least, would understand that.

The Wilder brothers of five years before would have passed the time cracking jokes. Inappropriate jokes, but jokes nonetheless.

They would have been busting into laughter, shushing each other, elbowing each other into a more appropriate silence. But that was before. As Levi Wilder lay on his deathbed, imparting wisdom or simple goodbyes to his youngest son, his three older sons stood around the tiny room, shoulders tense, jaws tight. Cash wandered over to the vending machine, inspecting its contents before walking away, only to repeat the process every two minutes or so. Hayes picked up a magazine, flipped through it, and set it back down, then repeated that process with a different magazine, apparently finding none of them interesting. And Sterling paced, four strides to one side of the room, four strides back.

Finally, Travis emerged, eyes and nose red, his sadness so palpable, Sterling could feel its weight pressing down on him. Travis didn't know a fraction of what Sterling knew. Cash went in next. Hayes continued his repeated examinations of the magazines. Travis blotted at his eyes and nose, soaking through the two tissues he'd brought out with him. On one of his laps, Sterling grabbed two more tissues and handed them to Travis, who sniffed and thanked him.

Sterling felt for the kid. In a way, he wished his dad's death impacted him like it did Travis. But no. He felt sadder for himself—for the lack of connection he felt with Levi. Cash came down the hallway, his eyes dry, but his mouth set in a grim line. It was the same trying-not-to-cry expression he'd worn since he was a little kid. A wave of affection rushed over Sterling at that. He almost cried, himself, as he remembered Cash making that face one day when all four of them had played a series of pranks on their dad. They put plastic wrap over the hole in his shampoo bottle, taped a tiny piece of index card over the sensor on his computer mouse, replaced the salt in the shaker with sugar, stuffed napkins in the toes of his boots ... Sterling couldn't remember what else they'd done, but from morning 'til night, Levi was cursing and carrying on as prank after prank befell him. Sterling, Hayes, and Travis kept straight faces, held their shit together as Levi stomped around demanding to know "who masterminded this bullshit."

But poor Cash couldn't do it. During Levi's first round of questioning, Cash avoided eye contact and pressed his lips together, eyes twinkling. Throughout the day, his ability to play it cool decreased. By evening, he was all-out laughing as Levi demanded to know who'd put sugar in the salt shaker and "ruined his goddamned mashed potatoes."

Despite stern looks from his brothers, Cash laughed and laughed. Naturally, Levi blamed him, even though all four boys had participated equally. Cash refused to tattle on the others, even as he received his spanking with the wooden paddle. He'd worn that same look then, mouth in a straight, wobbling line.

Hayes went in next. Knowing his turn was coming up, Sterling became even more restless. The pacing wasn't enough to dispel his nervous energy. He wanted to scream, go outside and run as fast as he could through the parking lot, punch a hole right through the wall in the lobby. Just like Cash, Hayes returned looking grim. He made eye contact with Sterling and gave him a little nod, and suddenly Sterling felt like throwing up. It had been five years since he'd seen his father.

The man lying in the hospital bed was recognizable only thanks to his startling blue eyes. Otherwise, he was but a withered, frail version of the larger-than-life, charismatic-but-intimidating Levi Wilder. In movies, when someone lay dying, their curtains were closed to keep the room dark. But Levi Wilder did things differently. The full, blazing midday sun shone through the window, throwing into relief every bony joint, his dark veins showing through his paper-thin skin, his hip bones visible through the blanket.

He lifted one hand in greeting, croaked out a sound Sterling assumed was his name, and then dropped his arm and died. Sterling knew he was dead. He watched the life go. In movies, people always rushed forward, calling out the name of their loved one, checking their pulse or shaking them. For Sterling, there was no need. He did smooth the crisp white blanket over his dad's chest and place a hand on his shoulder for just a few seconds. He did say goodbye and open the window to let Levi's spirit out. And when he walked out to the lobby, he simply said, "He's gone."

Travis pressed a fist to his chest, like the news physically hurt him. The other two just nodded. They'd all expected Levi to go after they'd said their goodbyes.

Sterling knew they'd want to do something together—dinner or drinks or both—but he found he couldn't bear the idea of anything even remotely close to a celebration. He retreated to the anonymous safety of his hotel, ruminating over the fact that his dad had spent several minutes talking with each of his brothers, only to die before saying anything to Sterling.

Knowing he was going to die, Levi planned his own funeral, and had his people take care of everything. All Sterling had to do was show up. For reasons Sterling might never understand, the funeral took place at a funeral home, not the ranch, and Levi requested a cremation.

The sound of a car horn honking outside the Great Falls hotel brought Sterling back to the present day. The day he was planning to head back to Sweet Springs Ranch after more than five years away. Despite the dread that weighed heavily on his body and his consciousness, Sterling felt a strange sort of anticipation at being home again. Sweet Springs Ranch had given him a magical childhood, even if Levi Wilder himself hadn't.

"God, I love that place." He zipped his suitcase and left the room, checking out on his way to the curb and the car he'd ordered.

The driver, a burly man in his twenties—Sterling suspected he moonlighted as a bouncer at a fancy club—hopped out to take his suitcase. "To the airport, sir?"

"To the airport," Sterling said.

Money couldn't buy happiness, Sterling knew. But it could pay for this ride to the airport in a car so high quality, he couldn't hear even the slightest road noise. It could pay for these cushy seats and the cold bottled water in a fancy bucket attached to the back of the center console.

"Where are you off to?" the driver asked as they sped along.

Sterling sighed. "Home."

"Where's that?"

"Sweet Springs Ranch in Prescott, Arizona."

"I can't say you look like the ranching type," the driver said. In the rearview mirror, Sterling saw his eyes crinkling at the corners.

"For the past five years, I've tried not to be," Sterling said. "You can take the man out of the ranch…"

"I hear you, man," the driver said.

When they pulled up at the airport a while later, Sterling whistled. "Geez, is it Thanksgiving or something?"

The driver laughed. "Nah, man. It's just a Friday in summer. Airport's like this every weekend, pretty much."

Sterling groaned. He hadn't even realized it was Friday. He ran his business seven days a week.

"You wanna leave?"

"Yes," Sterling said, "but I can't. My brothers are expecting me. Family meeting."

The mere idea of a family meeting made nausea swirl in Sterling's stomach. He'd been holding onto a secret for the past five years, and chances were it was about to come out. His brothers would probably kill him—rightfully so.

"Bummer," the driver said. "I mean, family meetings are cool. If you've got a family, which I don't. But if you traveled on a different day, like Saturday, you probably wouldn't be stuck in this horde of people."

Sterling nodded. "I'm sure you're right. But I'm here now. Might as well go in, right?"

"Right." He put the car in park and winked at Sterling in the rearview mirror. "Let's get to it."

They met on the curb, the driver handing Sterling his suitcase and Sterling handing him a crisp one hundred. The driver's eyes widened when he saw it. "Thanks, man," he said, and Sterling grinned at him before walking away, suitcase in hand.

Chapter Three

Inside her house, June wasted no time making a reservation for the next available airport shuttle and scheduling a ride share to get her to the shuttle stop before throwing a bunch of clothes into a suitcase. She told herself she planned on going to Arizona just for the weekend, but she packed so much, she had to sit on her suitcase to get it zipped.

The ride share arrived right on time. When he saw her coming, the driver, a guy about June's age, jumped out of the car and opened the trunk. He made one gallant attempt to lift her suitcase, but it wouldn't budge from its spot behind his car. On the second attempt, he managed to get it off the ground, but couldn't hoist it over the bumper.

"I think this might require a team lift," June said, her face burning. She blamed her overpacking on Timothy Alexander, his push-broom mustache, and his penchant for ice sculptures in July. Because of him and his ridiculous demands, she couldn't think straight.

Once she and the driver were in the car, he looked at her in the rearview mirror. "I'm taking you to the airport shuttle stop on McCormick Street, right?"

Rendered mute by humiliation, June nodded.

He cleared his throat. "I'm pretty sure there's a weight limit for suitcases. You might consider bringing two. You know, splitting up your stuff so each one's lighter."

"That's not a bad idea," June said, "but I'm afraid I don't have time. I'll just take this one and hope for the best."

The driver shrugged. "Okay."

When they arrived at the shuttle stop ten minutes later, they hoisted the suitcase out of the trunk together. "Good luck," he said, and she swore there was an unspoken "You're going to need it" in there somewhere. Then he was gone. She didn't blame him—he probably wanted to gain as much distance as he could, as soon as possible.

Several people had already lined up under the shade structure. June joined them, but not without having to wrestle her suitcase up onto the curb while they watched.

"Where are you headed?"

June offered what was surely a weak smile to the man in front of her. "Phoenix."

His face contorted with disgust. "At this time of year? Arizona just made national news for record temperatures."

The woman he was with—June hoped she wasn't unfortunate enough to be his wife—gave him a gentle slap on the arm. "Westley, that's not a very nice thing to say."

"What?" he said,

June shrugged. "At this point, I want to be anywhere but here."

He didn't have a response to that and fortunately, the shuttle came barreling up to the curb, belching diesel fumes. The doors opened and passengers disembarked. June wondered if they were coming home or arriving in Great Falls for a visit.

After what seemed like ages, the shuttle driver hollered, "All aboard," and the line inched forward.

Perhaps when she was packing, June should have anticipated the difficulty she'd experience when pulling her enormous suitcase up the shuttle's stairs. But all she could think about was getting out of Montana.

The shuttle driver was at the top of the stairs, taking the suitcases from the couple in front of her (June noticed with some disdain that the Phoenix-hating guy didn't help his traveling partner). She stepped up onto the first stair and yanked on her suitcase handle, but it didn't budge. On the second try, she was able to lift it just a couple of inches off the ground, and it fell onto the bottom step with a crunching sound.

"Um, Miss? A wheel just fell off your suitcase," said the older woman behind her.

"Let me help you with that." Without waiting for June's response, the shuttle driver reached down and grabbed her suitcase handle, hauling the monstrosity up the stairs and swinging it onto the luggage rack.

Because the passengers behind her were making their way up the stairs, June didn't have time to assess the damage to the wheel— she moved down the aisle to the first open seat.

Damage control. She had to do it. Although Maya had probably done her best with Timothy, he was the type to blast people on social media ... June had seen it when she performed her social-media-stalking protocol on him after his initial consult.

She texted Maya: *I'm headed to the airport. Could you check Timothy's accounts and see if he's blasted us yet?*

Maya: *He has.*

June: *You checked already?*

Maya: *I did.*

June: *I admire your efficiency.*

Maya: *It's why you hired me, right?*

June: *Right. Ok, thanks. I guess I need to text my parents. My mom met some influencer in Paris and now she's all into Insta.*

Maya: *Insta?*

June: *Exactly.*

Maya: *Headed to the airport, huh? Because I didn't know about this, I assume it's an impromptu trip.*

June: *Very much so.*

Maya: *Where to?*

June: *Arizona.*

Maya responded with a sweaty-faced emoji.

June: *LOL. I'm heading north, to Prescott. It's in the mountains.*

Maya: *The desert is the desert, as far as I'm concerned. I've canceled your meetings for today—should I do Monday, too?*

June: *No thanks. I'll be back.*

Maya: *Ok. Safe travels.*

June: *Thanks.*

Next, June tapped on the text conversation with her mom. How to begin?

June: *I fired a client today. Figured you should know.*

There, that should do it. No dancing around the issue. She stared at her screen, waiting for a response, but then realized that with the time difference between Montana and Paris, her parents were likely asleep. "Probably for the best," June muttered.

By the time the shuttle pulled up to the departures area, June's stomach churned. She wasn't sure whether to blame her queasiness on the shuttle's top-heavy anatomy, the driver's driving, or her texting while riding, but she did know she couldn't wait to get off.

Only when she did, after the driver forcibly handed her the suitcase, she remembered about the wheel. Half-dragging and half-rolling the albatross along behind her, she weaved through the thick crowd to get inside, where she discovered an even thicker crowd. How could all these people have somewhere to go on the same day?

As if in protest, her suitcase suddenly stopped moving along with her, and its dead, immobile weight caused her to stop, too. That caused someone behind her to slam right into her with the force of a freight train and a masculine grunt that shouldn't have turned her on, but did. She turned around to give the guy a piece of her mind—he should watch where he was going, honestly—and found herself face to face with the most gorgeous man she had ever seen.

Like, movie-star gorgeous.

Swoon-worthy.

Sizzling.

Mouthwatering.

She noticed his eyes first. They were the lightest blue she'd ever seen, with thick, dark lashes. Although a manly scruff covered his jawline, she could tell it was strong and defined. He wore a white dress shirt with a few buttons open to reveal tanned skin and a little bit of dark chest hair. June swallowed as she took in his torso and hips, his strong, jeans-clad thighs and expensive-looking loafers. Her gaze traveled back up his perfectly sculpted form and landed on a pair of very kissable lips that were set in a definite scowl. Right. She'd come to a complete stop, apparently right in front of him. Of course he was aggravated.

"I'm sorry," she rushed to say, coming to her senses and wondering just how long she'd ogled him. Not that anyone would blame her, but still.

"It's fine," he said, his voice husky enough to conjure up images of his mouth on her neck and his hands on her skin.

What is going on, here?

"It's just that my suitcase broke." She stepped back, awkwardly, and looked down at the offending wheel—only to see that the second wheel had broken off, too. "I guess the second wheel fell off."

His lips twitched, and her body responded by creating a tingling sensation in her lower belly.

"You were pulling it on one wheel?"

June shrugged. "Trying. It's too heavy to carry, so I was half-dragging it."

"Where are you headed?"

"Phoenix."

The full-on smile he gave her then was completely disarming. If they hadn't been in the crowded departures area, she would have thrown herself at his feet.

"I mean, which airline? I assume you need to check this thing." He gestured at her deformed suitcase.

"Oh." Her laugh was awkward. "Um, I don't know yet. I don't even have a flight. I was hoping to buy a ticket here."

She had no idea what he found so amusing, but still smiling, he inclined his head toward the Western Airlines counter. "Let's try over there. I know they've got daily flights to Phoenix."

Like some kind of hormone-saturated zombie, June nodded. She'd follow him anywhere.

"Good idea."

"I'll take that." He reached across the front of her body to grab her suitcase handle and she caught a whiff of his scent: sandalwood, for sure, and maybe citrus. She inhaled deeply, saw him notice, and immediately held her breath. Something passed over his features, then. Interest, possibly, but she couldn't be sure. She didn't even know the guy.

But you'd like to.

She smiled at her own internal voice before realizing she hadn't let go of her suitcase handle and the guy was still waiting for her to do so, his body so close to hers, she could feel the heat coming off it.

"Oh! Sorry! Yes, thank you so much." She released the handle as if it were burning hot, and took a step back, only to bump into someone else.

Lips twitching again, June's new hero said, "Quite all right. Shall we?"

He started to turn toward the counter, but she put a hand on his arm. "Wait. I didn't even get the name of the man who was kind enough to help me."

"Sterling," he said, flashing that knee-weakening silver-screen smile again. "Sterling Wilder."

"June Cartwright," she said, giving him a nod.

"Pleasure," he said, and the word traveled over her skin, its undertones making their way to her very bones.

Then, as if that damned heavy suitcase was filled with feathers, he picked it up and gestured with his head for her to lead the way. Feeling a bit uncertain about what to do with her hands now that they were empty—she'd slung her purse over her shoulder to carry the offending suitcase—she gave him an awkward little curtsy and headed for the ticket counter, where the line was absolutely commensurate with the crush of people in the terminal.

They stepped into the queue. Sterling smiled at her again. "And to what do I owe the pleasure, June? Business or leisure?"

June cleared her throat. "I'm sorry?"

"Well, is this a work trip, or are you traveling for fun?"

"Oh!" June laughed, the sound high and unnatural, bordering

on crazed lunatic. "Right. Well, a little bit of both. I'm traveling for fun—to get away from business."

Eyes twinkling, Sterling said, "So you're running away. But that doesn't explain this." He hefted the suitcase and June could see his bicep flex under his crisp shirt.

"What about you?" She didn't care that her change of attention was obvious.

He shrugged. "Neither. I'm going back for family." His eyes pinched, just a little at the corners, when he talked about family.

That piqued June's curiosity, but she didn't have time to ask any more questions because in some cruel twist of fate they'd reached the front of the line, which meant their conversation was coming to an end.

With a wide, gallant sweep of his arm, Sterling said, "Ladies first."

June moved to the counter and Sterling hauled her suitcase up next to her.

"Tickets?" said the lady at the counter, whose name tag read *Tammi* with a little heart over the i.

June shook her head. "Not yet."

Sterling's voice was loud and clear when he said, "But we'd like to buy some. Two seats on your next flight to Phoenix."

June felt her mouth drop open as her head swiveled toward this man-god who'd just asked for two tickets on the same flight. Just as fast as shock set in, June realized perhaps Sterling had a traveling companion. A female traveling companion. Was it possible June had overlooked her because she was so smitten with Sterling?

Now her head whipped to the right and left, searching for his mysterious, behind-the-scenes other half. But she was nowhere to be found. Tammi tapped away at her keyboard, her shiny, bubblegum-pink fingernails dancing as she looked up the flights. Her gaze found June's eyes first, and then Sterling's. Her plump, pink lips turned downward, her frown exaggerated. "I'm sorry to say, we only have one seat left to Phoenix today. That flight leaves in two hours."

"He can have it," June said at the same time Sterling said, "She can have it."

He grabbed her elbow then, looking at her with an intensity that made her feel like they'd known each other for years, not minutes. "I insist. You're trying to get away, and I'd rather not go. Honestly. You go. I'll get a flight for tomorrow."

The burn of tears stung June's eyes. The realization those tears resulted not from his kindness, but from the fact that she so wanted to spend more time with him surprised her. She blinked a few times and nodded. "I can't tell you how much I appreciate this. I've only got a weekend, and I'd hate to wait 'til tomorrow."

Sterling's body seem to gravitate toward June's, almost as if it had a mind of his own. She could've sworn his arm started to lift, like he wanted to hug her. Her body responded to the idea of an embrace with a gravitational pull. His hand was still on her elbow and he ran it up to her shoulder, leaving behind a trail of warmth.

"You're welcome. Do me a favor and make the most out of your weekend, okay?"

Unable to speak, June nodded. "Okay," she managed, her voice barely more than a whisper.

And just like that, he was gone.

"Great!" Tammi said. "Let me reserve that seat for you. Do you have your ID?"

June handed it over, her throat still tight, and Tammi continued typing at a furious pace. At first, June watched her every keystroke, ensuring she entered her details correctly. That lasted only a few seconds, because June found she couldn't resist the urge to look for Sterling. Where would he go? Where would he spend the night? She knew next to nothing about the man, but she could think of nothing else.

Before she could get an eye on him, Tammi clapped, just once. "All right, Ms. Cartwright! I've got your seat booked. Just set your suitcase on the scale and we'll get it checked."

June nodded absently, her mind on Sterling spending the night somewhere. She wrapped her hand around the suitcase handle and tried to lift, but nothing happened. Focusing, she tried again. Still nothing. Tammi smiled expectantly, her hands still clasped together at her sternum.

Someone behind June took pity on her: a man's voice said, "Let me help you with that."

A burly body appeared next to June's, gently nudged her out of the way, lifted the suitcase, and plopped it onto the scale. At which point, a horrible zipping noise erupted from it as the zipper split, all the way around, spilling her clothes all over the scale.

"Oh, my," Tammi said, both hands now pressed flat against her chest. "Oh, my."

June's face burned hotter than it ever had before. She was certain that if she could see herself right now, she'd see flames flickering off her skin.

"I'm sorry to say that unless you can find a way to close that suitcase and secure it right away, I'll have to refund your ticket." Tammi's voice rang loud and clear through the space.

June felt like the whole terminal went dark and someone illuminated a spotlight on her as she crouched down to gather up her things. The people in line were the audience, and she was the fool onstage.

Chapter Four

The powers that be were giving Sterling a second chance. He'd cursed himself as he walked away from June Cartwright, The Most Beautiful Woman He'd Ever seen. That's how he would remember her for the rest of his life. He should have asked for her number. Or her snap, at least. Wasn't that what the kids did these days? But, no. He couldn't get a woman's number or snap or business card. Women wanted to settle down and stay in one place, and he never planned to do that.

He should have insisted they find a different airline, one that had two tickets to Phoenix, right then and there. He should have said they'd share a seat, just so he could spend a little more time with her.

Quite unexpectedly, he envisioned June on his lap in an airplane, facing him, her big brown eyes on his, his hands on her waist, their lips meeting.

Why had he been so stupid?

He cursed again, earning a few looks from other travelers. "Sorry," he muttered, and then pulled out his phone to call for a car. As he spoke to the scheduler, he decided to get a hotel nearby rather than going all the way back to his apartment on the other end of town. He stowed his phone in his (small) messenger bag, laughing again at June's monstrosity of a suitcase.

Having left the job site and then his apartment in such a rush, Sterling hadn't used the bathroom, and he figured he may as well do that while he waited for the car to show up.

When he reemerged, he glanced over at the Western Airlines ticketing counter, knowing it was unlikely June was still there, but hoping he'd get to see her just one more time. He did—but instead of excitement, Sterling experienced a rush of concern.

June wasn't walking toward the security checkpoint wearing the expression of someone who couldn't wait to take off for the weekend. No, she was kneeling on the floor next to her suitcase ... which had somehow split open and spilled clothes all over the place. Was it wrong to be intrigued by the swatches of colorful, lacy fabric he spotted in the pile as he strode over to her?

Only when he knelt next to her did he hear her murmuring, "Stupid, stupid, stupid."

She stilled when he said, "I wouldn't say 'stupid,' but I would say someone overpacked her poor, unfortunate suitcase."

The corners of her mouth lifted, just a little, and she turned to face him. "I may have."

She'd taken her mane of honey-blond hair and wound it into a messy bun on top of her head. The result—a clearer view of the elegant lines and angles of her face—was stunning.

"Let me guess." He scooped up a silky piece of fabric and shoved it back into the suitcase. "Tammi said that if you can't get this fixed immediately, she's selling your seat."

"Pretty much."

"I hate to say it, but I'm fairly convinced you can't get this fixed immediately."

For a moment, Sterling was afraid he'd said the wrong thing—that June would burst into tears then and there. Her bearing seemed so ... fragile. But rather than bursting into tears, she burst into laughter as she continued shoveling clothes, and clothes continued falling out.

"I'm fairly convinced you're right."

"Look," he said, tenderness overcoming him. "I just ordered a car to take me back to a hotel for the night. What do you say we take the car, go buy you a new suitcase and repack, and then go back to my hotel, have a nice dinner, maybe a drink, and come back tomorrow. I'll put you up in your own room."

Tammi looked over the counter at them, and June gave her a little wave. Her voice still strained with laughter, she said, "Go ahead, Tammi. Give me a refund and sell my seat. There's no way I can fix this in time."

She giggled while he scooped up her suitcase, clothes and all, and marched back out to the curb. She giggled while he loaded the trunk, colorful swatches of cloth visible flapping in the breeze, and when he opened the door for her. She was still giggling as she sank down into the plush seat. By the time he'd walked around the back of the car and gotten in on the passenger side, she'd stopped giggling and was running her hands over the velvety upholstery, her eyes wide.

"This is the fanciest ride share I've ever been in."

The air conditioner lifted little wisps of her hair away from her face, and he admired the way her cheeks had grown rosy in the short time they were outside.

"That's because it's not a ride share," he said, opening the cooler and offering her a cold water.

"That sounds very ominous." She took the water, opened it, and drank before looking over at him. "I just realized I've gotten into a car with a strange man—*two* strange men, actually—and have no idea where we're going. We could be going back to your secret underground lair for all I know."

In the rearview mirror, Sterling saw the driver raise an eyebrow. For his part, Sterling laughed out loud. "I'll have you know, madam, that as strange as I may be, I won't hurt you. I'm fairly confident the driver won't hurt you, as my car company vets all the drivers before hiring them. But I promise I'll protect you if he tries. As for my lair, I think you'll find it's quite a lavish place, and the exact opposite of underground. If not a bit overpriced."

"You have a car company?"

"I do," he said.

"Fancy."

Because he wanted to stare at June, take in and memorize every perfect detail, Sterling looked out the window as the car sped along.

Her gasp when they pulled up at the hotel was satisfying. Her face turned a whole new shade of red, and he wondered if she was embarrassed about her secret lair comment, or just surprised he'd chosen such a nice place. Her movements were slow when he offered his hand to help her out of the car, and she looked at the ground as she followed him to the trunk.

"Chin up, June," he said as he lifted her suitcase, holding the top shut. "I took the liberty of ordering you a replacement and it should be here soon. I hope you'll forgive me—it's been such a long day and I couldn't stand going to a store and being surrounded by even more people."

"You ordered me a replacement?"

He couldn't tell if she was elated or on the verge of being pissed off, so he acted casual, shrugging one shoulder (despite the massive amount of weight he held in each hand). "Yeah. I hope that's okay. Same color, different brand."

She slid her arms around his waist and squeezed, sending a pleasant little buzz through his veins. "Thank you. So much."

Sterling couldn't decide whether to loathe the suitcase for preventing him from hugging her back, or to love it for putting him in this position in the first place. June released him and stepped back, and he ached at the absence of her body against his.

"I'm sure we can leave this with the front desk while we have dinner," he said. "I hear they have a killer restaurant here."

"That would be great," she said. "Would you mind dropping it off while I run to the restroom?"

"No problem. I'll meet you in the lobby."

A few minutes later, June waited in the lobby, her back to him as she studied the water fountain on the wall opposite the front desk. He took a moment to study her: the way she stood so still, hands clasped behind her; the curve of her waist where his hand would fit just perfectly; the many layers of color he could see in her hair in the lights from above—browns and golds and maybe a little red. Because he couldn't resist touching her, he placed his hand on the small of her back as he came to stand next to her.

"I have an idea," he whispered, his mouth close to her ear. He was insanely pleased when he saw goosebumps rise on her neck.

She turned toward him, her eyes already crinkling at the corners with a smile. "I'm intrigued. Do tell."

"You want to get away, right?"

"Right."

"And I want to avoid where I'm going."

"Right."

"So what do you say that for just one evening, we pretend we planned this? We pretend this you're not running away and I don't have anywhere else to go and we're here, together. We pretend that having a couple of drinks and dinner is exactly what is supposed to be on our joint agenda. For just tonight, we avoid the things we want to avoid and enjoy each other's company."

A flame of interest flared in her eyes. She uncrossed her arms and her shoulders relaxed. "I love that idea. But can we lay a few ground rules?"

"Sure," he said. "Should we do it over a drink?"

For the first time that evening, she gave him a genuine smile— one he imagined she gave her friends. The affect was disarming. "Let's."

Sterling had heard rave reviews about the restaurant here, but the sleek, posh decor still caught him off guard. Everything was black, except for the carpet, which was a pale, shimmering silver. Each booth was sunken into the floor, its seat backs high for privacy. There were no freestanding tables. This was a place people came for privacy. Sterling liked that.

June led him straight to the bar. Its black surface was so shiny, he could've seen his reflection in it if the lighting was any brighter. She ordered a glass of red and he went for bourbon on the rocks. Once the bartender poured their drinks, he melted into the background.

June's reaction to her first sip of wine—her head dropped back, her eyes closed, and she sighed and licked her lips—made Sterling hope, fervently, that her first ground rule would be that they go up to a hotel room and make use of the bed.

"I needed this," she said, eyes still closed. "I'm not one to drink on flights, but I would have, today."

"Was it rough, even before I ran into you?" Sterling was surprised at how deep his voice sounded. Like he was on the prowl. Was he?

She sat up straight and opened her eyes. "Rules," she said, her gaze sharpening on his face. "Let's not talk about our days or our jobs or our current lives. Let's truly pretend none of that exists and live just this one evening, together in our own little world."

Sterling held out a hand, and June took it. They shook. June picked up her glass again and took another sip of wine. "So, Sterling."

"June."

Her eyes were impossibly deep, serious. "Tell me about your perfect day."

She watched as he sipped his bourbon. He took his time because he realized he liked the way she watched him: like he was the only person in the world, and she couldn't possibly be more interested in his every movement. "The sunrise wakes me up." He'd only just met the woman, but in his vision of the perfect day, when the sunrise woke him up, she was in his bed. Not that he'd say so. "Then, I go into the kitchen, where my coffee's ready and waiting."

"Coffee guy, huh?"

"Aren't you?"

"No. I'm a tea girl."

Sterling feigned shock. "I don't think the two of us can co-exist in our own little world."

"Just for tonight?"

Something about the genuine need behind her lighthearted words made him want to reach out and draw her closer to him. "Fine. Just for tonight though. Tomorrow, you drink coffee, or we go to our separate worlds."

"Fine." She sipped her wine, uncrossed her legs and crossed them again. "Go on."

"I sit at the counter and read a good book while I drink my coffee."

"What's a good book?"

"Something with excitement. A thriller. Fight scenes, a little gratuitous sex."

She raised her eyebrows.

"Just in the book. Not in real life."

She smiled. "Then what?"

"Then I go for a run. Along the river. I don't live by a river," he added quickly, omitting the fact that he didn't have a permanent address. "But it's my perfect day, and on that day, I walk down to the bank and start running."

"I love it so far. Then what?"

"Then I'd shower." Why did he say that? Now he was picturing himself in the shower, June in front of him, her skin slippery as he ran his hands from her hips to her breasts, his mouth on hers.

"Are you blushing?" she wanted to know.

"It's the bourbon," he lied, signaling for another.

The bartender reappeared and poured him another shot. June held up her glass and he refilled it before once again disappearing.

"Then I'd make breakfast."

Another couple came into the restaurant. Sterling watched them, wondering if they were together, or co-workers, or friends, or two strangers like June and him.

"What would you make?"

"Glad you asked. I'd make eggs. With veggies. Bell peppers, mushrooms, onion."

"A man who can cook. I like that."

He shouldn't be basking in her approval like a puppy basking in praise, but there he was. "Then I'd buy a coffee and head out to visit all the antique stores I could. If my riverside town had an antique mall, I'd go there."

"Antiques, huh? That's unusual."

"I have a soft spot for old things—things that hold stories within them. Houses, cars, clocks, dishes."

"You're full of surprises, Sterling."

"I'm deciding to take that as a compliment."

"You should."

"Also, this bourbon's going to my head. I think we should eat. Want to get a booth?"

June glanced around the restaurant and, apparently seeing a booth that earned her approval, she nodded. "Let's see if we can get that one in the corner."

He took the opportunity to touch her again, offering his hand to help her off the barstool and then his arm for her to hold onto. They walked back over to the hostess stand and Sterling asked if they could have the corner booth. Her eyes on June, the hostess replied that of course they could. She picked up two menus and led them back to the booth.

"They're very accommodating here," Sterling said once they were seated.

June's eyes sparkled with humor. "They are. Anyway, doesn't this booth feel secluded? We could be the only two in this restaurant."

"I wish we were."

"Only then, we couldn't eat," June said. "Unless we wanted to cook for ourselves. Which I now know you can do."

He picked up his menu, surprised at the weight of it in his hands, and impressed by the fancy dishes he had to choose from. "I can, but I don't think I could make these seared scallops or roast duck."

"Well, you're in luck, because the chef is in tonight. That server just brought out a tray of food, and it looks amazing."

"It does look amazing," Sterling said. "And it smells even better."

June nodded. "It does. I've read rave reviews about this place."

"You've never been here, either?"

A server dressed in all black brought them water.

"My answer to that question falls on the other side of the line we've drawn with our rules, I'm afraid. So why don't you tell me what you'd do after spending part of your perfect day at the antique mall?"

Sterling was intrigued, but in favor of honoring their rules, he said, "Well. I'd probably kill the entire day looking at antiques, and I'm sure by then I'd be hungry. So I'd go my favorite restaurant for dinner."

"What's your favorite restaurant?"

Another server materialized table-side. "Can I take your orders?"

He could have sworn June hadn't looked at the menu at all, but she rattled off her order—a steak salad with balsamic dressing—as if she knew it by heart.

"I'll have the prime rib," Sterling told the server.

Once she was gone, he told June, "My favorite restaurant is this fondue place in a little town in northern California. I rarely make it out that way, but this is my dream day. I might even teleport."

"Ooh, fondue," she said, her body again releasing like it had on her first sip of wine, and his reacting the same way. "I love fondue."

God, what he wouldn't give to be there with her. "Tell me about your perfect day."

"Wait," she said. "Yours isn't over. What do you do after fondue?"

Sterling wrapped his hands around his bourbon tumbler. "Well, now it's freezing. Starting to snow. So I go home, make myself a hot toddy, and light a fire in the fireplace. I sit in front of the fire and read. Or watch a movie. I'm not sure. What if you're there with me? What do we do?"

She raised an eyebrow at him over the rim of her wineglass. His entire being reacted, flooding with a desire that made his jeans tight and had him shifting in his seat. Typically, he'd break eye contact, but something about June Cartwright made him want to maintain that connection, simmer in it while all the flavors came to life.

The server returned with their food and when they both looked up, Sterling felt the absence of June's gaze on his like he'd taken off a sweater.

"Now," Sterling said when the server left, "tell me about your perfect day."

Chapter Five

When June told Sterling her perfect day would end with dancing—in a classy, upscale spot—she hadn't expected him to pull out his phone and say, "I've found just the place, and it's within walking distance. Want to go?"

Anticipation thrummed throughout her body, creating a rhythm.

"I'd love to," she said. "As soon as we pay the bill."

"Already taken care of."

He stood and offered his arm again (she could get used to that) and they walked out of the Hotel Cartwright, her home and place of work (not that he needed to know that). The summer evening was still warm, the air humid and dewy on June's skin.

"When's the last time you went dancing?" Sterling asked her, looking down at her like there was no one else in the world.

"I can't even remember," June said. "I don't want to break our rules of engagement, but my job usually occupies pretty much every weekend. This?" she flung out her free arm, encapsulating the night-time scene, the two of them out on the town. "It's a fluke."

"Then we should make it a night you'll remember forever."

We already have.

They walked south, their strides in sync as they passed a couple of other hotel properties and restaurants. When they came to Keys, a Piano Bar, June gasped. "How did you know? I've wanted to come here since this place opened!"

"I wish I could say I knew. But it was luck."

Keys had been the talk of the town, all the buzz, since it opened a month ago. She couldn't help herself: she squealed. Sterling laughed as he pulled open the door. When he whispered, "I'm not sure this is the kind of place for squealing," his breath hot on her ear, she nearly came undone. She could shiver right out of her own skin and into his, just to be that close to him.

Inside, June could see right away what all the hype was about. Everything was on key (June laughed at her own pun). Lamps around the room illuminated the space, just bright enough to see, and just dim enough for romance, ambience. A giant, shiny grand piano sat in one corner. The pianist, a young man wearing a tuxedo, played with passion, his eyes closed as he swayed with the notes.

Immediately, June envisioned the kinds of events she could organize here. Bachelorette parties, milestone birthday parties, office parties. Oh, how she would love the freedom to plan events somewhere other than the hotel.

High-top tables lined three walls, while a bar lined the fourth. A dance floor occupied most of the open space.

"What do you say to a dance?"

June nearly groaned with anticipation. How many times had she wished for a man who would ask her to dance, no expectations, no strings attached?

She was practically purring when she said, "That would be wonderful."

His hand found hers. When their palms touched, she experienced a deep sense of knowing at her very core. Within a few strides, they were on the dance floor.

And then she was in his arms.

She intertwined her fingers behind his neck and rested her forehead on his. His hands were on her hips. He moved his thumbs up and down, stroking her rib cage in a way that felt completely erotic.

"Can I go back and revise my perfect day?" he said. "Because I would definitely add this. I had no idea just how it would feel to dance to piano music with the most beautiful woman I've ever seen."

His words is sent a thrill through her.

"You already finished your perfect day, but I guess you can add on to it. Just this once."

In her mind's eye, June zoomed out, took a wide-angle view of the two of them on the dance floor. To anyone else, they undoubtedly looked like a couple. She felt like they were a couple. So much so, she had to remind herself they weren't. This was a one-night deal, an escape for both of them. Temporary.

"Where'd you go?"

She forced her eyes to focus as she looked at him. "I'm right here. I guess I just got lost in the moment."

He pulled her closer, wrapping his arms around her waist so their hips touched. She laid her head on his shoulder and they swayed.

"You know," she said, hearing the dreaminess in her own voice. "I think I'm going to go ahead and add this to my perfect day, too."

His chuckle rumbled in his chest. "Perfect."

One song melted into the next. The two of them remained on the dance floor as other couples came and went. June couldn't get enough of the way his body felt under her hands. The planes of his abs and pecs, the curves of his biceps, made her wish she could tear his clothes off then and there. At least they weren't in the Hotel Cartwright anymore, where the staff would definitely keep tabs on her. But, they were only a few doors down. As close as they were, she hoped no one in Keys would recognize her. Not that she'd take any chances in public, so close to where she and her parents made their living.

"Would you like another drink?"

Again, the sound of his voice in his ear, and his breath on her skin, sent little jolts of energy zipping all over her body. "That would be nice."

He took her hand and she relished in the idea that he needed to maintain contact as much as she did. They joined a few others at the bar, but June paid them no attention—she couldn't take her eyes off Sterling. He'd called her the most beautiful woman he'd ever seen. As she watched him chat with the bartender about which wine he recommended, she reckoned she'd return the compliment. He was, hands down, the most handsome man she'd ever seen. He belonged in an ad for cologne or luxury travel. Despite his designer jeans and expensive-looking shirt, there was something rugged about him, and it wasn't just the stubble on his face. His left hand bore a couple of scars, and he had one right through his eyebrow.

"Want to try the merlot?" He broke through her study of his physique.

"Sure." She wondered what she'd missed in the bartender's description, what had made Sterling select it. She wanted to know what made him tick.

Glasses in front of them, June pinned him with her stare. "Would you rather have the ability to fly, or use telepathy?"

His laugh, loud and carefree, caught her off guard. "Fly. No question. I can't tell you how many times my brothers and I tried it. I may or may not have broken my arm after jumping off the barn roof to see if a higher starting point helped my cause."

"Aw," June said. "How old you were you?"

Another bout of hooting laughter filled the space. "I know you're thinking I'm going to say six, or maybe eight. But, no. I was fifteen."

At that, June laughed out loud. "Fifteen?! What were you thinking?"

He shrugged, his smile looking a little abashed. "Like I said, I figured a higher starting point might make the difference. We'd just seen a new superhero movie—Superman or something, I'm sure— and we thought, you know, maybe there was a way."

June shook her head. "Maybe it's a good thing this is a one-night relationship. I mean, no offense, but you don't sound like the brightest crayon in the box."

"Tell me you never did anything stupid as a kid."

June sipped her wine and felt her eyes go round. "This is good."

"I think so, too," Sterling said. "Bartender said it's from Bordeaux."

Feeling exponentially bolder than usual, June said, "I wasn't listening."

He picked up on what she was putting down. She could tell from the way he raised an eyebrow and let his gaze skim down to her mouth.

"Anyway. I've done a handful of stupid things," June said, remembering. "Haven't we all?"

Sterling smirked. "Some more than others. As one of four brothers, I can almost guarantee I've done more, stupider stuff than you."

June smiled. "Maybe. When I was little, there was a cat in our neighborhood who was super friendly. He would do all the cat things: rub against my legs, lean into my petting, purr. I wanted to keep him, but my mom wouldn't let me. Obviously. He belonged to someone. I *really* wanted a cat of my own. But my mom was allergic. Very allergic. That year, in second grade, I had a binder with kittens on it, a backpack with cat ears, a kitten pencil box, you get the idea."

Sterling's lips twitched. "I have a feeling I might know where this is going."

"I happened to sit across from this girl, Mindy. We bonded over our love of cats. And then one day before Halloween, Mindy came to school, so excited. I mean, she squealed the second she saw me walk in the classroom door."

"And that's when the squealing started," Sterling said.

"Indeed. So, she tells me her cat had kittens the night before. She says her mom said they would have to find homes for them. Eight kittens, can you believe it?"

Sterling couldn't believe it. He said so. "On the ranch, it's an anomaly for a cow or horse to have more than one calf or foal."

Ah. A clue into Sterling's past.

"We did have barn cats, but we didn't pay them much attention until they were bigger and could hunt rats. Anyway, carry on."

June made a mental note to learn more about his life on the ranch. "Of course, I told Mindy I would be happy to take one."

"Of course."

"I didn't have a plan," June said, throwing up a hand. "It was stupid. All I knew was that I wanted a kitten, always had, and Mindy had eight she needed to get rid of. I was helping her out, really."

Sterling inclined his head. "Doing a good deed."

June laughed. "Exactly. So the day comes when Mindy's mom says the kittens can go to their new homes. I used to ride the bus after school."

Sterling raised his eyebrows in disbelief.

"I did. I took the kitten on the bus. Mindy's mom brought it after school and I stuck it in my backpack and carried it to the bus. You know how loud buses are. The driver had no idea she had a kitten passenger on board. On the way home, I walked to the corner store and bought cat food. I got everything set up in my bedroom."

"I can't wait to see how this story unfolds," Sterling said. He leaned back, made a show of getting comfortable, his elbows on the armrests.

"Well, sadly, the story is almost over. My first foray into cat ownership did not last very long."

He waited for her to speak and again, she noticed his complete focus on her. There could be one hundred other women in this piano bar, and he wouldn't notice a single one. She might be in love.

"Cue the honeymoon phase. I told my mom I was reading or playing with Legos or whatever, and I spent all my spare time in the bedroom playing with my cat."

Grimacing, Sterling said, "You named him, didn't you?"

"I did," June said. It was hard to believe, but she still experienced a pang of sadness when she remembered little Hairy (she'd found that name so clever).

"He was so playful. I made toys for him out of stuff we had around the house. Ribbon, yarn, old toys. Within a few days, we had a little routine where he slept with me all night, curled up between my shoulder, neck, and pillow. God, I loved that little guy."

Sterling leaned forward and put his elbows on his knees. "You're about to break my heart, aren't you?"

"I am," June said. "It breaks my heart to think about it, even now. Sure enough, my mom got suspicious. I didn't typically hang out in my bedroom that much. And even though I kept Hairy in there, she started having allergic reactions to *me*. As tiny as he was, his cat dander was powerful. It affected her because it was on my clothes. She kept thinking she was getting sick, but I knew it was allergies."

"I can tell you felt bad."

"I did!" June said. "I felt so bad. But I kind of figured, it's just mild. It's just a bit of a stuffy nose and a light cough. And the payoff was so, so great. Anyway, one day when I wasn't home, she went into my bedroom to look for something. And there was Hairy, comfortable as a king in the nest I'd made for him out of the decorative pillows on my bed."

"No," Sterling said.

June loved how invested he was in her story. "I'm afraid so. And that was the last day I had Hairy. Or any cat. When I got home from school, my mom made me put him in a cardboard box and we took him back to Mindy's house."

Years had passed, but the memory of handing Hairy to Mindy, his purr vibrating against her palms, broke her heart all over again.

"Geez," Sterling said, twirling his wine glass. "I was anticipating a stupid-funny story, but that was just sad!"

June laughed. "Sorry. It *was* sad. And that's why it was so stupid. There was no other potential outcome, really. I should have known better. I never should have taken that cat or gotten attached to him."

Sterling signaled for two more glasses of wine and the bartender poured them. "I think we need to wash that one down with a funnier story from the early days of June Cartwright."

"Hmm," June said. "A funnier story ... how about the time I read the recipe wrong when I made cookies for my first boyfriend and swapped the sugar and salt amounts."

By the time she'd finished, describing how her sweet boyfriend ate an entire cookie with a brave face, raving about delicious it was—before she had one and realized her mistake—the two of them hooted with laughter. "Okay, that was a much better story."

June wiped tears from under her eyes. The bartender came over to tell them the bar was closing.

"Is it two a.m. already?" Sterling sounded incredulous.

June checked her watch. "It is. Time flies, I guess. I mean, I think my suitcase's official time of death was at six p.m. or so, which means we've been having the time of our lives for eight hours, give or take."

"That long? Feels like mere minutes."

They sat there in their barstools, looking into each other's eyes as staff members turned off the lamps one at a time.

"Speaking of my suitcase," June said, "I still have to repack. I hate to say this, but maybe we should go back to the hotel and get some sleep. Didn't Tammi say we should get back to the airport by six a.m.?"

"She did," Sterling said. "That Tammi. I'm going to give her a piece of my mind when we see her."

His use of the word "we" sent yet another thrill through her body ... and then a wave of sorrow. They were "we" for now, but by the next morning, they'd go their separate ways.

"Chin up, June. We've still got four hours."

Apparently filled with a renewed sense of excitement, Sterling hopped off his stool and offered June his arm. They walked out of Keys and into the summer night.

"Tell you what," he said. "Let's go back to the hotel, go to bed, and then tomorrow morning, we'll wake up and go to the airport together. After we buy tickets, we can have breakfast."

June squeezed his arm. "Great idea."

She knew the Hotel Cartwright's only on-duty front desk attendant would be in the office unless he saw a new guest come in, and was grateful when they walked into the lobby and made it to the elevators without seeing anyone else.

"Our rooms are on the tenth floor," he said.

The tenth floor? That's where all the suites were—the fanciest rooms in Hotel Cartwright. Sterling must have money. He must be *loaded*. Interesting, though, how he didn't let on that he'd gotten them suites until now.

He pushed the button. "I picked up the keys when I dropped off your suitcase, which, by the way, should be waiting in your room." Pulling his wallet from his pocket, he slid out a couple of keycards and handed them to her. June knew the elevator's speed as if she'd ridden it every day for the past twenty-six years, and she knew they were already approaching the tenth floor. Sure enough, the elevator stopped and gave them a friendly ding before the doors slid open.

"You're in room six and I'm in eight." They stepped into the hall. "We're next door neighbors."

Six and eight? What did this man do for a living? He must have the bank account of a gambler or mobster or a guy with a very high credit card limit. They turned right, heading for their rooms. June's legs felt like they were moving through molasses ... heavy and sluggish. Not because it was after two a.m., but because she didn't want the evening to end.

"Here we are." June detected a heaviness to his tone that matched the one in her body.

He'd stopped in front of her door. "I can't tell you how much I want you to invite me in," he said. She opened her mouth to reply, but he shook his head. "But don't. You're special, June. All night, all I've been able to think about is how, if I ever planned on settling down, you'd be exactly the kind of woman I'd settle down with. You're clever and fun and a great conversationalist, and so goddamn beautiful."

Her throat tight, she tried to smile. "But?"

"But you deserve more than me, June. You deserve everything. You deserve someone who can give you that."

She wanted to ask him why he couldn't give her everything, but the truth was, they barely knew each other. Right now, in this moment, it seemed impossible that he wouldn't be enough. But thinking logically, after one night together, she simply couldn't know if he was The One.

Still, she didn't want to think logically. Not after this perfect night. She wanted to think with her heart, act with her heart. So she took Sterling's face in her hands and brought her mouth to his.

Their lips touching ignited a fresh round of longing in her body, which manifested as a pleasant heat between her legs. He must have felt it, too. He growled, low and deep and unbearably sexy, and backed her up against the wall next to the door.

June's mind flashed on images of the screens in the security room—cameras in every hallway monitored activity and sent imagery to one of about a dozen screens. Whichever security guard was on duty tonight, he'd undoubtedly recognize her.

For once in her life, she didn't care.

She moved her hands into Sterling's hair, and he tightened his grip on her waist.

Chapter Six

How many times had Levi Wilder said to Sterling, "Sometimes life just ain't fair, son"? Sterling couldn't count, but parting ways with June that morning had felt beyond unfair. He had an actual lump in his throat, for God's sake.

While he waited in line to board his flight to Phoenix, his mind wandered back to that morning waking up next to June—the only thing that made getting just three hours of sleep even somewhat bearable. They caught the hotel shuttle back to the airport, where Tammi was not working the Western Airlines ticket counter.

There was one first-class seat available on the first flight out, and Sterling insisted June take it, even though they could have flown together two hours later. He watched her war with herself over whether to postpone her mini-vacation for a little more time with him. Knowing he would bring her nothing but pain, he told the ticket agent she'd take the first flight and slid his credit card across the counter. He couldn't stop thinking about her. The exact feel of her skin under his palm, the precise color of her eyes in the careful lighting at the piano bar, the musical sound of her laughter as she talked about Hairy the kitten. He scrubbed a hand over his face, sighed.

"Early morning, right?" The guy next to him in line sported a scruff of whiskers and dark circles under his eyes.

Desperate for the distraction, Sterling smiled. "Yeah. And a late night. At least I'm bound to sleep on the plane."

Sure enough, as soon as he sat down and buckled his seatbelt, he crossed his arms, tilted his head back, and went to sleep. He woke briefly when the engines roared and the wind rushed over the wings during takeoff, but went straight back to dreamland when they were airborne and didn't emerge again until they touched down in Phoenix.

Upon waking, dread filled his veins, cold and sludgy. He was almost glad to see that the weather *looked* hot. The sky was a dingy blue and Sterling imagined the dirt and grease from the tarmac had evaporated and hung in the air. Sweat stained the shirts of the baggage handlers and ramp agents. Sterling closed his eyes again.

He didn't want to meet with his brothers. If they knew that he'd known, all along, about their dad and his shenanigans, he'd be cast out. Taking a deep breath, he reminded himself that he had to do the family meeting, and the best way to eat an elephant was one bite at a time.

To start, he would get off the plane. Then, he'd rent a car and drive up the mountain to Prescott. The pilot came over the loudspeaker and announced the temperature outside was one hundred and fifteen degrees. Several people on board groaned and a few whistled. Sterling resolved to get out of there as quickly as he could.

Still, when everyone finally disembarked, he spent some time looking around the terminal. June left Great Falls two hours before he did, which meant she'd likely already come and gone. But he couldn't let himself leave without being sure. He made it all the way to the rental car counter without seeing her and disappointment made his shoulders slump even though he knew it was childish.

Treating himself to the fastest car they had in stock, he zipped up the interstate, making the drive in an hour and a half instead of two. A rush of emotions, all jumbled up, hit him as he drove into town. Nostalgia, grief, joy. Driving past the old, stately courthouse and the surrounding plaza, Sterling remembered many summer

Sundays spent on the lawn with a frisbee. Somehow frisbee always ended up devolving into roughhousing, and someone usually ended up with a bloody nose or a split lip. That was before he uncovered his dad's secret, before his mom left, before everything went bad.

Just outside of town, he looked up to the giant sledding hill he and his brothers went to every time it snowed. He remembered the snowball fights and snow fort building, the laughter and sometimes the fighting. He knew that now, in summertime, a healthy creek bubbled along at the bottom of that mountain. If he wanted to, he could catch a couple of crawdads, although Hayes and Cash had been more into that than he had. Sterling always said crawfish required too much work for too little meat, something his brothers never stopped ribbing him about.

Beyond town, the houses thinned out. He could feel the pull of home despite the past five years and all the time he'd spent thinking he didn't care if he ever saw the place again. It didn't look like much from the road. In fact, even the little sign announcing the entrance to *Sweet Springs Ranch, Established in 1924*, had seen better days. It canted to one side and the paint on the motto, *Life is sweet here*, had chipped away so the words blended in with the sign's background.

Sterling turned off the main road. The shade trees lining the driveway were thicker than ever. He could feel the temperature difference as soon as he drove under the canopy, and he emerged on the other side where the property opened up before him. Off to his left, the big arena stood empty as it had for a while. Years had passed since Sweet Springs hosted any events. The main barn stood behind that. Sterling figured it was empty too, although he didn't know for sure.

The driveway curved around behind the barn, giving Sterling a close-up of the building. It didn't look like it was going to fall over any minute, but he'd give it a month. Two, tops. After another several seconds, the main house—which the Wilder family referred to as the big house—came into view. Whenever Sterling had pictured the place over the past five years, he'd imagined it as it was in its heyday. Bright white. The pillars on the front porch scrubbed to shining. The windows sparkling. As he approached though, he quickly realized that heyday was a thing of the past.

One of the four pillars had broken at the top and leaned to the right. Sterling had no idea how it hadn't fallen. The steps leading up to the front door were missing a few bricks, and those had tumbled down to the ground where they lay, half-crumbled. The flower baskets still hung above the porch rail, but instead of bright blooms cascading down, Sterling saw only dry, brittle leaves and petals. His throat tightened. How had the place come to this? He had a few ideas, but that didn't make seeing his childhood home in disrepair any easier.

With a start, Sterling realized he was so caught up in being back —being home—that he'd forgotten the details of his meeting with his brothers. He put the car in park, grabbed his phone, and scrolled through their group text.

Hayes: *Meet at the big house at 3 p.m.*

Everyone had responded with thumbs-up emojis ... except Sterling.

He swore. It was only two and his eyes felt grittier with each passing minute. He debated how to best pass the hour he had to kill, and although his stomach growled with hunger—he blamed his obsession with June for making him forget to eat all day—he decided the best course of action was to explore the ranch. That would keep him awake and plus, if the disrepair was widespread, he'd rather see it while he was alone than when he was surrounded by his brothers.

He got out of the car and stretched. Despite his nap on the plane, his body felt achy from exhaustion. The sound of his car door shutting was loud on the silent property. The big house might look different, but so much was the same, too. Sterling could smell the sweet honeysuckle, and was relieved to see the vine had survived in its spot on the trellis at the end of the house. He made his way around to the side, where the old tire swing still hung from the oak tree. The rope looked rotten and Sterling made a mental note to cut down the tire before anyone tried to use it.

A bird trilled from the branch of the sycamore tree. It was the same call he'd heard every summer of his childhood. Just below the tree, he saw the carcass of one of his mom's old bird feeders—she hung them there so she could see them through the kitchen window. The whole scene conjured up memories of relaxing on the back porch after chores.

One summer, Hayes had gotten the idea to make homemade lemonade, and after they'd all tried it the first time, they begged him to make it every summer day. Sterling could still taste it—the tartness of the lemon, the sweetness of the sugar as the granules ran across his tongue.

Back then, they kept the weeds trimmed and the yard tidy. Now, plants grew waist-high, devouring the walkway as if it had never been there. Sterling waded through them to get a closer look at the porch, where he found sagging boards and a broken swing. After seeing the big house, he wasn't sure he wanted to see the rest of the place, but he forced himself to follow the curve of the road to the other buildings.

The small family barn was only in half as bad a shape as the big barn. It could use a fresh coat of paint, but it looked structurally sound. The neighing he heard from inside surprised him as much as he had apparently surprised the horse. The sliding door opened easily, and Sterling was relieved to find the barn stocked with hay and alfalfa just like it had been when he lived here. On autopilot, he went through the mental checklist: the water bowl was full and the bubbles rising on one side showed him the watering system was in good order. The tack hung neatly on the south wall. The stalls were clean. Someone had mucked them that morning or maybe the night before. Fly traps hung on the outside corners of the space. Everything was as it should be.

The horses approached the center aisle, their ears pricked and their eyes bright with curiosity. Sterling closed the distance and said hello, then talked about the weather to let them get used to his voice before he reached out so they could sniff his palm. These must be Travis's horses. He was the one who'd stuck around.

Regret was like a knife to Sterling's gut. He didn't even know the names of his brother's horses, or whether they liked carrots or apples or those molasses treats. The horses didn't seem to mind.

They leaned into his neck scratches as if they'd known him for years. Although he could have stayed in the barn for the rest of the afternoon, Sterling figured he'd better complete his tour. On the main road again, he noticed with some relief that here, too, things remained the same. The old cottonwood trees still lined up as sentries and their branches still swayed in the gentle summer breeze. The cicadas still sang, their screeching song a comfort. The next house he came to—he assumed it was Travis's now—was in great shape. So all was not lost.

A little lawn lay like a welcome mat in front. Tall, colorful flowers made a border around the grass. Unlike the other buildings he'd seen so far, this one did have a fresh coat of paint, light yellow with white trim.

As he continued his once-over, the front door opened and his brother stepped out. "Hey, stranger."

If Sterling had to choose which one of his brothers to see first, it would be Travis. He felt himself smiling, a wide-open smile he hadn't felt in ages. An unfamiliar energy, a buzzing, swirled around his body and he recognized it—barely—as joy. He quickly tempered it though, so he wouldn't be blindsided if Travis and the others called Sterling out for keeping his giant secret.

"Hey, man." He bounded up the front steps and wrapped Travis in a bear hug.

"Good to see you." Travis patted his back a little too hard. His baby brother stepped back, holding him at arms' length. "You look good. Tired, but good. Want to come in?" He hooked a thumb toward the house.

Sterling shrugged, his hands tingling as his fight-or-flight response calmed down. He seemed to be in the clear. "Sure."

The house was as immaculate as the yard. The surfaces were tidy, the floor was clean, and the sink was empty.

"Nice place," Sterling said.

Travis, on his way to the kitchen, stopped and turned around to grin at Sterling. "You've seen it before, haven't you?"

"Yeah," Sterling said. "But not since you moved into it. And compared to the rest of the property, it's a sight for sore eyes."

"Want a beer?"

Sterling checked his watch. "Our meeting starts in fifteen minutes. You think Hayes or Cash will judge me for showing up with a beer?"

Travis made a dismissive gesture. "Screw 'em if they do."

Travis took out two bottles and removed their caps. He handed one to Sterling and they clinked the necks together.

"To family reunions?" his expression, eyebrows raised, smile so wide it was a grimace, made Sterling laugh. "To family reunions."

They drank, and the cold beer felt exceptionally good going down.

"How was your trip?" Travis wanted to know.

Sterling shrugged. "It was okay. I tried to get a flight last night but everything was full."

"Where were you coming from this time?"

Was there an edge to his brother's voice? Sterling studied Travis's face and decided there wasn't. Just making conversation. "Great Falls, Montana."

"Yeah?" Travis said. "How is it? I've always wanted to check it out."

"One of the nicer places I've been."

"What are you working on?"

Sterling told him about the old house, and how he was remodeling it for modern family living. Travis listened intently, his eyes on Sterling's. Sterling found himself leaning into the conversation, adding details like he hadn't in years. The fifteen minutes passed quickly and the conversation ended only when an alarm went off on Travis's phone. "That's our cue. The meeting's about to start. Should we had over?"

As they walked out, Travis shutting the door without locking it, a memory of Sterling's only encounter with coyotes came to mind. As a little kid, he'd found their nighttime howls and yipping nerve-racking. The fact that he never actually saw them made their calls even more eerie. One night he was riding his horse, Trusty, along the tree line at dusk. Trusty froze, his entire body going still, except for his ears, which turned this way and that, and his nose. His nostrils flared as his ears twitched.

"What do you see, buddy?" Sterling asked him.

That's when he spotted them. A whole pack of coyotes, just a few yards to the east. They sensed Sterling and Trusty—he knew because they also stood statue-still, staring. Then they started pacing, trotting this way and that, eyes on Sterling and Trusty. Would coyotes attack a horse? Sterling didn't know, and he didn't want to wait around to find out. He didn't want to turn his back on them either, so he put the horse in reverse, having him back up so he could keep an eye on the coyotes. They had the same idea: their gazes followed Sterling and Trusty's every move, even as they kept pacing.

Once he figured they'd given the pack enough distance, Sterling swung Trusty around and kicked him into a gallop. After a few seconds punctuated by the sound of his heartbeat in his ears and the sound of Trusty's hooves punching the ground, Sterling risked a look back. The coyotes were gone. Disappeared. Just like that.

Present-day Sterling, on his way to meet with his brothers, felt the same way he imagined the coyotes felt all those years ago. On edge. Nervous. Too energized to be still. Not for the first time, he lamented the fact that all his brothers knew what this meeting was about and he didn't.

He wondered if Travis could sense that feeling, because he said, "You ready for this?"

Sterling winked at him. "Of course I'm ready."

Two trucks were parked outside the big house by the time Sterling and Travis walked over. If Levi had imparted any wisdom other than the fact that life is unfair, it was that a person should always be on time. Punctuality was one of his main tenets.

"I guess we're meeting inside," Travis said.

"Think it's safe to walk across the front porch?" Sterling wanted to know.

"I'm inclined to say it's not," Travis said. "But Hayes seems to think it is."

"And if Hayes says it is, then it must be so," the two of them chorused.

They were still laughing when they came around the front of the house. Sterling was still smiling as he walked gingerly across the rotting boards. But his smile faded when he made it to the open doorway. The place was a mess. Sterling stopped just inside the front door to take it all in. They always called it the big house, but it wasn't actually big. At the moment, as messy as it was, it looked downright small. Levi had lived alone for the past five years, with no one to clean up after him (or nag him to clean up after himself). Piles of clothes covered the back of the couch. Dishes overflowed from the sink and took up every available square centimeter of counter space. A stack of dirty plates even sat on the TV tray next to Levi's recliner. The kitchen trash was so full, the lid stood open. Several full bags, tied shut, surrounded the trashcan.

"You look a bit shellshocked, my man," said Cash, striding toward Sterling from somewhere in the back of the house. He reached out a hand to shake, and Sterling took it. The welcome was warmer than he anticipated. Which was good, but also meant he'd have to spill the beans at some point. Nerves and nausea returned.

"Understatement of the year. The decade, even."

A hoot of laughter came from behind him and Travis was at his side, patting him on the back again. "I couldn't decide whether to warn you."

Sterling shook his head. Then Hayes was there at Sterling's other side, punching him in the arm. "Place is a shithole, right?"

"Maybe *that's* the understatement of the year," Sterling said.

"I'd say we should sit at the kitchen table," Cash said, "but I'm pretty sure we'd be taking the rats' spots."

"Smells like shit in here anyway," Sterling said. "Why don't we go outside?"

"Good thinking," Hayes said. "I'll grab us some beers. You know that as bad as this—" he circled his forefinger in front of his body in a rapid, comical motion — "gets, our old man kept the fridge stocked."

Within minutes, the four of them had settled into the back of Hayes's pickup truck, a six-pack of beer center stage. There was no toast this time, just four men guzzling beer, softening the sharp edges of what their father left behind.

Sterling downed half his bottle. "So, is that what this meeting is about, then? You wanted to show me the place?"

"We wanted to play rock, paper, scissors to determine who has to clean it up." Travis smiled, but his eyes glittered. Sterling shook his head, rolled his eyes.

"Nah, man." Hayes's mouth was a thin, straight line. "The meeting is a little more serious."

"More serious than that?" Sterling jerked his head toward the house.

"Afraid so."

"Turns out," Cash said, "Dad was behind on mortgage payments. If we don't come up with what he owes in the next thirty days, it's going to foreclosure."

Sterling ignored the stab of panicky pain at his center and said, "Who cares? Have you seen the place? Let it."

He saw the hurt flash in Travis's eyes and immediately regretted his words. He guzzled some more beer and reached across the bed of the truck to give Travis a gentle punch on the leg. "I'm sorry, man. I can tell from your house that the place means something to you. We'll get this figured out. How much does he owe? I can put in some money."

His brothers looked at each other as if they'd not only expected him to make this offer, but also talked about it. Not for the first time, Sterling felt like the odd man out. "What? What are you guys thinking?"

Travis cleared his throat. "We don't want your money, man."

"Why not? I could fix this foreclosure problem." He snapped his fingers. "Just like that."

Cash shook his head. "Look. You already resent Dad enough as it is. If you have to put up your own money to fix his mistake, you're going to resent him even more."

"And," Hayes said, "you might resent us, too. We don't all have the cash you do, moneybags. This is something we all need to do together. With that in mind, Callie came up with an idea."

Although his knee-jerk reaction was to deny he resented their dad and that he could ever resent the three of them, Sterling considered. If he put up all the money to save the property and down the road, they fell behind on payments again, maybe he *would* resent them.

His other knee-jerk reaction was to remind his brothers Callie wasn't family. But she was. In addition to being Hayes's fiancée, Callie was also their childhood friend. They'd all grown up together and for all intents and purposes, she *was* family. And anyway, she was smart as a whip. If she had an idea, it might be worth listening to.

Chapter Seven

June heard someone holler her name as soon as she stepped out of the baggage claim area and onto the curb in arrivals, her new suitcase rolling smoothly behind her. She turned toward the voice and saw Callie standing outside the drivers door of a cherry red Corvette, waving her arms above her head, her smile practically glowing in the dim lighting. Involuntarily, June broke into a run and before she knew it, she was caught up in Callie's arms, the citrusy scent of her perfume a cloud of home sweet home.

"Look at you," Callie said. "The heiress of Cartwright Hospitality, fancy suitcase and all."

A fierce heat blossomed on June's cheeks and she was grateful they were on the airport's below-ground level, where almost zero natural light filtered down.

Always one for action, Callie grabbed June's suitcase and started rolling it toward the back of her car, only to stop and put a finger on her chin when she got there. "I'm not sure this thing is going to fit in the trunk. We might have to team lift and put it in the backseat. Geez, you said you were only coming for the weekend. Seems like you packed for a year or something."

June wondered if her strangled laugh conveyed the complicated range of emotions she felt over that damn suitcase.

Once they wrestled the behemoth into the backseat and hit the road, Callie grabbed June's hand. "Listen. I know you're only here for the weekend. But something's come up and I need to take care of some business while we're in Prescott. I'm so sorry. I can't get out of it. Want to come along, or do your own thing?"

"Are you kidding? Mountain breezes, the pine trees swaying, and time with my college bestie? Of course I want to come along."

"I was hoping you'd say that. Not only because I want to spend time with you, but also because the thing that came up? I might need your help. I'm going to take you to lunch and tell you all about it."

Butterflies fluttered in June's stomach as she wondered what Callie could possibly need help with. Her friend was a brilliant family attorney and the epitome of self sufficient.

"First things first. We're getting out of this Phoenix traffic. Can you wait to eat for forty minutes?"

"Sure," June said. "I'm more sleep deprived than anything."

"What'd you do last night after you couldn't get a flight out?"

"Oh, you know. This and that."

Callie turned her head just long enough to give June a look. "I *don't* know, actually. What are you not telling me?"

June laughed. Callie had always been able to see right through her. "What I didn't tell you yesterday was that as soon as I decided I'd come to Phoenix, everything went wrong."

She filled Callie in on her flat tire and broken suitcase. Callie grimaced and winced at appropriate intervals in the story, and when June got to the part about a rugged, handsome, swoon-worthy man in designer jeans swooping in to save the day, Callie pressed a hand to her heart. "A real-life hero! Please tell me you got his number."

June shook her head. "We agreed not to exchange numbers. He said he never stays in one place too long and isn't looking to settle down. I'll probably never see him again. But I haven't even told you the best part."

By the time June was done telling the story, Callie was practically swooning right there in the driver seat. "I cannot believe you didn't get his contact info. June Cartwright, I'm very disappointed in you."

"I know you're joking, but I'm disappointed, too. For real. Like I said, he's not looking to settle down and he moves around a lot. Which obviously I can't do because I will be under the thumb of the Hotel Cartwright for the rest of my life."

Callie pulled into a parking spot in front of a diner where a sign boasted the best pie in the world. She put the car in park. "I don't know, June. You just left the hotel in the middle of a client meeting, after firing said client. And you haven't even told your parents yet. If you can do that, I think you're on your way to being able to do anything."

Ah, there it was. Guilt, which had hidden behind the curtain for the past twenty-four hours, poked its head out and gave June a little wave.

"Oh, no!" Callie grabbed her arm. "I didn't mean to make you feel guilty. It's written all over your face. You deserve this, June. You shouldn't have to put up with all these crazy clients. I mean, maybe this is just the impetus you needed, the kick in the pants to get you to finally tell your parents you'd like to work elsewhere. Have more freedom. Let your brilliance shine."

June's stomach roiled. "Let's go eat. Before I lose my appetite altogether."

When they came around the hood of the car, Callie slid her arm around June's waist and put her head on her shoulder. "Don't worry, June. Your parents don't have to know you left for the weekend. But I do think this would be an excellent time to tell them how you feel."

Blinking back tears, June told herself it was lack of sleep making her emotional, not the roller coaster of emotions she'd experienced since the day before.

The scent of fresh-baked pie greeted them when they walked in and June suddenly felt very hungry. Her mouth actually watered.

Once they sat down and ordered, Callie fixed her laser-bright gaze on June. "So. The thing that came up this weekend is a meeting at Sweet Springs Ranch."

"Aww," June said. "Isn't that Hayes's ranch?"

Callie's whole bearing went soft around the edges at June's mention of her fiancé. "It is."

"I can't wait to see it," June said.

"Well, don't get too excited." Callie held up a hand. "The thing is, it's kind of falling apart. And, worse, it's about to get foreclosed on. Apparently, the Wilder dad, Levi, had stopped paying the mortgage a while back. He died recently, and the boys—Hayes and his brothers—found out they have thirty days to come up with the money or they'll lose the ranch."

"Oh, no! But isn't that their childhood home?" June asked, her emotions still close to the surface and putting her on the verge of tears.

"It is. And this is where you come in." She paused while their server set their food on the table. Ravenous now, June picked up her sandwich and took a big bite.

"I proposed to Hayes that they host a big fundraising event. The Prescott community always comes together for people, and I know it will do the same for the Sweet Springs Ranch."

Awareness dawning, June swallowed her bite and took a drink of her water. "And you want me to help with the event."

"I want the best event planner I know to help make it a smashing success, yes."

Smiling, June said, "And how do Hayes and his brothers feel about this?"

"That's the thing," Callie said. "Hayes thinks it's a good idea, but he wants me—us—to present it to his brothers today."

June felt her eyes go round. "To *present* it?! Like, with a slide show or something?"

Callie squirmed a little in her seat. A half-laugh escaped. "Well, no. It's nothing that formal. I first came up with the idea a couple of days ago, and when you called and asked if you could come out, it was like an *aha* moment. It's serendipity, isn't it? Fate? Right after I thought of having a fundraising event, you called. It's meant to be."

"I hope Hayes and his brothers feel that way. I happen to know men get a little prickly when it comes to asking for help. And you're proposing that they accept help, not just from you and me, but from the entire community. Are we walking into a war zone?"

Callie's laugh was high-pitched and maniacal. "I hope not, June. I sure hope not."

A couple of hours later in Prescott, they pulled off the main road where a sign indicated Sweet Springs Ranch was established in 1924.

"I'm in love already." June smiled across the console at Callie. "This is so cute."

She slipped into event-planner mode as they drove in. The place looked exactly like she'd imagine: old-growth trees lined the drive and the whole property was fields and rolling hills. They passed by an old barn and arena, and the surrounding area looked like a good place to set up a fundraising event. They could do a silent auction and maybe a dinner ... she wondered if she could find a local chef to donate services if the Wilder family could cover the cost of the food. Yes, the arena area had plenty of space for tables and chairs, and maybe a live band.

"You're seeing it, aren't you?" Callie said.

June nodded. "Yep. This could work."

"We just need buy-in," Callie said. "And now, we're going to get it."

June looked out the windshield to see a house with so many loose parts, it looked like it might actually fall down. "Oof. That house has seen better days."

"Yep," Callie said. "Sure has."

A sports car and a couple of giant pickup trucks sat in front of the house. Four men sat in the back of one of the trucks, and June whistled at the ones who faced Callie's car. "Wow. They sure make them good looking in Prescott."

"Sure do." Callie grinned and put the car in park as one of the men—June recognized him as Hayes even though she'd met him only a couple of times—raised a hand in greeting and swung his body over the side of the bed to come jogging toward them. Callie threw open her door and Hayes swept her into a hug that made June weak in the knees. And then he was coming around the car and before June knew it, he was pulling her out of her seat and hugging her, too.

As June shook hands with two more Wilder brothers, Cash and Travis, she saw the fourth brother stand up in the bed of the pickup truck. She was glad he faced away from her. She was positive her thought—*Boy, does he make those jeans look good*—was written in giant, bold script across her face. Awareness prickled at the edge of her consciousness. There was something familiar about those legs in those jeans. In fact, she was fairly confident she had burned that image into her mind just that morning.

But no. It couldn't be. By the time he finished his rotation, her gaze had traveled up his torso and when their eyes met, she realized he wore the same disbelieving expression she did. The scene around them seemed to stand still as they both realized they were, in fact, once again in the same space. She was vaguely aware of the others looking at Sterling and then at her and then back at Sterling, but most of her attention was on the smile that transformed his face and then on his body as he put one hand on the rail of the pickup bed and leapt nimbly down to the ground. June expected him to run up to her, hug her, something. But he seemed to suddenly remember they had an audience and stopped short, a foot in front of her. "June?"

Because the hope and despair in his eyes were too much, June laughed out loud, the sound strangled. "It's me." she said.

Callie spoke first. "Wait. That handsome hero from the airport. This is him, isn't it?"

Mute, June nodded.

"It was *Sterling*?" Callie said, and Hayes guffawed. "Handsome hero?"

Cash barked out a laugh. "Bro," he said to Sterling. "It was almost like you weren't sure if she was real."

Sterling blinked. Shook his head. "I wasn't."

Travis leaned over and in a stage whisper he said to Cash, "I think we have a situation here."

For his part, Sterling looked shellshocked. The sparse details he'd shared with her ran through her mind. He hadn't wanted to reach his destination which was obviously this family meeting. Had he known the family ranch was about to go to foreclosure? He hadn't hinted at it, but maybe that was one of the things he wanted to forget when he proposed they spend the evening together.

Despite the unfiltered joy she'd seen in his eyes just a second before—she *knew* she wasn't mistaken—June watched as something closed off inside him. The eyes she looked into now were quite different than the ones she'd looked into just that morning when they said goodbye.

"So you've met," Callie said. "Which means you probably already know June is a kick-ass event planner. I'm sure she didn't brag about how great she is, because she's humble like that, but she's seriously the best. I'm sure the guys mentioned we were thinking we could have a fundraising event."

Sterling's eyes, now steely, slid over to Travis. "No, they hadn't gotten there just yet. They were waiting for you."

"Oh." Callie's eyes darted to Hayes, who didn't quite smile, but gave her a little nod. Callie cleared her throat and licked her lips. "Well. I had the idea that we could hold a community fundraiser, just to raise the money we need to keep Sweet Springs from going to foreclosure. And when June called to ask if she could come for a visit, I knew it was serendipity. Who better to help us plan a successful fundraiser than someone who plans events for a living?"

June hadn't taken her eyes off of Sterling the whole time Callie talked. His expression hadn't changed, but his eyes had gotten increasingly more distant.

"I don't think it's a good idea," Sterling said, his eyes on some faraway point.

How could this possibly be the same guy with whom June had spent twelve of the best hours of her life? *Unbelievable.*

Hayes came to stand next to Callie. If June wasn't mistaken, there was actual laughter in his eyes. "I'm sorry, bro, but I have a feeling you're going to be outvoted on this. All in favor of Callie's great idea, with the silver lining that her college best friend here also happens to be an event planner extraordinaire?"

All three of Sterling's brothers raised their hands, and all three of them flashed movie-star grins. As one, they said, "Aye."

Chapter Eight

Sterling felt like he'd been punched in the gut. For a few hours the day before, June had been his respite. His escape. His time with her had allowed him to forget (almost completely) about the meeting with his brothers and everything that had transpired in the past five years.

He'd kicked himself about a million times for not getting her number, for wanting to keep that time with her sacred. Every time he kicked himself, he wished he could see her again, told himself he'd do things differently, that maybe they could build something together, despite his flaws, despite his past.

But not like this. The absolute last thing he wanted was for June to be tangled up in the mess that was his family. He looked around at the little circle the group had formed. Each and every one of his brothers looked smug, their "aye" votes echoing in the air.

For her part, June looked as shocked as he felt. She also looked hurt. He'd watched her expression show the exact emotions he'd experienced: disbelief, hope, joy, confusion. And now he saw pain. Which he had caused.

"Guess I'm outvoted."

Then he did the absolute worst thing he could do. He stalked over to his rental car and got in. Just barely suppressing the urge to spin the tires and throw gravel, he drove around the big house, past the main barn and arena, and down the driveway. He had no idea where he was going. He only knew that he had to get away from Sweet Springs, from his brothers, and from the woman he wished he could change for.

He found himself at A Cold One, the bar where he'd spent many a long night with his friends—and his brothers—throwing back beers, dancing with girls, and playing pool and darts. He pushed open the old-fashioned saloon doors. A Cold One was always cool and dark, and he appreciated that about it.

A voice from way in the back said, "Do my eyes deceive me, or is that Sterling Wilder, returned from the dead?"

Despite all the feelings swirling around inside his body, the corners of Sterling's mouth tugged upward. Here, too, he received a warmer welcome than he expected. "Your eyes do not deceive you," he said. He broke into a jog to reach the bar and held out a hand to the place's owner, Jerry. "Good to see you, man."

"Tell me what I can get you, and then tell me how the hell you've been. When's the last time you came around?"

More at home here than at his actual home, Sterling felt the tension slip out of his body as he slid onto a barstool. "I'll take a Budweiser. For old times' sake."

Jerry grunted and pulled a beer glass out of the freezer under the bar. He stepped to his right to fill it from the tap. "Start talking."

Sterling nodded and pulled the beer toward him when Jerry set it on the counter. "It has been a long time, hasn't it? I'm sure you've heard I started a restoration company. I restore old buildings. Houses, hotels, restaurants, that sort of thing."

Jerry set to work slicing limes on a small cutting board. "I hear you travel all over the country. People ask for you. Pay big bucks to bring you in."

"Yeah?" Sterling wondered who had told him that.

"Your daddy was real proud of you."

Sterling doubted that, but was too polite to say so. "Keeps me pretty busy. But my brothers called a meeting, so I had to come back."

Empathy shone in Jerry's eyes as he paused his task and looked at Sterling. "I hear the place might go to foreclosure."

"News travels fast." Sterling took one long drink of his beer.

"Anything I can do?"

Even as his mouth formed a hard line, Sterling nodded. "Maybe. Apparently, my brothers, cream puffs that they are, are planning some kind of fundraising event. Callie Barrett—you remember her."

"Big-time attorney these days. Your future sister-in-law."

"Right. Well, she's our official cheerleader, apparently. Kind of a Pollyanna, if you ask me." Sterling hated himself for mocking someone who'd been a friend, damn near family, all these years. But he also didn't want to look like an idiot in front of Jerry. "She seems to think that if we can get the whole community to come together, we can save the ranch."

Fortunately, Jerry's eyes held humor, not the disbelief or anger Sterling felt like he deserved for abandoning his family, his home, and his community. "It's not a bad idea."

Sterling shook his head. "I know. It's just—it's humiliating. After what my dad did. Asking people to share their hard-earned money with us. And not only that, but inviting people out to the place. Have you seen it?"

Jerry's gaze was steady on his. "I've seen it. But remember, you're not asking for money for your dad. You're asking for help—for you boys. Your dad might be a damn fool, but that's not your fault."

Quite unexpectedly, Sterling felt the sting of tears. Jerry might feel that way, but he was probably in the minority. He'd been a friend of the Wilder family forever. He could forgive the Wilder boys for their father's sins. But forgiveness might not come so easily to everyone else.

"I'm not saying it's the only way, son," Jerry said. "But it might be best way, right now. I know you resent what your dad did, and I can't say I blame you. But do you really want to lose the place over it?" He set the lime slices in a square container and wiped down the counter. "It's been in your family for a century."

Sterling gulped down half of what was left in his bottle. "No. I mean, I could let it go, but I don't know if the others could."

The light changed behind him; he knew those saloon doors were opening by the way the shaft of light widened and then narrowed again.

Jerry lifted an arm in greeting. "Whole crew's here."

Sterling suppressed a groan as his brothers descended on the bar like a murder of ravens, and when he asked for another beer, they all ordered "whatever he's having" before practically carrying him to a booth in the corner.

"So," Hayes said, as if this were just a continuation of their earlier conversation and Sterling hadn't just walked out on all of them. "We have two weeks. Two weeks to put together a fundraiser that brings in a shit ton of money."

"Has anyone considered hiring strippers?" Travis asked, and Cash punched him in the arm.

"What?" he said. "Don't you think that would bring in a decent amount of money? We could have it here. I'll bet Jerry wouldn't mind. Would you, Jerry?"

Jerry didn't answer—he couldn't possibly have heard what Travis said.

"Be serious," Hayes said, and Travis giggled.

"We could have a casino night," Cash supplied, and Hayes punched him in the arm. "Too soon, man. Too soon."

"Sorry."

"I wish the arena was in better shape," Hayes said. "We could have a rodeo. Remember how much fun those used to be?"

Just like that, Hayes's words transported Sterling back in time to the days when Sweet Springs Ranch hosted the best rodeo events in town. Cowboys and cowgirls came from all over the country to compete and the place was packed with trailers and RVs and livestock. Vendors came to sell food, and you could smell the meat cooking all day long as the music played and the horses' hooves kicked up dirt.

"Those were the days," Sterling said, the nostalgia softening him a bit. "But you're right. The arena's in no shape for an event."

He looked at Travis and realized he was glaring when Travis

held up his hands. "I'm sorry I didn't keep up with it. Taking care of dad basically used up all my resources."

"It's not your fault," Sterling said. "If he'd been paying the mortgage, we wouldn't be here."

"I should have known he wasn't."

"This conversation's getting a bit heavy," Cash said. "I'm sorry for punching you when you brought up the stripper idea. Can we get back to that?"

Just like that—and just like old times—Sterling's brothers had smoothed things over. Not *everything*, but the awkwardness of their meeting, anyway.

"What's up with this June girl?" Hayes wanted to know, and all the awkwardness came whistling back through the air like a torpedo missile.

All three of Sterling's brothers stared at him, expectant.

"What do you mean?"

"I think you know," Travis said. "Handsome hero, wasn't it?"

"You had to use the air quotes," Sterling said. "I'm handsome, aren't I? If not, then neither are the three of you assholes."

This got them laughing, but not distracted.

"Tell us about your heroics at the airport, man," Hayes said.

"Nah," Sterling said. The more they knew, the more they'd believe he and June could have a future. They should know he couldn't have a future with anyone.

"The less you talk, the more we want to know," Cash said.

"And the more we want to know, the longer we'll wait," Travis said.

"And the longer we wait, the more we'll drink," Hayes said. Looking toward the bar, he lifted an arm, then held up four fingers.

"The more we drink, the more you'll want to talk," Cash said.

"And the more you want to talk, the less resistance you'll have," Travis said.

"And little by little, you'll tell us everything, anyway," Hayes said.

Cash and Travis nodded, eyebrows raised with mock wisdom.

"So you might as well save us all the drinkin' and start talkin'," Cash said.

Jerry came to the table, four bottles on a tray. "This round's on the house. It's good to see you four together again."

It was good to *be* together again (better than Sterling expected, actually) but that didn't mean he had to spill his guts, did it? They should talk about how they'd barely spoken since Sterling left town, or how he'd been the one to uncover their father's misdeeds and create a huge family rift.

But he didn't want to talk about any of that, either. "Let's talk about this fundraiser."

Ultra-casual, his beer dangling from his loose grip, Cash said, "Well, if there's nothing to talk about regarding June, I think I'm gonna move on that."

Anger flashed, hot, in Sterling's veins. He ground his molars together, and Travis pointed at him across the table. "See, man? You got all pissed off, like, real fast. There *is* something to talk about."

"I did not get pissed off." Teeth still tight together, he picked up his beer and took a drink.

"And I didn't ditch Jenny Wasco to take Sherrilyn Bruner to the prom junior year because I thought I had a better chance of getting to third base." Cash grinned.

"Are you serious?" Travis said. "You're a dick, man."

"Hey," Cash said. "That was a decade ago. You can't hold it against me."

"That's what Sherrilyn said, right?" Hayes said. "You might have had better luck with Jenny, seeing as how she gave it up to me that night."

Cash punched Hayes, and Sterling hoped he'd escaped talking about June. Until Cash circled back around. "So. You acted like the fundraiser idea was okay. Then you saw June and bolted. We followed you here to find out why, and you said there's nothing to talk about. Only, when I talked about June, your jaw got all tight and your face got all red and you tried to change the subject."

Travis held up his pointer finger. "Unsuccessfully, I might add."

"I think we should take a swig of beer every thirty seconds until he spills." Hayes took his phone out of his shirt pocket and turned it over on the table. "I'm setting a stopwatch. And, go."

All four of them watched the phone screen like it was counting down to an explosion. It reached thirty seconds and Hayes, Cash, and Travis drank. Sterling watched them, hoping they were properly reading his expression, which said, *You guys are idiots.*

Silence while another thirty seconds passed, and then Hayes said, "Drink up, fellas."

The three of them were going to be dead-ass drunk if he didn't start talking. Maybe he could fabricate something. Something so outlandish, they'd forget they were playing this silly drinking game. Maybe he could get up and leave. Go somewhere so far, they couldn't follow. Only, he had to stay ... had to help them save the ranch even if he was ninety percent certain he never wanted to see it again.

His brothers drank for a third time. He decided to join in. They all snickered before their attention returned to the phone screen.

"Drink," Hayes said.

They all drank. Sterling didn't know how long he could hang with them. He rarely drank anymore, and knew he'd be beating himself up the next day if he didn't slow down.

"Fine," he said, hearing the toddler-like pout in his own voice. "I'll tell you."

The three of them looked at one another, wearing triumphant expressions.

"Drink."

Sterling shook his head and drank again despite his knowledge he'd regret it. "I heroically saved June from her monstrosity of a suitcase in the Great Falls airport. Just so happened, we were both headed for Phoenix last-minute, and neither of us could get flights. So, I bought her a new suitcase, we spent the evening together at a hotel—"

"Wait. Stop right there." Cash held up a hand, which wobbled.

"Spent the night at a hotel?" Hayes said. "That's not really your style, is it? That's more like Cash, here."

"We didn't *spend the night,* spend the night," Sterling said, drinking again even though Hayes hadn't instructed them to. "We had dinner, went dancing at a piano bar—"

"Wait. Stop right there," Travis said, mimicking Cash's gesture.

"A piano bar?" Hayes repeated. "Drink."

As that gulp of beer went down Sterling's throat, a little shy of cold now, something occurred to him: June might not like him telling his brothers what transpired that night. Although, she must have said something to Callie, since Callie had called him the handsome hero from the airport.

"You guys aren't on empty yet?" Travis held his beer up to what little light there was so he could see how much he had left.

"Almost," Hayes tipped his bottle back, finished off the beer, and belched before signaling for another round.

"A piano bar," Sterling said. "We ended up going back to the hotel together, where we slept for three hours before heading back to the airport. There was one seat available on the first to Phoenix, so I let her have that. Because even if I'm a gentleman, I'm not a hero. I figured I'd never see her again."

Jerry set down four more beers and picked up the empties. "You guys might want to slow down a little bit. Your daddy's last name wasn't Wilder for nothing."

"Cheers, boys," Hayes said.

The borderline animosity between them forgotten—at least temporarily—they all clinked their bottles together and drank again.

"But here she is," Cash said, picking up right where they'd left off. "And your reaction to her tells us that you hoped you'd see her again."

"Drink," Hayes said. Then, "Let me guess: you told her you move around a lot, so it was nice knowing her."

"But," Travis said. "Judging by the way you looked at her when Callie brought her to the ranch, you were real torn up about it. And you couldn't believe your eyes, or your luck, when you saw her there."

"And you'd like to go to a hotel and *not* sleep with her," Cash had a wicked gleam in his eye that made Sterling want to punch him in the mouth right then and there. "But you already told her things could never work out."

The alcohol had hit Sterling's bloodstream full force, and he felt giddy all of a sudden.

"How right you are," he said to Cash. "That's the full truth. And you put it so succinctly, too. I'd love nothing better than to not sleep with June Cartwright the next chance I get. However. There will not be a next chance. As soon as she hears the full story, and sees the whole picture, she will want absolutely nothing to do with me—at least, not beyond this fundraising event."

Had he just blurted out all that?

He had.

He'd just spilled his guts, exactly like his brothers had wanted him to.

They'd goaded him into it, plied him with beer, and forced him to tell them what he was really thinking. The strange thing was, he felt a bit better for it. He could have heard a pin drop at the table. All three of his brothers blinked back at him.

"Our little Sterling has feelings," Hayes said, his words meant to be humorous, but his eyes conveying more empathy than Sterling had seen from him in ages.

"Yeah," Cash and Travis said.

"Drink," Hayes said.

"I mean, is it possible you might be wrong?" Travis winced as he spoke, making Cash giggle.

"No," Hayes and Cash said, making Sterling giggle. "Never."

"Is it possible she may be interested in you, too? And that she may overlook the family drama and the rundown property and the growly reception you gave her and actually want to not sleep with you, too?"

"I don't know," Sterling said. "But for now, I think the safest route is to keep things strictly professional so we can get this fundraiser done."

"You don't want to mix business and pleasure?" Travis said. He wiggled his eyebrows.

"I don't, no," Sterling said.

"Drink," Hayes said.

"I'm calling a vote," Cash said, and Sterling's spidey senses started to tingle. "All in favor of having Sterling take lead on this project?"

As if it it were the most brilliant idea they'd heard, Travis and Hayes's faces lit up. All three of those jerks chorused, "Aye."

Sterling's brothers were not going to take it easy on him.

Hayes said, "You know what? I'm going to propose we have a family dinner tomorrow. It's been way too long. I'm going to text Callie. We'll invite her and June."

Sterling swore, not nearly quietly enough.

"What?" Hayes, all innocence, grinned. "I assume you don't mind spending time with June."

Sterling wanted to punch *him* in the nose. He could still remember the satisfying crack of fist to face that time in high school when they both had dates and they fought over who got to use the car (he smiled as he remembered they'd ended up sharing it and turned the evening into a double date, which they both attended with bloody lips).

"I don't want to spend more time with her than I have to."

But Hayes wasn't listening. Thumbs on his phone's keyboard, he typed out a message, hit send. "What were you saying?"

Sterling shook his head, and Cash said, his voice babyish, "He doesn't want to spend more time with June than he has to."

Eyes gleaming, Travis rubbed his hands together. "And that's why this is going to be so much fun."

"Callie said they'll be there," Hayes could barely contain the humor in his voice.

Sterling cursed again, and Hayes added, "Also, Cal wants to know if you'll take June on a tour of the ranch before that. Help give her some ideas, you know?"

Chapter Nine

After Sterling drove away from Sweet Springs Ranch, leaving June and Callie in the dust, literally, his brothers remained standing in a circle, mouths hanging open.

Then Hayes said, "Well, I'd guess he's gone to A Cold One. Should we go?"

He gave Callie a perfunctory peck on the lips and they were off, one of the pickup trucks roaring to life and zooming around the house and back down the driveway.

In the still silence that followed, Callie rubbed June's upper arms, fast, like she was warming her up. "You're in shock. I should see if I can find one of those foil blankets they give to marathoners at the finish line."

June blinked, realizing her eyes had glazed over. "I *am* in shock. But who can blame me?"

"Not me," Callie said. "If they're going for drinks, we're going for drinks. Get in the car."

June obeyed, her mind so overrun with all things Sterling, she couldn't think for herself. God, he was so handsome, it hurt to look at him. And he might not want her here—she could tell that from the transformation in his expression—but he needed her. That was obvious, wasn't it? The evening before, when they'd *not* talked about their personal lives, he'd been in pain. Maybe, by being at Sweet Springs Ranch, at his home, she could help ease that pain.

As they zipped back onto the main road to head toward town, Callie glanced at June. "Do you want to talk about it?" The question pulled June out of her ruminating.

It—the Sterling situation—was all June could think about, but talking about it wasn't going to help. She shook her head. "Let's get down to business."

"Okay." Callie nodded, both hands on the wheel, gaze focused. "So. I don't know how your genius works. Do you want to brainstorm together? Do you sit down and make a list? Do you need music? Wait. Have you even agreed to do this? I guess I should back it up. Do you think you can do it? I mean, who am I kidding? If anyone can do it, it's you. And by do it, I mean create an event that raises enough money to cover everything the Wilders owe on that place."

She inhaled like she had more to say, but June reached across the cab and put a hand on her shoulder. "Hold on."

Callie's laugh in response bordered on breathless. "Sorry. Go ahead. Answer one or all of those questions."

"I see that nothing has changed when it comes to you talking a mile a minute."

Her friend's lips twitched. "That's true. It's one of my specialties in the courtroom. But do go on."

"My first instinct," June said, "is to run away. Far, far away. I left the Hotel Cartwright to get away from drama, but now it seems I've stumbled across more."

She didn't say that Sterling's cold reaction to her broke her heart into a million tiny pieces.

Callie opened her mouth, raised her eyebrows, and June held up a hand. "Hold on. Let me finish."

Callie snapped her mouth shut.

"But as soon as we drove onto that property, I could see it." June's heart sang with the possibility of hosting an event on that lush, green, picture-perfect ranch. "Yes. I can do it. Yes. I *want* to do it. But here's the thing. We need buy-in from all four Wilder brothers. It's going to be all hands on deck. I can't do it on my own. But if we get help, then I'm fairly confident we can pull it off."

Callie squealed.

Smiling at that point, June said, "The caveat is that I have to clear this with my parents. As much as I'm ready for bigger, more exciting projects—exactly like this one—I can't in good conscience leave my parents in a bind."

Callie took June's hand in a death grip. Her eyes were wide. "What do you think they're going to say?"

Dread, acidic black smoke, curled in June's stomach. "I don't know. I'm not sure."

"Well, maybe we put that as the first item on our brainstorming list. How to get you time off of work without upsetting your parents."

Callie parked the car and only then did June realize they'd come to a building with a patio out front. Umbrellas in every color provided shade, and string lights hung around the perimeter.

"This place is cute," June said.

"And their wine is to die for. It's the tasting room for a nearby winery. I'm warning you: you might never want to leave Prescott after this."

Callie opened the car door and stood up, and when Jun did the same, they looked at each other over the top of the car.

"Is that an evil gleam I see in your eye?" June wanted to know.

Callie did her best evil laugh. "You bet it is. You might think Sterling will start angling for you to stay. But it's me you have to watch out for."

Inside, they each ordered a glass of the local Merlot, and then went outside to wait on the patio.

Once they were seated, Callie folded her hands on the tabletop and looked at June. "I'm so excited to see you work." She held up a hand to interrupt herself and said, "I know. First we have to talk about getting you some time off. But then. I'm so excited to see you work."

Laughter bubbled up inside of June. "It might not be as spectacular as you're thinking."

The wine arrived. Callie's eyes lit up. "Try it. Take a couple of sips. I'll wait."

June did, and moaned with pleasure. "Oh, wow. You're right. This is incredible. I can taste all the flavors. Cherry, vanilla, oak. I'm in love."

"Told you," Callie said. "It's one of my favorites." She took a sip as well and closed her eyes in ecstasy. "However long you stay, you'll have to take a couple of bottles home with you."

June nodded. "Maybe we should buy a bottle now and take it home with us. Where are we staying tonight, anyway?"

Callie laughed. "I have no idea. It's about as mysterious as your upcoming leave of absence."

They both fell into peals of laughter at that.

Suddenly, clarity hit June right in the gut. "Maya."

"Who is Maya, and how can she help? Should we send her a bottle of this wine?" Callie held up her glass.

"She's my assistant. And as amazing as I am, she might be more so. I think maybe, just maybe, she could handle things while I'm gone."

Callie was nodding. "So. We call Maya. We brief her on the upcoming events. We get *her* an assistant. And then you're home free."

Callie finished off her first glass of wine and picked up the menu, although June was fairly certain she had it memorized.

"Hmm." June paused. "I like your thinking. So when we're done here, I'll call her and feel her out. After the blow-up with Timothy Alexander yesterday, this idea will probably terrify her. I'm putting her in charge of ice sculptures in summer."

"Ice sculptures in summer?"

"He's the groom." June tipped back her own glass and drained it. "He's planning the wedding. Exclusively. Should give you an idea of what we're dealing with."

Callie raised her eyebrows.

"Winter is his favorite season and although he let his betrothed choose *one thing* about the wedding—she chose the month of July—

he won't budge on anything else. So they're having a winter-in-summer theme."

Callie laughed out loud. "I'm getting hot just thinking about it. In fact, I'm going to adjust the umbrella."

She set down the wine menu, then stood and began tilting the umbrella to create more shade for their table.

"As bad as he's been to work with," June said, "I can't imagine what it would be like to marry the guy."

"Oof. So that's what we'd be leaving Maya with." Callie sat back down.

"Right."

"Well, I think Maya can handle it."

June laughed. "You haven't even met her yet."

"Yeah, but if you say she rocks, then I know she can handle it. Next. How does your genius work? Do you want me to help you brainstorm? Do you need quiet alone time? Tell me what you need to unleash your creativity and I shall make it happen."

"Do you still need music, a scented candle, and a cup of tea to unlock your genius?" June asked.

"I sure do," Callie said. "In that department, not much has changed."

"Let me get us another glass of wine, and then we'll start brainstorming. I have some ideas. What would you like?"

"You pick."

Inside at the bar, June asked the bartender for his recommendation. He asked her a series of questions about what she liked to eat and drink, and then suggested she try the carmeniere.

While he poured, he asked, "Are you visiting?"

"I am."

"From where?" He slid the glasses across the shiny wooden bar.

"City."

"How long are you in town?"

Suddenly exhilarated with the possibility of staying, she decided to commit. "A couple of weeks. I'm helping put together a community fundraiser for the Sweet Springs Ranch. You know it?"

"Of course I do," he said. "That place is a fixture in Prescott."

"Oh, wonderful," June said. "The friend I'm here with is the fiancée of one of the Wilder boys. Hayes. She asked me to help out."

"Great!" the bartender said. "Let me know how I can help. We can put flyers on our bulletin board, get the word out."

"Wonderful, thank you." June picked up the glasses. "I'm June, by the way."

"I'm Walter. Nice to meet you."

"Likewise."

Back on the patio, June said to Callie, "I just made it official: I told the bartender, Walter, we're throwing a fundraiser."

Callie's eyes went round and she snatched one of the glasses from June's hand. June sat down and they took simultaneous gulps.

"I guess we're really doing this thing," Callie said. "Now. About your genius."

"So, I'm thinking a barn dance. Right around Fourth of July."

"I love that idea!" Callie sat up straighter, and June could see the energy and excitement buzzing around her body. "That is perfect! It's so Prescott. And, the cherry on top: you'll be here for the big Fourth of July party."

"That sounds fun."

"It's the funnest," Callie said. "Now. Back to the fundraiser."

"I think, to make money, we've got to make it *bougie* Prescott. We've got to do a dinner and wine and dancing. A silent auction with some really big prizes. A raffle. You know?"

Callie nodded, lips pressed together, thoughtful. "I see where you're going with this. We might have a hard time convincing the guys on the bougie angle, but I think if I can get Hayes in on it, he can persuade the others. Maybe I'll offer him a BJ if he agrees to convince the others."

June laughed out loud. "Perfect."

"Now. Let's address the elephant in the room."

"What elephant?" June, knowing full well what Callie was talking about, looked around wildly, as if there were really an elephant on the patio.

"Sterling."

June sighed, that icky smoke-curling feeling in her stomach

again. "I know. He's a sexy elephant, isn't he? But it's clear he wants nothing to do with me. Our time together? That was a one-night thing. Don't worry. I can keep things strictly professional." Her voice cracked when she added, "I'll just pretend last night never happened."

Even as she said the words, her body remembered the feeling of him curled up behind her while they slept, the warmth and sturdiness of him against her. Her traitorous memory reminded her of his woodsy scent, which she'd inhaled and memorized while they danced. His calloused hands on her bare arms. His breath on her neck. His mouth on hers.

"Good luck," Callie said. "You ain't forgettin' that any time soon."

"Ain't that the truth."

"Okay. Before we get any further, I think you've got to talk with Maya. See if she's willing to cover for you while you're here. And then you've got to tell your parents."

An electric jolt came from inside June's body and zapped every square inch of her skin when she imagined actually telling them. Thinking about it was one thing. Coming right out and saying it was another. It felt bold, audacious, and terrifying.

June took out her phone. Took another sip of wine. Navigated to Maya's contact info, and made the call.

"June." Maya sounded breathless. "Are you okay?"

"I'm perfectly fine," June said. "Better than fine."

Callie winked at her. She smiled.

"I have a big favor to ask."

"Anything," Maya said. "As long as you come back."

"Well, that's the thing."

Silence.

"I'm coming back!" June rushed to say. "After a couple of weeks. Can you hold down the fort?"

More silence. A grimace from Callie.

"By hold down the fort, you mean ..."

June took a gulp of wine, swallowed, and laughed manically.

"Oh, you know. Just do my job for the next two weeks. I'll hire an assistant for you."

"June—"

"I know I'm asking a lot."

Maya scoffed. "We have two weddings in the next two weeks, and one of them is Timothy Alexander's."

"I fired him."

"Um, well, he's already called your parents and insisted we un-fire him. I debated whether to call you, but it seemed like you needed a break..."

"He called my parents? In France."

"In France."

June put her forehead on the table. If he'd called her parents in France, then they'd have a heads up things were amiss at Hotel Cartwright. They wouldn't know—yet—that she'd left town, but they would know she wasn't acting like herself.

The Cartwright Family Empire's Cardinal Rule Number Four: Always be the one to break important news.

"June?"

"I'm here." She sat up again and pinched the bridge of her nose. "I'll call him and re-fire him."

"You can do that?"

"Today, yes."

"June? If you fire him and get me an assistant, I'll take over for two weeks. But it's only because I'm pretty sure you were on the verge of a mental breakdown."

"Deal. I'll get back to you."

They hung up and Callie grinned at June across the table. "What time is it in Paris?" she wanted to know.

June checked her watch. "Midnight. They're probably still awake. My parents have become real party animals on this vacation."

Wrinkling her nose, Callie said, "Should you just call them now? Get it out of the way?"

June's whole body started to vibrate with nerves. "What, exactly, should I say?"

Callie, the epitome of confidence, shrugged. "Just tell them what's up. Inspired by all the fun they're having in France, you took a quick mini vacation."

June grimaced. "They don't even know I've left Great Falls."

"Well, break the news!" She flung out an arm. "Then tell them you got here and I needed help with a client. You've got everything at the hotel covered, thanks to Maya, and you'll be gone for two weeks. They love me. And they love you. So they should be fine with it."

"Okay." June nodded, closed her eyes, and did her best to absorb some of Callie's confident energy. Opening her eyes, she dialed her mom. Sure enough, she picked up right away. Before she spoke, June heard talking and laughter, music, and the clinking of dishes.

"June! How are you, honey?"

"Hi, Mom. I'm fine. How are you guys?"

"Oh, we're wonderful! Your dad and I are at another lovely little bistro. All we've done here is eat and drink. And—well, you know what two married people do on vacation."

Despite her nerves about the conversation she was about to have, June laughed, a genuine belly laugh that eased some of her tension. "You don't have to tell me about that, Mom."

"Oh, I suppose not. But why are you calling, honey? It must be important. You haven't really called since we've been gone."

"I just wanted to let you know that I'm in Arizona for the weekend."

Callie, who'd been scrolling on her phone, paused and looked up at June.

June's mom said, "Arizona? What are you doing there, sweetheart? Isn't it hotter than Hades?"

Fighting back a sigh, June closed her eyes and tilted her head back. "Actually, the temperature is just about perfect. I'm in Prescott. You remember, that's where my college roommate, Callie, lives part-time."

"Oh, that's right. Yes, Maya might have mentioned that. How is Callie? We really like her."

Callie winked at June.

"She's great, Mom."

"Good, good. A lawyer, didn't you say?"

"Yep."

"Oh," her mom said, suddenly remembering something. "Listen. Speaking of Maya, she also mentioned that you and our client, Timothy Alexander, had a bit of a misunderstanding. He called me, too. He seems to think you canceled his wedding."

Although her mom's voice held nothing but curiosity, maybe a little incredulity, June felt a ton of pressure in her stomach. She might actually throw up. "Yeah. That wasn't a misunderstanding. He's terrible, mom. I did tell him he should find another venue for his wedding."

Callie had set down her phone and was watching June.

"That just won't do, Junie. His wedding is in a week. There's no way he can find someone as accommodating as you—as the Hotel Cartwright—by then."

Callie's eyes went round. In this case, June knew *accommodating* meant "a pushover," because her parents insisted she give in to almost every demand, no matter how crazy said demand might be.

"That's because no one should be as accommodating as the Hotel Cartwright," June said.

"Well, honey, the Cartwright Family Empire Rule Number One is that the customer is always right. If he wants a winter-in-summer theme, then that's what he shall have."

June tapped the mute button on her phone and groaned. "Can you believe what you're hearing?"

Callie shook her head. June unmuted her phone.

"Well, agree to disagree. I'll let you work the details out with Maya. Anyway, that's the real reason I'm calling. Callie's fiancé and his brothers, they're about to lose their family ranch to foreclosure. Long story, but their dad wasn't paying the mortgage, he died recently, and they just found out. They've asked me to stay and help with a fundraising event." When her mom didn't answer right away, she plowed ahead. "I'll be here for two weeks. I've already called Maya and asked if she can take over my duties while I'm gone."

For a long couple of seconds. June's mom didn't speak. The

festive sounds from the bistro gradually faded, and the sound of footsteps replaced them. June could picture her mom, tall and elegant, her long hair flowing behind her as she walked out of the bistro and down the sidewalk to find a quiet place to talk. Which scared her. She wasn't going to accept this idea easily.

"Junebug."

June closed her eyes. "Mom."

"We need you at the hotel. There is no one who can plan an event like you."

"Maya—"

"Maya is great, but she's not a Cartwright."

"I know, but she's—"

June could tell her mom was doing her absolute best to keep her tone light and even. "We need you home, Junie. Make it a long weekend in Arizona if you must, but come back for the Alexander wedding. Leaving Maya in charge just won't do. Anyway, I've got to go. I just left your dad at the bistro. If I'm not careful, he'll give all our cash to the band. The live music is incredible here. You really should make a visit. I love you."

Her mom disconnected. June set her phone on the table and put her head in her hands.

"Well?" Callie said.

"They need me back, she said."

"What are you going to do?"

June didn't know, and that's what she told Callie. "But, I'm not going back right away. Let's at least start brainstorming."

Concern etched on her features, Callie nodded. "Okay. If you have to go back to Montana, I totally understand. I wanted you to hold our collective hands while we raise money to save the ranch. But you can make a plan here and then hold our hands by phone and email."

June shook her head. "No. I want to hold your collective hands in person, too." Her mind flashed on Sterling. His big, strong hands.

"I'm so glad you're saying that. But June? Can I be honest?"

Her gaze was direct, and June's stomach lurched. "Of course."

"I remember how, in college, you talked about your dream of starting your own event planning company."

June nodded. They used to sneak onto the roof of the dorm building and talk about their college friends and crushes and about their biggest plans for the future.

"You said you wanted to start out at your parents' hotel, but branch out. It seems like that desire hasn't changed. Is that correct?"

"Yes, that's correct. And by the way, I'd never guess you're a lawyer."

Callie smirked. "Right. Just wanted to confirm. Here's the thing, June. I totally get feeling like you have to do something because it's the family business, or because your parents want you to. But at the same time, I hope that one day, you'll gather up the courage to tell your parents that you're going to pursue your dream—and then do it. I see big things in your future."

June's throat felt tight all of a sudden. Her eyes misted over. "Thanks, Cal. It means a lot."

Callie's phone chimed. "It's Hayes. Can we do dinner tomorrow? He's calling it a family planning dinner."

June bit back a groan. She was certain dinner together was the absolute last thing Sterling would want.

Callie gave her a knowing smile. "All right. I'll tell him yes. And then we'll start planning. And June?"

June gulped her wine, waited.

"Don't worry about Sterling. He'll come around."

Chapter Ten

Sterling had to admire Callie's style. The morning of his tour with June, Callie—in her bright red sports car—came zipping into the driveway, practically pushed June out the passenger door, and zipped away, leaving Sterling and June alone and surrounded by twittering birds and a nice summer breeze that rustled the leaves.

"I guess she's not sticking around," Sterling said by way of greeting, doing his best to keep his tone playful. Because the sight of June at the ranch in the early morning light made him picture her standing in the kitchen of the big house, wearing that little white tank top she slept in, setting the tea kettle on the stove while he poured himself a cup of coffee.

June smirked at him and he felt like they were sharing an inside joke. "Since I've known her, Callie has moved at a million miles an hour—has she always been like that?"

"Yeah," Sterling said, thinking of their childhood and how Callie was always a doer, bouncing from one activity to the next, fashioning a working crawdad trap, jumping off the rope swing into the swimming hole, building a fire to roast s'mores. "I guess she's always been like that."

They stood there looking at each other and Sterling kicked

himself for noticing the way the dappled sunlight played on her chest, her collarbones. "Are you ready for your tour?"

When she nodded, she captured her lower lip between her teeth. Like she was nervous. Like she had something to say, but wasn't quite ready to say it. Like she wanted him to kiss her. Before he could act on that, Sterling inclined his head toward the entrance. "Let's walk."

She fell into step beside him and he found that even though he'd experienced it for only one night, he missed the security of her hand tucked into the crook of his elbow.

They'd come almost to the main road when she said, "Sterling, I think we should talk." He stopped and turned toward her. They probably did need to talk, but what was he supposed to say?

I'm sorry I didn't tell you what a mess my life is. I'm sorry I didn't act happier to see you. I'm sorry we can't give us a try. Want to run away together? Can we start over?

Fortunately, she spoke first. "Based on some of the things you said the other night, I know you don't want to be here. And I could tell from your reaction when I showed up that you don't want me to be here, either."

He felt like an asshole. He prepared to speak, to defend himself, but she held up a hand. "I get it. The other night—for both of us, I think—was like a respite. A break from reality. It was wonderful." The smile she gave him, full of warmth and understanding, made him weak in the knees. "And then you dragged yourself here and as soon as you're immersed in that mess you were dreading, I show up. Your two worlds collide. Am I right?"

Is this woman a damn mind reader?

He nodded. "You're right. The other night with you was the best I've had in a long time. The best date, planned or otherwise, ever." He watched her face as he spoke, noticed the way her pupils dilated when he talked about their night together. "But nothing has changed with regard to what I said before. I don't plan on settling down. You deserve someone who does. And, to tell you the truth, I'm certain that once you've spent two weeks with the Wilder family, you won't want anything more to do with us." *With me.*

June nodded, swallowed. He wanted to reach for her when she looked off into the distance. "I think we can get through the next two weeks. Obviously, I agreed to help Callie before I realized you'd be here." Those words were like a knife to his heart and she must have seen as much because she rushed to say, "Not that I would have turned her down if I knew you were involved. I'm just saying, my intentions are pure. I'm just here to help. And—" she tilted her head and gave a little nod, like she was admitting to something. "Also, I really did need to get away. I might get into some trouble at work for staying longer than a weekend. But I just had to do it."

Sterling nodded. "I understand, believe me. And I appreciate you being here." He had to force out his next words. "I think that while we're both here, we should just stick to being friends and colleagues. Co-conspirators."

She raised an eyebrow. "Co-conspirators. I like that." She put out her hand to shake. "Deal."

He took her hand and in that instant, it was as if his soul recognized hers. The sense of connection, knowing, hit him like a physical force, knocking the air out of his lungs. He dropped her hand and held out his, palm up, sweeping it toward the ranch's entrance. "Shall we?"

Her smile made everything fall away—the stress, the anxiety, the fear—just for an instant. Side by side, they finished walking the length of the driveway, the sounds of their shoes crunching in the gravel generating yet another round of long-forgotten memories: running up the driveway after getting off the school bus, hearing his uncles pulling onto the property on holidays and rushing out to greet them, jumping in giant puddles after a summer monsoon storm. *Finding out his dad was willing to throw away everything they all worked so hard for.*

June followed his lead as he stepped onto the shoulder of the main road, where he could view the sign.

Once again wracked by humiliation, he said, "That sign? It didn't look like that the last time I was here, five years ago. We should probably do something about that before the fundraiser." He scratched the back of his neck. "Anyway. I don't know why I had you walk all the way over here just for that. But there you have it. Should we go back in?" They trudged along for a couple of minutes before reaching the arena and the big barn. More memories: music, cheering, cows lowing.

"Again, the arena and barn weren't in this bad of shape the last time I was here. We used to have events out here. Rodeos and stuff."

June was at it again, worrying that lower lip. Sterling told himself he wouldn't be human if he didn't have to fight the urge to cover her mouth with his.

He flung out an arm, gesturing vaguely in the direction of the rest of the property. "You've seen the big house. And Travis has another house beyond that, with a smaller barn. We don't have to walk all the way over there if you don't want to."

June turned to face him and took both of his hands in hers. He expected some sort of jolt, electricity. But all he felt was a sudden calm enveloping him.

"Sterling." Her gaze was on his, intense but kind. "This tour—it's not just to show me around. It's to give me a feel for what Sweet Springs Ranch could be like. What it *was* like, in its heyday." She let her gaze roam over the property. "Just in my short time here, I can tell it's a special place. It's bursting with memories. Tell me how you feel when you see the sign, the arena, the barn. Tell me what you remember. Those glory days of summer when school was out—what did you and your brothers do? What about when the whole place was covered in snow? I need to know what it feels like here when things are great. That way, I can help recapture that magic for the fundraiser."

While she spoke, Sterling's memory went crazy, dredging up long forgotten clips of life at Sweet Springs Ranch. Long trail rides with lunch in the little apple orchard. Summer days in the above-ground pool. Riding the horses around the arena. Racing. Always racing. The Wilder parents laughing, doing sneak attacks with water balloons. Building snow people in the front yard.

As much joy as these images produced, they also brought up grief. Life wasn't like that anymore. Sterling had burned it to the ground when he left. He shook his head. "I don't know if anyone can ever bring that back."

June blinked and didn't respond. He didn't blame her. *He* didn't even know what to say.

"Show me, anyway." And then, with a gentleness that made his heart ache, she did tuck her hand into the crook of his elbow and led him toward the big house. Hadn't he spent the past five years tamping down these memories, these feelings, every time they rose to the surface? And they did—he and his brothers had a magical childhood, a wonderful, golden youth there.

But it was fragile, wasn't it? A house of cards ... and how many times had he kicked himself for being the one to remove that singular card, the one that sent the rest of the cards fluttering to the ground?

Could he be the one to rebuild it?

His voice sounded a bit croaky when he said, "The big house used to be something to look at. My mom kept it sparkling clean and decked out with plants and flowers. I never took it for granted—I loved seeing it there, knowing it was my home." Throat aching, he went on. "And our rodeo events? They were the talk of the town. People came from all over and had so much fun."

Once he started, Sterling found he couldn't stop. He led June all over the property, showing her the site of his first broken bone (he'd fallen off the tire swing), the spot where he and his brothers used to catch crawdads, and the window they used to climb out onto the roof and look at the sky. He even showed her the trail that led to the big field between Sweet Springs Ranch and Hendrickson Farm, where the Wilder boys and the Hendrickson boys used to meet to drink beer and hang out.

"There was one time where we somehow procured a forty-pack of beer. Forty cans between six boys. Boys will be boys, you know, and we decided to see how fast we could drink them. We used our knives to cut holes in the sides and we chugged those things. Beer sprayed everywhere, but I'm confident most of it ended up inside our bodies. We were as sick as dogs. Every single one of us except Hayes. To this day, I don't know how he avoided it. We went home reeking. Our mom was so mad, we did extra chores for a week. My hands still hurt from the blisters I had after digging ditches for a full day."

June's eyes sparkled. "Seems like you had a pretty good life here." They came back to where they'd met at the start of the tour.

Sterling nodded, looking around at his childhood home, some of the pain falling away as the tightness uncurled, just a little, in his chest. "I guess we did."

"I grew up in the city, so all this seems so idyllic. Magical."

Watching her react to his stories, he felt another deep pang of grief. "It was."

"So what happened?" Her gaze was direct.

"It's a long story." *And a humiliating one.* "Suffice it to say, everything changed five years ago. And now, asking for help from the community—even though we grew up in it—doesn't come naturally. Especially for me. Maybe for the others, since they stuck around, but not for me."

He swore he could see the questions in her eyes, so he led her back to the big house, where Callie waited, engine idling. Watching June's graceful movements as she got into the car, Hayes found he was actually looking forward to their big group dinner that night.

When he arrived, he knew it wasn't coincidence that the only open seat was next to June. She sat up straight, her hands clasped in her lap as if she were afraid of taking up too much space or making a move that would cause the Wilder brothers to send her packing.

Sterling leaned close and whispered, "You can relax. If our family dinners are anything, they're fun."

He saw goosebumps rise on her neck, and wanted to place his lips there. She smiled at him, and the worry lines between her eyebrows eased.

For all the times Hayes had accused Callie of being bossy, he sure looked at her with unadulterated adoration when she tapped her spoon against her glass and said, "You will all be happy to know that June has some wonderful ideas for the fundraiser."

Sterling thought he'd relaxed, but at talk of the fundraiser, his stomach churned, just as it had been off and on since he arrived in Phoenix.

Cash, who sat on his other side, leaned close and whispered, "Better listen up, buddy. You and Miss June Cartwright are going to be working real closely together."

Sterling ground his teeth, hating the idea that his brothers were going to have front-row seats to his work with June. All the more reason to kill his feelings for her—throw water on that fire so only steam remained.

"So, June." Cash threw a glance at Sterling to make sure he was watching, and then he pinned June with an intense stare. Sterling knew exactly what he was doing.

"Yes?" June's smile wasn't quite genuine—her eyes didn't crinkle at the corners, like they had earlier that day during the tour, or the night when the two of them shared wine at the piano bar.

"You're an event planner."

Way to state the obvious, Cash.

"Yes."

Cash smiled, his most dazzling, adorable, dimpled smile. The one that had gotten him out of countless consequences when he was a little kid. All he had to do was say something funny, show those dimples, and he was off scot-free. Apparently, it worked on the ladies, too. Sterling could literally feel June's energy shift. Calm.

"I apologize," Cash said. "This was starting off like a job interview. I just wanted to get to know you a little bit."

She was already charmed. "Of course. You can ask me anything."

"Anything?" Travis said, his own mischievous grin competing with Cash's on the megawatt scale.

June's face flushed and it was at once the hottest thing Sterling had ever seen (he wondered if her face flushed during sex, and then gave himself a mental hand slap) and made him want to stand in front of her and beat his chest to ward off anyone who might make her uncomfortable.

Cash elbowed Travis.

June cleared her throat. "Okay. Not *anything*. But anything related to event planning."

"What kind of events have you planned?" Cash asked.

"I work at a hotel and plan all the events there. Mostly weddings, but also baby showers, birthday parties, holiday parties. A little bit of everything."

"Have you ever done a fundraiser?" Cash asked.

June nodded. "A few local nonprofits have their fundraisers at the hotel every year. Usually they have their own event planners, so I stand by to help with whatever they need. And the day of, I'm part of the team, making sure everything runs smoothly."

"If you don't mind me asking, which hotel is it?" Hayes asked.

June glanced at Sterling, and he saw a flicker of something—guilt, maybe?—in her expression. She cleared her throat again. "Hotel Cartwright in Great Falls."

Sterling nearly choked on his water.

Hayes's eyes narrowed as he looked at Sterling. "Is that where you—" Callie elbowed him. "What?"

That brief exchange gave Sterling time to recover as he worked through the realization in his mind: she worked at the hotel where they had dinner and drinks, and where they'd slept for those few precious hours in one of the nicest rooms.

This time, it was Callie clearing her throat. "June's parents actually own the hotel. So, she's excited to expand her horizons, plan an event somewhere else."

A fresh wave of color made its way up June's neck and into her cheeks, and Sterling wanted to gather her up in his arms.

Her parents owned the hotel? And she wanted to branch out? Suddenly, Sterling understood why, when he saw her in the airport, June had the frantic energy of someone running away. She was. Just like he'd run away five years before. No wonder they got along so well. They were kindred spirits and hadn't even known it. As close as they sat to each other, he could reach out and put a hand on her thigh, to brace her, to let her know he understood. But there was no way he could do that without his brothers seeing—and he'd never hear the end of it.

"I'm really looking forward to spending some time here," she was saying. "To tell you I needed a change of scenery is an understatement."

Callie leaned forward, hands on the table, a conspiratorial look in her eye. "Did you guys know one of June's clients wanted a winter-in-summer theme for his wedding? With ice sculptures! In July!"

"Wait," Cash said. "Did you say a guy? The *guy* is planning the wedding?"

Every head at the table swung toward June for confirmation. "Yep. Timothy Alexander. The biggest groomzilla I've ever had the pleasure of working with. He wanted a mini ice-skating rink at one point, but we couldn't get it to work. Thank goodness."

As June told horror stories—the bride who wanted her bridesmaids to stand at the back of the audience throughout the ceremony so she'd be center stage, the groom who surprised his bride by wearing a camouflage tux to the wedding, the couple who agreed to break up in the middle of their vows—she had the whole group laughing.

She fit in so well, Sterling had to remind himself that he'd promised to keep their interactions strictly professional. June had enough going on at home. She certainly wouldn't want to immerse herself in the tangled mess that was the Wilder family.

Still, it didn't hurt to imagine, just through dinner, that they could be together. His brothers were obviously smitten with her, and so was Callie, the only woman who planned on joining the Wilder family.

What if they were all cursed, like his dad?

Chapter Eleven

For June, remaining in Prescott and working closely with Sterling was already proving to be a sweet torture. The morning after the big family dinner, June woke in the spare bedroom at Hayes's place thinking about how much she enjoyed being around him. Obviously he was beyond pleasant to look at—gorgeous, actually. His quiet, calm nature put June at ease and she found herself gravitating toward him.

She could hear Callie and Hayes talking out in the kitchen, and felt a stab of jealousy. Since they reconnected over Christmas the year before, they'd fallen madly and deeply in love. His fun, easygoing nature complemented Callie's supercharged personality. They brought each other balance. June stretched and let herself imagine having that kind of balance with Sterling.

What would they talk about in the kitchen every morning? Would he want to hear about the events she was planning while she whipped up pancake batter? Would he talk about his latest projects while he snagged a piece of bacon off the plate?

If only.

While it didn't hurt to daydream, she had work to do. And she couldn't let her subconscious get any ideas—she had to remain the picture of professional as they worked on the fundraiser. Steeling herself with that idea, she got out of bed, pulled up the covers, and got dressed before heading into the kitchen. Callie jumped up from the kitchen table, grabbed the coffee pot, and then replaced it. "Tea."

"Tea," June said.

"Do we have tea?" Callie turned to Hayes, whose eyes twinkled.

"We do have tea. Let me get it."

While he rummaged in the pantry, Callie set a pot of water to boil. Hayes put a little box on the table and Callie pressed a mug of hot water into her hands. "Good morning."

"Will you marry me?" June said.

Hayes cleared his throat. "I'm afraid she's already spoken for." He grinned. "But I happen to have three single brothers."

Callie gestured for June to follow her as she returned to the table and gave Hayes a playful swat on the shoulder. "Knock it off. She's here on business."

Still smiling, he said, "Maybe she doesn't mind mixing business with pleasure."

Callie rolled her eyes, but June could see her amusement dancing around her mouth.

"I'm feeding you breakfast," Callie told June. "There's a quiche in the oven. What's on the agenda for today?"

A little zing of energy ran through June's veins. "I'm meeting with Sterling to get down a solid plan for the fundraiser."

She didn't miss the look that passed between Callie and Hayes.

"Yeah," Hayes said. "I'm sorry I can't come to that meeting. I have lots to do today. Lots to do."

Callie gave him a sideways glance and turned to June. "Do you want me to tag along?"

The oven timer beeped and Callie got up to check the quiche. June was grateful Callie couldn't see the blush that crept into her cheeks. "No, that's okay. You told me you had some files to go through. But I would love it if you would look over our plan this afternoon or evening, see if there's anything else you can think of."

Callie stood up, the baking dish in her hands. She used a hip to shut the oven and set the quiche on the counter. "Sure. I'd love to."

While the three of them ate, June considered what to wear to her meeting with Sterling. Although she probably wouldn't want to go through the broken suitcase debacle again, she thanked her past self for packing such a good variety of outfits. Even if they were professional co-conspirators and co-conspirators only, she wanted to look good. She wanted to make Sterling pine for her the way she did for him. Was it a little devious? Maybe. Smiling to herself, she decided on a sundress she knew flattered her figure.

"What are you thinking about?" Callie demanded. "If I didn't know you better, I'd say that smile is pure evil."

"This is really good quiche," June said.

Callie, a lawyer through and through, raised an eyebrow. "We'll come back to this."

Hayes laughed out loud. "She doesn't let anyone get away with anything. Might as well just tell her what you're thinking."

"Nah," June said. "I'll keep it to myself for now."

An hour later, June walked into the lobby of the Granite Mountain Resort. Having grown up in a four-star hotel, it took a lot to impress her. But this did. The main doors stood directly across from a wall of windows, which overlooked the most stunning rock formation June had ever seen. The front desk stood off to the right, and a bar with a generous seating area occupied the space between where she stood and those gorgeous windows.

"Pretty great view, right?" Sterling's voice sent shivers over her skin. As much as she'd dressed to impress him, she had to wonder if he'd done the same. He wore a white button-up shirt tucked into dark jeans that fit him so well, all she could think about was getting him out of them. He hadn't shaved that morning and his dark scruff made his eyes a startling shade of blue. A lock of his still-damp hair lay across his forehead and June had to clasp her hands together to keep from brushing it back.

"It's a remarkable view," she agreed.

"It's probably a little early for drinks, but we could go sit in the bar and have coffee. Well, I can have coffee and you can have tea."

Should it thrill her that he remembered she was a tea drinker?

Once they were seated, drinks in front of them, Sterling said, "So, tell me what you've got."

More nervous for this meeting than she'd been for any other client meeting, June pulled out her notebook and opened it to the page where she'd started listing her ideas.

"From what you told me yesterday, Sweet Springs Ranch was a place people thought of for fun. Good, old-fashioned, dirty fun."

Sterling raised an eyebrow at her, and too late, she realized the innuendo. When she did, she laughed out loud. "You know what I mean." She laid out her ideas: the barn dance, a big family-style barbecue dinner, and the silent auction. While she spoke, he leaned back in his chair, his posture casual, his eyes intense. His expression remained neutral and she would have killed to know what he was thinking.

"The only catch is that we're going to need to set up a space. You have the barn and the arena, I know, but they're—"

"Dilapidated." He took a drink of his coffee.

"I didn't mean to imply—"

"No implication necessary. It's plain as day without you having to say anything."

June felt her nerves in her chest, tendrils of that smoke curling against her collarbone. She decided to pursue the solution rather than talk about the problem. "You're a builder, right?"

"Right," he said.

"One of your brothers said you make old things new again."

Sterling nodded and again, she wished she could read his mind. "That's accurate."

June debated for a half-second before blurting out, "I researched you. Online. I know you can transform a property in a week. I read some of the reviews. What did one of them say? 'Sterling Wilder took my place from falling down and overrun with weeds to a sparkling vision of home.'"

One corner of Sterling's mouth lifted, and he gave a little grunt. "Max Hooper. To be fair, his place *was* falling down. Anyone could have improved it."

"But could anyone have turned it into a sparkling vision of home?"

He lifted a shoulder. "Nah. I'm good at what I do."

"So can you create a space for this fundraiser? Out of something we already have, or maybe even from scratch?"

"Of course I can."

The sudden change in his expression—from broody to cocky—surprised June ... and delighted her. She imagined him smiling at her in bed, looking up at her from between her legs, and immediately chastised herself. She should *not* be thinking about Sterling Wilder like that. Although it didn't hurt to fantasize.

He seemed to realize his effect on her and his smile got even wider. "Is that not what you were expecting me to say?"

Blushing furiously at that point, June feigned an interest in her tea cup. "Actually, it was. I should have asked if you're *willing* to create a space for the fundraiser."

That sobered him right up. He shrugged again, his gaze sliding to the side, making him look so bereft, so adrift, she wanted to climb into his lap to anchor him there, to steady him.

"I guess."

Hoping to lighten the mood, June let herself laugh out loud. "Your enthusiasm is overwhelming."

It didn't quite work. He rubbed a hand over his face. "Sorry. I can do it. I *will* do it. But my enthusiasm level might not surpass its current level. I'm doing this more for my brothers than for myself. If it were up to me, I might very well let Sweet Springs Ranch go to foreclosure and to another owner. Let someone else make memories there, and enjoy the ones I have—the ones that aren't tainted."

June nodded. "I get that."

"Do you?" His gaze held hers, and in that moment, she wondered if she did.

The spent a few minutes going over particulars. June drew a diagram to show Sterling what she was thinking in terms of layout, and he took notes. She watched his calloused hand write in neat, tidy block letters.

"Look like I got everything?" He turned his notebook so she could read his writing, and she smiled. He'd written: *Build kick-ass dance floor with stage for rockin' live music.* Under that he'd written: *Need space for tables—eating and serving. Also tables for silent auction. Wiring for microphone?*

"You even got some things I didn't think of."

"Told you I could do this."

Suddenly she was picturing him as a broody little boy. She was charmed. "You did tell me. This looks great. When do you think you can get started?"

"I'll call my foreman today. My guess is he'll get the crew out here by day after tomorrow."

June felt her eyebrows shoot upwards. "That fast?"

Thinking about his foreman and crew seemed to relax him. "That fast. It's what we do. It's why Riggs is my foreman and why I have the crew I do."

God, why did everything this man said have to be so intriguing? June had a million questions. Why did he claim he didn't get along with his brothers, while managing to put together a crew of men who would come across the country at a moment's notice?

How could a man who spotted her at the airport, bought her a new suitcase, and danced the night away with her, cradling her in bed like a lover, be the same man who could let go of the property that had been in his family for a century?

She wanted to know everything there was to know about him. He had so many layers, and she wished she could peel away every single one.

But before she could lean in, before she could express that, he snapped his notebook closed and stood. "I'd better get going if I'm going to get the guys out here."

June rushed to stand too, and held out her hand for a shake.

"Come on," he said, shaking his head. "You're giving me a hug. Whether you like it or not, you're part of the family—or the family mess—now."

He grabbed her hand and pulled her against him and she closed her eyes and inhaled his woodsy scent and wished they could be more than co-conspirators.

* * *

June hadn't even made it to her car in the resort parking lot when her phone rang.

"Maya."

"Hey, June. Got a minute?"

The fact that Maya's voice held none of its usual warmth made June's mouth dry. "Sure."

"Timothy Alexander is a complete nightmare," Maya said.

Despite the seriousness of the situation, June laughed out loud. "I know you didn't call to tell me something I already know."

"He's back on the ice skating rink. Now that he got your parents involved, he thinks he has leverage. They'll let him have whatever it wants, and he says he wants the ice skating rink or else."

June sighed as she opened her car door. A blast of heat hit her, and she rushed to sit down and turn on the ignition and air conditioning. "Where are we even going to put it?"

"I don't know," Maya said. "The Lakeside Room, maybe?"

Leaning her head against the headrest, June squeezed her eyes shut and opened them again. "There's another event in there that same day. A baby shower or something. Check the schedule."

The sound of Maya's computer mouse clicking came through June's earpiece. A curse followed. "You're right."

"He can't have the ice skating rink. I'll call my parents to warn them."

"I'm so sorry, June," Maya said. "I was trying to leave you alone. I've been on the phone with him all morning. I keep saying no, and then he calls back with another line of reasoning."

Eyes closed again, June said, "I'll take care of it."

They disconnected and June jumped when someone knocked on her window. Her eyelids flew open. Sterling's face was level with hers and his lips twitched with amusement as she rolled down her window.

"Everything okay?" he asked.

"Everything except the fact that you almost gave me a heart attack." She felt herself smiling even though she'd been stressed to the max just a moment before.

"Sorry. You looked stressed."

"I am. Groomzilla strikes again."

His lips went from twitching to smiling broadly. "What now?"

"The ice skating rink. My assistant's covering for me, and he thinks he can walk all over her. He called my parents and threatened to expose us on Insta if they don't give him what he wants. And now that my mom has apparently discovered the power of Insta influencers, she's scared to death. She wants me home."

Although humor still showed around Sterling's eyes, she also saw compassion there. He rested his elbows on the doorframe. "You don't have to stay here. You could just give me your notes."

She raised an eyebrow at him. "You're going to run the fundraiser?" He returned her raised eyebrow and she said, "Not that I think you couldn't, but I get the feeling you're not the most enthusiastic Wilder brother in the bunch."

"Of course I wouldn't run it. I'd give your notes to Callie. *She* would run it."

"Ah. That might work."

They stared at each other, grinning, until Sterling seemed to remember he'd been on a mission. "Right. Well, I've got to call Riggs, my foreman, and see about getting the crew over here. Let me know what you decide to do."

I don't want to leave. It hit June like a freight train. "I'm staying." Her words sounded decisive, but even as she said them, she imagined her mom's reaction. *You have to come home, Junie. We need you. The client is always right.*

Sterling grinned and rapped on the roof of the car. "I hoped you'd say that. You'll be here for July Fourth. You're going to love it."

"I've heard." Her heart raced, pumping exhilaration through her veins.

He nodded. "All right. I'll see you later."

She watched him saunter off, admiring his muscular legs in those form-fitting jeans.

"What a view," she said to herself. Then she rolled up her window, turned up the air conditioning, and headed for downtown Prescott. If she was going to stay for a couple of weeks, she was going to need her own place.

Chapter Twelve

Travis had offered up the spare bedroom at his place, but Sterling needed his own space, away from Sweet Springs. After leaving June at the resort, he headed downtown, choosing one of the historic hotels in the heart of Prescott. He loved the creaky wood floors and the views of the courthouse plaza.

Clothes unpacked, laptop set up, Sterling picked up the phone. As he expected, when he called Riggs and asked when he could be in Prescott, his friend whooped with excitement and said he'd have the whole crew there in a couple of days.

Nerves mixed with his gratitude. Sterling wondered what the guys would think of his childhood home ... especially the mess he and his family were in. But there was no one else he'd rather have onsite with him. After hanging up, he stood at the window, watching people peruse the booths at an art fair on the plaza.

A family walked down the sidewalk, ice cream cones in hand. Sterling remembered their mom taking them to the shop on the corner and the agony of having to choose just one flavor when they all looked so good. Sometimes they'd make deals—Hayes would get bubblegum and Sterling would get peanut butter chocolate and they'd take turns licking both.

The fountain stood in the same place as always. Water spilled from a bowl in the hands of a mostly naked stone woman. Oh, how he and his brothers had giggled over that the first time they realized "she has boobies." Tears leaked from his eyes and his stomach ached from laughter. Their mom had done her best to shush them, but they were little boys after all, and couldn't get past the hilarity. They cracked up every time someone remembered the realization. On the way home that day. While mucking stalls that afternoon. At the dinner table, where their dad threatened to take them behind the woodshed if they didn't shut up and eat. Even now, years later, Sterling felt laughter creeping up from his center.

He sobered up quick when he remembered the time the four of them had been playing frisbee during a fair like the one he was watching. He'd thrown the frisbee to Cash, but the wind picked it up and it sailed right over Cash's head and into one of the booths, knocking over a woman's jewelry displays. Necklaces and earrings and bracelets toppled off their stands and onto the grass below while the woman looked around, wild-eyed, for the monsters who'd thrown the frisbee. Across the distance, Sterling and Cash looked at each other. Cash's eyes were so big, Sterling would have laughed if he wasn't worried about the woman chasing them down and wringing their necks. Instead, he yelled, "Run!" and the two of them met in the middle and ran to the corner of the plaza and out onto the street. They waited all day for someone to call their parents; Prescott was an even smaller town back then, and surely someone would ID them. But their luck held and they ducked their heads whenever that jeweler brought her wares to the plaza after that.

Those were the good old days. Although he loved his adulthood—traveling the country and breathing new life into once-loved buildings was a rush, every time—he missed having a place to call home... a family to call home.

His phone dinged. A message from Travis: *Drinks tonight?*

He started to decline, his knee-jerk response that he was too busy, had things to do, had to get to bed early. But before he even realized what he was doing, a craving to belong again had him deleting his message and starting again. *Sure. When and where?*

Travis responded, *The usual. 8?*

Sterling smiled and wrote back, *Sounds good.*

"You really do have shit to do, man," he told himself then, and tore his gaze away from the window.

Sitting at the little desk, he opened his laptop, pulled up his blueprint software, and got to work. Within a few hours, he'd designed a stage and a dance floor and ordered all the lumber his crew needed to build them. His stomach growled, reminding him dinnertime had come.

As he approached the hostess stand at the restaurant downstairs, he saw June coming toward it from the other direction. Her face lit up when she saw him, and he wondered if his lit up, too.

"Fancy meeting you here." Her eyes crinkled at the corners.

He pointed at the ceiling. "I'm staying upstairs."

"Same."

His heart did a little happy dance even while his brain reminded it that another coincidence bringing them together meant nothing.

"You're not staying with Callie?"

She shrugged. "Once I committed to staying two weeks, I figured I'd better get out of Hayes's hair."

"He needs a haircut anyway."

The hostess reappeared from wherever she'd gone. "Two?"

Sterling and June looked at each other and shrugged. "Two."

"Right this way."

So what if he snuck a look at June's trim waist and peach-shaped butt as he followed the women through the dining room and to a secluded table in the corner? He was a man, after all, and she was a woman—the only woman he'd ever felt this attracted to.

"Is this all right?" When the hostess gestured at the table, June's gaze found Sterling's. The smile she offered him made him feel like they shared a sacred secret. Just like he had on the first night they met, Sterling decided to let himself pretend he and June were a couple, like this dinner date was typical for them, like he was the luckiest guy in the whole damn world.

"This is perfect." He maintained eye contact so June knew he was referring to that moment and not to the table.

As they sat, she winked at him and nodded at the hostess, who set down their menus and said, "Your server will be with you soon."

For just a moment, the two of them sat there looking at each other. The light from the candle in the center of the table flickered, casting warm light on June's skin. Involuntarily, Sterling envisioned June naked and bathed in candlelight, straddling him, moving with him, calling his name.

"How was the rest of your day?" June asked.

Casual. As if they did this all the time. As if he wasn't getting aroused right here at this table. As if he deserved a relationship with her. As if being here, together, was the most natural thing in the world.

"Good." He swallowed to release the tension in his throat. "I called the guys and they'll be here in a couple of days. And I ordered the lumber for the stage and dance floor."

June nodded. "What's good here, do you know?"

"I haven't eaten here in forever, but I have a feeling anything you order will be good. They used to be famous for their ribs, but I don't see those on the menu."

After a couple more minutes while she perused her choices and he watched her, completely absorbed in her movements, she set down her menu. "I think I'll try the chicken marsala. What are you going to have?"

He couldn't admit that he hadn't been focused at all on the food, so he glanced down and chose the first item his eyes focused on. "I'll get the ribeye."

"Can't go wrong with that."

They set down their menus and Sterling found himself speechless. She was just so beautiful.

"Has it really been five years since you were in town?"

Tension coiled in his chest. "Five years."

"Wow," she said, looking dreamy. "I can't imagine getting a five-year break from the Hotel Cartwright."

"Five years may be a bit much. Since I came back, I've been hit with a deluge of memories. It borders on overwhelming."

"Any good ones?"

This woman. He'd expected her to throw a bunch of questions at him about why he'd been gone, but she seemed to sense he didn't want to talk about it.

"Lots of good ones," he said. "In fact, I spent some time reminiscing today while I looked out the window at that fair on the courthouse plaza. God, we were troublemakers. One of the buildings used to have this old fire escape ladder—I'm certain it wasn't fit for use anymore, but the four of us would climb it and hang out on the roof. Once, we made paper airplanes and threw them off the roof at people. We thought we were so funny. I hadn't remembered that in years."

"You guys must have had a blast growing up."

Another barrage of memories hit Sterling then. Evenings around the bonfire, the wood popping and sparks flying. He and his brothers, lying on their backs in the bed of the old pickup truck, stargazing and talking about girls and school and teachers. The discovery he'd made five years ago that turned his family upside down.

"For the most part," he said. "What about you? What was it like growing up in that four-star hotel?"

She sighed. "I have to admit, when I was a kid it was pretty magical. I had the run of the place, of course. On weekends and holidays, I had so many kids to play with. There was always someone in the pool or on the playground. As I got older, I loved to check out the boys who came through. Not that I ever did anything with any of them, but it was fun to squeal to my friends about how cute they were." She laughed, and he was enchanted, picturing her as a giddy teenager. "When I went away to college, I realized how many opportunities are out there beyond the hospitality business. I hadn't really realized it before, and I certainly hadn't considered it, but suddenly, the whole world opened up, and all I could think about was doing my own thing."

"Only, your parents wanted you to stay."

She nodded. "Right."

The server came to take their order and after he left, June said, "My first summer back, I brought up the idea of starting my own business. I don't think my parents meant to discourage me, but they basically made entrepreneurship sound like a slog. They told me how fortunate I was to have an established family business to work for and eventually take over. They made it sound like I'd be crazy to branch out. And as young as I was, I listened. I always figured, 'Oh, I'll just wait a few years and then venture out on my own.' The years passed, and here we are."

"I can definitely relate to that," Sterling told her. "Growing up, the four of us staying here to run the ranch was a given."

"But you left." She looked thoughtful, contemplative.

"I left."

"And now?" she asked.

"And now ..." he sighed with gratitude when the food came, but she was still looking at him, waiting for his answer, when the server walked away. He picked up his knife and fork and cut a healthy bite off his steak. "I have mixed feelings about being back."

He put the steak in his mouth, hoping to end the conversation there ... at least for the time being ... because she was one of the reasons he had mixed feelings.

* * *

Three days later, Sterling stood on the site of his childhood home and latest project, watching the guys from the lumber yard unload boards and beams onto the open field next to the old arena. The whole scene glowed in the afternoon sunshine and for a moment Sterling was able to forget everything that happened in the past and look at what lay before him as nothing more than a job, a place to transform, to make beautiful despite everything humans and time had done to it.

He heard the sounds of vehicles turning off the main road and onto the driveway, and all those questions swirled back up to the forefront of his mind: What would his crew think of the place? What would they think of him after seeing it? What would they think of his family?

But then they pulled up and parked and jumped out of their

trucks and jogged up to him, giving him hugs and handshakes and smiles. His throat tightened with unexpected emotion, and he hoped no one noticed his eyes tear up.

"Hey, boss!" Riggs brought up the rear, wrapping his massive arms around Sterling as the others broke into small groups and checked out the stacks of lumber and the blueprints Sterling had laid on a table nearby.

"Thanks for coming," Sterling said, half hoping Riggs couldn't hear the tightness in his voice and half hoping he could; it was a better expression of gratitude than he could put into words.

Riggs patted his back and then stepped away and put his hands in his pockets. "Wouldn't miss it, man. A chance to learn more about your mysterious past? I'm here for it."

Did his guys think he had a mysterious past? Sterling laughed off the comment, but it stuck with him.

"I was thinking you guys could set up over there." He gestured at an open area between the sites of the stage and dance floor.

Riggs nodded. "Looks good, boss. When's the tour?"

The tour? Sterling hadn't planned on showing them around, but he should have. Of course they'd want to see his childhood home. His hackles rose, fueled by shame, as he pictured the rundown big house, main barn, and arena.

"It's kind of a mess, man. I haven't been here in five years, so..."

"Still," Riggs said. "It'd be cool to see it all. We won't judge, you know that."

He did know that. With a curt nod, he said, "Tomorrow, then. First thing."

Body buzzing with stress, Sterling returned to the hotel that evening with a takeout pizza box and a six-pack of beer. He should walk it out—head to the courthouse and do laps. But he couldn't bear to interact with anyone else that night.

Still, as he sat at the little desk overlooking the plaza, grease dripping from his fingertips, the burn of the spicy pepperoni warm on his lips, he couldn't help but think of June and wonder what she was doing. He sipped his beer, which was half gone, and he swore he could feel the alcohol entering his bloodstream. It'd be easy enough to find her considering they were staying at the same hotel. The longing to be with her hit him hard and caught him off guard. He'd returned to his room seeking solitude, hadn't he? Yet, he wished she were here. Not in a passive way, like it would be nice if she were, but in a visceral way that made his bones ache for missing her.

Why had he been so bull-headed about getting her phone number?

Because you were afraid you'd be tempted to use it.

He could get up, wander the hotel, hope to run into her. As he downed the rest of his beer, he imagined himself walking the halls, calling her name. That vision produced a chuckle, and he knew with certainty he'd better stay put. He couldn't afford to make a fool of himself.

But. He could call Callie and get June's number. He could text her. That wasn't quite the same as having her here, in his room, in his arms, in his bed, but it was a connection.

Opening a second beer, he nodded. Yes, that's what he'd do.

He picked up his phone and pulled up his text string with Callie. *Can I have June's number?*

She responded with a smiling devil emoji and, *I think you have June's number.*

Sterling cringed. Debated whether to cut the conversation short or pursue his mission at the expense of his pride. Decided he was this far in, he may as well go for it.

Sterling: *Pretty please with sugar on top?*

Callie: *That's what she said.*

Sterling rolled his eyes, took a gulp of beer, and decided he'd better slow down on the drinking.

"It's just as easy to make a fool of yourself over text as it is in person," he muttered before typing, *Never mind. I'll ask someone else.* His face burned. Why did she have to make this so hard on him?

Callie: *No one else has it.*

He waited.

Finally, she wrote again: *I'm just messing with you. Here you go.*

She shared June's contact card, and while shaking his head Sterling wrote back, *Thanks*, hoping she could read his begrudging tone.

A smiley face showed up on his screen. *Be careful, Sterling. She's my best friend.*

He didn't know whether it was a warning or a plea, and he didn't know how to respond. A thumbs-up? Too sarcastic. A smiley face? Too friendly. Okay? Too flippant.

He settled on *I will*.

Chapter Thirteen

The early summer sunrise blinded June through her closed eyelids. She gasped, pulled the covers over her head, and cursed herself for forgetting to close the drapes the night before.

It's not your fault you were distracted.

She uncovered her head and smiled into her pillow as she remembered the unexpected way the evening unfolded. She was in bed, in pajamas, and in the midst of working up her confidence to tell her parents she didn't plan on going home for the Timothy Alexander wedding. Her thumb hovered over the call button on her mom's contact photo. A text notification popped up.

She didn't recognize the number, but her heart thudded happily in her chest when she opened the message and read, *Hey, June. It's Sterling.*

Grateful for the distraction, and more than a little pleased to see who it'd come from, she closed out her mom's contact and opened her texting app.

Hey, Sterling.

Yes, she had butterflies like she was a teenage girl again.

Yes, she was grinning so hard, her cheeks ached.

Yes, she let herself forget she'd been about to tell her parents not to expect her home.

Sterling: *What are you up to?*

Was he making casual conversation?

June: *Just getting ready for bed.*

Sterling: *This early?*

June: *Absolutely. I'm in my pajamas, sitting in bed with a good book and a glass of wine.*

Had she said too much? The unsolicited description of what she was wearing would certainly come across as a come-on. Especially because it was pajamas.

June: *I was also procrastinating on telling my parents I pre-paid for this hotel room and I'm not coming home.*

Sterling: *The relaxing part sounds pretty amazing. I don't envy you the other part, but I've been there. I'm in my room, eating pizza and drinking beer, people watching.*

June: *See anyone on rooftops?*

Sterling: *Ha. Not yet.*

June: *Excited about getting started tomorrow?*

He didn't respond right away. She waited, staring at her own words at the bottom of the screen. Antsy, she set down her book and got out of bed to walk to the window. The sky was mid-transformation, somewhere pale and violet between the bright blue of the afternoon and the deep blue of late night.

Despite the hour, people remained on the courthouse plaza. Some of them walked on the wide sidewalks, arm in arm or alongside a dog. Others lounged on the grass, pulling the warmth out of the day's very last rays. A rowdy group of boys threw a football back and forth, tackling each other at random, wrestling on the grass.

Sterling: *See those kids?*

June: *The ones playing football, or the ones lying in the grass?*

Sterling: *Football.*

June: *Yeah. Looks like they're having fun.*

Sterling: *They are. They don't even realize how much. Anyway. About tomorrow. I'm excited but nervous. Don't tell anyone I said so, though.*

June: *Don't want them to think you're too invested?*

She meant it as a joke, a gentle ribbing, but almost right away she worried he might not realize that. She rushed to add, *I'm kidding. I know you're invested.*

The football-playing boys had ended up in a heap on the grass, arms and legs and elbows and knees going every which direction.

Sterling: *I'm invested. For now. Just like I would be with any project.*

June couldn't say why those words made her feel sad, but they did. She changed the subject: they chatted about long summer days and rowdy boys and ice cream until her eyelids were closing of their own accord and she had to get back in bed.

And now it was morning and she hadn't called her parents and she had to work up her confidence from scratch again. She groaned.

"Just *do* it, June." She brought herself to sitting and groaned again. "Fine." She drew out the word for dramatic effect. "After tea."

The electric tea kettle she'd bought for the room took less than two minutes to boil and she was back in bed with a cup in one hand and her phone in the other. "It's now or never."

She'd lost her mind. Here she was, sitting in a hotel room alone, pining after a perfect-for-her-but-unavailable guy, afraid to call her parents.

In her mid-twenties.

"Just dial, June."

She obeyed herself and used her thumb to call her mom.

In an unusual turn of events, the phone rang and rang and finally went to voicemail: "This is Clara Cartwright. So sorry I missed you. Leave a message."

As the beep sounded, June cleared her throat. When it finished, she panicked. What to say? "Mom. Give me a call." God, that sounded ominous. "Everything's fine! Hope you're still having fun! Talk soon! Au revoir!"

Hands shaking, she hung up. She couldn't believe she was reacting this way to disobeying her parents—as an adult. She'd obviously misused her teenage years. That's when she should have gotten all this out of her system. But instead, she'd spent all this time doing exactly what her parents expected of her ... what everyone expected of her.

Funnily enough, she did what she expected of herself, too.

And she was tired of it.

Things were going to change—starting right away.

Although she'd planned to spend most of her day in town, asking business owners for silent auction donations, she decided to change things up. But first, she had to go shopping.

Two hours later, she pulled into the driveway of Sweet Springs Ranch.

"Wow," she breathed when she saw the buzz of activity near the old arena. Several pickup trucks with box trailers were parked in a neat row, and another row of pop-up shades stood over tables lined with tools. A bunch of men in jeans and work boots walked the site, measuring and staking and talking.

The place looked alive. It wasn't even her place, but June felt the emotion rise in her chest like a balloon filling with helium. She parked and got out, doing her best to be invisible. It worked for a moment as she walked the perimeter of the space where the stage and dance floor would be.

Her breath caught when she saw Sterling.

He was in his element. He'd shed all the memories and feelings that weighed him down here in his hometown, and he looked like the carefree man she'd met at the airport in Great Falls.

And that made him so damn sexy.

He didn't see her so she decided to spend a little time getting the lay of the land.

She should have known her invisibility would last only so long. A lone woman—and a stranger—in a sea of men stood out. As she walked around the outer edge of the industrious group, each set of men she passed quieted, until she'd made the full circle and created a near silence.

That's when Sterling saw her ... and his face lit up, which caused June's whole body to warm like she was sitting by a fire. She couldn't think of a time a man had ever looked so happy to see her, or that her entire being had reacted this way to it.

He surprised her by jogging over to her, the grin remaining, his eyes bright. She could have sworn he wanted to hug her, but he stopped himself short and offered his hand for a shake. It was all she could do not to laugh when she accepted.

"June!"

"Sterling!"

"What are you doing here?" She started to answer, but he kept talking. "I mean, not that you're not welcome here. It's just that I wasn't expecting—" He stepped back and gestured at her outfit. "Are you planning to work?" Again, before she could respond, he went on. "Not that we can't use the help. It's just that Callie mentioned you had errands today.

Was he nervous? He looked past her and ran a hand over the back of his head. He *was* nervous. Adorable. Also, he knew she planned on errands that day.

"I did plan on errands today, but I was excited to see you breaking ground here." She shrugged, as if her decision to be there, his reaction to her, and her reaction to him were no big deal.

"I'm excited, too. Here, come meet the guys."

The guys had stopped feigning lack of interest and were all now openly staring at her.

"Guys, this is June. She's in charge. June, these are the guys."

"Hi, June," the guys chorused, and she said, "Pleased to meet you."

The introduction seemed to break the spell and the guys went back to what they were doing.

"It's nice to see you here," Sterling said. "Are you really planning on working?"

"You sound surprised. I'll have you know, I can handle a set of tools as well as the next guy."

"I am surprised. Not only are you heiress to the Hotel Cartwright, but you can also handle tools?" He winked, and she flashed him her most self-assured smile. "You bet your ass."

"I'll put you to work then."

Within a few minutes, she had a post at the smart end of the measuring tape. Someone handed her pieces of wood with lengths marked on them and she measured and cut them. The repetitive simplicity of the work allowed her to listen to how Sterling interacted with his crew.

"How did Sarah take it when you told her you were coming out here?" Sterling asked his foreman, Riggs.

Riggs laughed, a big, hearty sound that made June think she could be friends with the guy. "Oh, you know. She said she's going to call up her boyfriend to keep her company while I'm gone. And then she insisted on a date night. We stayed over at that new hotel on Wallis Street."

"Sounds nice. Sorry to pull you away, man."

"Hey, it's cool." Riggs laughed again and June couldn't help but smile. "I got a night of hot hotel sex with my wife."

"Dude."

"You should try it."

"Hot hotel sex?"

"Romance, bro."

Sterling guffawed. "Thanks for being here. I know the girls have that summer volleyball league, too."

Sterling knew what Riggs's kids did? June measured, drew a line, waited to cut until she heard Riggs's response.

"No biggie, man. I figure I'll head home for their big tournament next weekend. The way everything works out, I only have to miss one game. Sarah will take video for me."

"That's good," Sterling said. "Wish them luck for me, okay?"

"I will, thanks." Riggs walked off, calling out to a group of guys who were mixing cement for the stage footings.

Another couple of boards showed up on June's workbench, and she measured each one and cut it. Until then, she'd been handing the cut boards to whomever showed up to take them. She hadn't looked up, but this time, she heard Sterling's voice.

"Pretty clean cuts, here."

She shot him a look. "Did you expect any less?"

"Nah. It was my way of giving you a compliment."

A hand on her hip, she said, "You know, you could just say, 'Nice cuts, June.'"

"Touché." His lips quirked into an almost-smile.

Because she wanted nothing more than to kiss them, she looked away, grabbed her next set of boards, and measured.

"Seems like we're making good progress today," she said, positioning the saw.

"We are," Sterling said.

The saw whined and sawdust flew. When she finished, she looked up to see that he'd turned around and was surveying the progress. God, what a view. Those jeans looked like they'd been made for him, and he could very well be featured in an advertisement for those boots. He was looking off to one side, and she decided his profile belonged on a statue. The early afternoon sunlight cast shadows that highlighted the muscles in his arms and legs.

He turned around to look at her again and caught her staring. She quickly closed her mouth and resisted the urge to slap a hand over it. She could swear he knew she'd been ogling him, based on the humor etched in the lines around his eyes.

"I hate to admit this." He came toward her. "But now that we've started, I can see the vision. And I might be a tiny bit excited about it."

June couldn't say why her heart beat faster at his admission. "I'm happy to hear that. I think it's going to be a fun event. And, obviously, successful. It doesn't matter how fun it is if it doesn't save Sweet Springs."

Sterling nodded and turned around again. "I'd better go make sure they've got the posts level in the footings."

Watching him go, June hoped she hadn't said the wrong thing. She'd always believed in keeping the goal top of mind. She cut a couple more boards before her phone rang.

Of course. Her mom had to call back right when she was sinking into the swing of things.

"It's now or never, June," she told herself and heaving a deep breath, she answered the phone.

"Junie! I know you said everything's fine, but your voice sounded strained in your message. Are you sure everything's fine?"

It's not going to be, when I tell you why I called. "Great, mom! Everything's great. Look, I know you wanted me to come home, but I'm going to stay here in Prescott. I've got a hotel. It's nonrefundable. I'll walk Maya through everything."

In the silence that followed, she chastised herself: *You completely abandoned your game plan.* Backpedaling, she said, "Remember how I told you Callie asked me to help with this project? Well, I've fallen in love with it."

And I might be falling in love with a certain man related to the project.

More silence.

"Mom?"

June's mom cleared her throat. "June, I'm so glad you've fallen in love with this project. I'm happy for you. But I'm worried about your duties at the Hotel Cartwright, honey. No one can do them like you can."

"Maya can do them just like I can!" June's voice was insistent. "Maybe even better."

From across the miles, June heard her mom sigh. She could picture exactly what her face looked like: disappointment showed in little lines at the corner of her mouth and a crease between her eyebrows. She tilted her head to one side, as if trying to puzzle through this sudden change in behavior—or character.

"Are you sure everything's okay, June? You're not acting like yourself." She gasped. "Have you been kidnapped?"

The only alternative to crying—her mom's response to her not doing what she wanted was to ask if she'd been *kidnapped?*—was to laugh.

"Of course not, Mom. I've just found a project I'm really excited about. It's only two weeks, and then I'll be home."

"You know, I saw something about this on Insta. Tell me something only you would know."

The pile of wood for her to cut was growing. She tucked her phone between her ear and shoulder and measured a a few sticks. "That's to prove it's really me. Do you think I'm an imposter?"

"Oh. Right. How do I know you haven't been kidnapped? You

know, we should have come up with a code word for this, knowing Dad and I were going to be halfway around the world."

"I'm fine, Mom. You're just going to have to trust me."

"June." Her tone hovered somewhere between pleading and trying to break a stubborn child out of her fit. "Can we compromise?"

As tempting as it was to look directly into the afternoon sun and blind herself so her parents would never expect her to work at the hotel again, she looked and focused on a fluffy cloud in the western sky. Her eyes watered.

"No, I'm afraid not. I've got to see this through, Mom."

At this point, her desire to see the Sweet Springs project through was equal only to her desire to win the argument.

"You can't miss the Alexander wedding, Junie."

I can't *not* miss it, Mom. The guy hates me. He's ridiculous. He doesn't listen to a thing I say. That wedding will crush my soul." June knew her mom wouldn't take any of those responses seriously. "I'll be there for Maya every step of the way. You won't even notice I'm gone."

Inspiration hit: she remembered a piece of advice her mom had given her when she was babysitting an argumentative little boy, David, one summer. "You don't have to win every argument, June. Just put an end to the conversation."

With that memory fresh in her mind, she cringed and said, "I've got to go, Mom. Love you."

She disconnected and dropped the arm holding the phone, tilted her head back, and managed not to scream.

"Everything okay?" Sterling's voice—in all its husky, rumbly glory, sent a wave of relief rushing through June's body. Looking at him, the concern evident in the squint of his eyes, she knew she'd made the right choice. He needed her here as much as she needed this fundraiser.

The bright smile she offered him was completely genuine. "Everything's okay. I just told my mom that I'm not coming back until after the fundraiser—not even for the groomzilla wedding."

"I can tell from your post-call expression that you're not accustomed to going against your parents' wishes. Are you okay?"

"I'm ..." An unusual feeling was swelling up inside her chest ... was it excitement? She'd declared her freedom. She'd given herself two weeks to do what she wanted. It wasn't the rest of her life, but it was two weeks—more than she'd ever had as an adult. "Great, actually. I'm great. I may have just given my mom a shock, but she'll recover." June's phone rang and she wasn't surprised to see her mom was calling her back. "You know what? I'm not going to answer. I've told her what's happening, I have a plan in place, and there's no more to discuss."

"I get the feeling I should offer you congratulations." He held out a hand to shake, and she took it and pumped it twice. "Thank you."

Chapter Fourteen

Something strange was happening to Sterling, and June Cartwright was behind it. She'd shown up at the job site that day in jeans and a plaid shirt with cut-off sleeves and work boots and he couldn't take his eyes off her.

God, she was beautiful. Her arms were toned and her hair shone in the sunlight and she moved with all the feminine magic in the world. She knew how to use a tape measure and a saw and she kept her head down and helped out and joked with the guys and barely talked to him all day.

When she'd hung up with her mom and he watched her expression go from defeated to exhilarated, he wanted nothing more than to whisk her away somewhere they could be alone and he could soak in that energy and show her how much fun it could be to do what she wanted. She might not know she wanted him yet, but he'd show her.

She probably had no idea she'd inspired him.

With her enthusiasm.

With her courage.

With those jeans he wanted to peel right off her legs.

Most of all, the interest she took in the ranch inspired him.

When his brothers showed up in the late afternoon, he kept seeing her talking with them. Hot flames of jealousy licked at his insides when she laughed at something Cash said or touched Travis's arm.

He pretended not to notice but always found ways to move so he was within earshot. June asked so many questions about the ranch: about growing up there, their favorite aspects of ranch life, their best memories.

And boy, were they anxious to share.

Cash, of course, talked about how much he hated chores in the wintertime. But he surprised Sterling by admitting to June that he looked back on those days with fondness; his memories of those dark, early mornings feeding the horses and cows and livestock were some of his favorite.

"We dreaded those chores," he told her, and Sterling felt his own lips twist into a rueful smile. All four of them did dread those chores, but Cash always complained the loudest. Cash went on, "But the older boys, they made it fun. They made up these stupid songs..."

As his story went on, Sterling remembered those stupid songs, and how they'd laugh and laugh as they sang them, each of them adding a phrase or line or word until they had a full (if nonsensical) song.

Oh, we hate the cold, we hate the snow, we hate how slow the golf cart goes.

We hate the hay, we hate the wet, we hate that asshole Barry Burnett.

Barry smells like stinky cheese. The hair is thickest on his knees.

Sometimes he and Hayes would sing about Cash and Travis, and a good-natured fist fight would delay the chores getting done. Twice or three times, they'd finished so late, they had to skip breakfast to catch the school bus.

"Fortunately, neither Sterling nor Hayes could function on an empty stomach—still can't—and they focused their songwriting on kids at school after that," Cash was telling June.

They *had* grown up having fun here. Sterling wandered away from the job site and over to the old arena.

For years, they'd lived a magical existence. Maybe that's why it hurt so bad when their mom left and Sterling discovered their dad had a serious gambling problem and risked losing everything.

He hadn't told his brothers the whole story but after the falling out with his dad, he'd taken off and started his own, separate life—one nobody could ruin but him.

For the past five years, he'd lived that life indignant and self-righteous, telling himself he didn't want or need his family or the ranch or anything associated with them.

But there he was, his feet sinking into the dirt in exactly the way he remembered, the afternoon sun shining through the leaves on the cottonwood trees in exactly the way it always had, and his heart falling into the ranch's rhythm as if he'd never left.

None of those things erased what had happened, but he could feel them starting to heal him. For the first time since coming home, he could envision the property fixed up again. He reached the old barn and ran through a mental checklist of what he'd do to restore it: he'd have to replace a couple of beams in the ceiling and probably all the boards on the east side of the building. The sun had done a lot of damage there. Although the roof was in pretty good shape, it could use reinforcing.

He was so immersed in his thinking, he didn't sense Hayes coming up behind him until his brother was at his side.

"Hey, man."

Sterling jumped. "Hey. You should really warn a guy if you're going to sneak up on him like that."

"I didn't sneak. You were deep in thought."

"You're right."

"You and your guys are making great progress already." Something unfurled in Sterling's chest at that. He hadn't literally been holding his breath, but he suddenly felt like he could breathe again and the realization struck him that he'd been nervous about how his brothers would react to his work.

Merging these two parts of his life—present and past—was terrifying. Despite the fact that he'd barely talked to his brothers recently, their opinions meant the world to him.

"Thanks." He kept his tone nonchalant because to reveal how much the compliment meant would spell doom.

Hayes punched him on the shoulder. "I'm glad you're back, man. Place isn't the same without you."

"Wait." Sterling turned to face him, his face breaking into a smile. "Are you saying you missed me?"

"I'm not saying I didn't." Hayes's smile faded. "Listen, man. Not to get all mushy or anything, but I'm proud of you. I've never said it because you left angry. Angry at us. But I've been keeping up with you—we all have—and everything you've done? It's pretty cool, dude."

He clapped Sterling on the arm, then, which Sterling figured was as close to a hug as they'd been in forever. The gesture gave him a funny feeling in his core, one that made his throat tighten.

"Thanks," he managed. "I wish I hadn't left under the circumstances I did, but I've enjoyed having something of my own. And it's pretty cool to be able to bring that back here and—hopefully—help out."

Hayes smiled again. "I think with your skill set and June's vision, not to mention her skills with a set of tools, we should be able to pull this thing off."

"If you and Callie weren't already getting hitched, I'd say you have a thing for June."

"That's just jealousy talking, bro. She's great. She's smart and funny and drop-dead—"

"Stop it!"

Hayes's eyes sparkled. "What? I'm just saying. I guess *you* have a thing for her."

Sterling ground his teeth, didn't answer.

Just like he'd have done when he was a teenager, Hayes jumped away from Sterling, eyes wide, smile wider as he pointed at him. "You do! You have a thing for her. I knew you guys hooked up or whatever—"

"We didn't hook up. We spent one evening together in Great Falls."

"Right." Hayes situated his features into something resembling a serious expression. "You spent one evening together in Great Falls. But think about it. Isn't that a crazy coincidence? You both show up in the same spot in the same airport at the same time and don't have flights and then end up going to the same place? It's a one-in-a-million chance, right? And she shows up to *work* today. I think the universe is trying to tell you something, bro."

"I don't know."

Hayes rolled his eyes. "You *don't know?* Dude, what's wrong with you? It's obvious you guys have the hots for each other."

Sterling shot him a dark look.

"I mean, it's obvious you share a connection." He wiggled his eyebrows.

"So what? After the next two weeks, we'll never see each other again. She's got to go back to her hotel, and I've got to get back to work. I never stay in one place long. It's not conducive to a relationship, even if I wanted one, which I don't."

"Huh."

"Yeah. Huh."

"Have you ever considered that it doesn't have to be that way?" Hayes crossed his arms and looked over at the crew. "You could have a home base. You could travel with your significant other. You could—"

"I know what I could do."

"Bro. Seems like you told yourself five years ago that you'd never settle down. And you've held yourself to that, ever since."

Sterling grunted. Hayes didn't know how close to the truth he was.

"But that June..." Hayes said. "She might change it all."

"Knock it off."

"Fine." Hayes grinned, relaxed his posture. "Whatever. But just know, I'm rooting for this you-and-June thing. I might start taking wagers."

"Don't bother. What are you doing here, anyway? Don't you have something better to do?"

"As a matter of fact, I don't. I've got it on my schedule to hang out with you this afternoon. Want to put me to work?"

"Yeah, so you'll stop talking. Why don't you go dig ditches?"

"For real?" Hayes hated digging ditches. "I hate digging ditches, man."

"Gosh, you sound exactly like you did when you were twelve." Sterling whistled to get Riggs's attention. "Hey, Riggs."

"Yeah, boss?"

"Get my brother a shovel, will you?"

"One shovel, coming right up."

"Asshole," Hayes said.

Sterling grinned. "Same to you."

In the middle of his stalking away, Hayes paused and turned around. "Hey, Sterling?"

"Yeah?"

"I think it's time you tried dating. And we have the perfect candidate right here."

Sterling flipped him off and he sauntered over to where Riggs waited, holding a shovel.

Hayes was right. There was no reason Sterling should avoid dating *forever*.

Maybe the universe *was* trying to tell him something: that he and June could be good together. Opening that door now didn't mean he had to marry her, for goodness' sake. But wouldn't he regret it if he never took the chance? Yes. He would.

That realization fortifying him, he went in search of June. Her cutting station was empty, but finding her wasn't difficult. The sounds of conversation and laughter punctuated the industrious hammering and drilling, and there she was, in the center of it all, laughing right along with his guys while she held up boards and and checked their fit, just like she'd been doing it all her life.

He cringed when some of his guys obviously mistook his determination for anger and scampered out of the way when he approached. Even June's smile froze.

Geez, you'd think I yelled at these guys all the time.

Or, maybe they're worried because they're all socializing with the good-looking newcomer.

That perspective put the ease back in his stride and he noticed everyone else relax, too. "Cartwright," he barked. He jerked a thumb over his shoulder. "Can I get a word?"

At that point, she grimaced and Sterling wondered if she felt guilty for distracting his crew. He led her over to the old arena and leaned against the fence.

"Am I in trouble?" She put her hands on her hips and looked up at him, an uncertain smile on her face. He wished, desperately, that they were alone, so he could kiss her senseless and show her just how very much trouble she was in, but he could sense Riggs and the crew listening, watching, their movements slow and careful so as not to disturb the air.

"Listen." His voice was barely louder than a whisper. Her eyes widened in fear. Guilt swamped him. He put a hand on her shoulder. "Relax. I was going ask you out on a date, not criticize your workmanship."

This was not how this conversation was supposed to go. Now his own heart pounded, forcing blood and adrenaline through his veins, making his hands shake.

Fear turned to a surprise and she said, "You were going to ask me on a date?"

"Yeah. I was going to do it with a lot more finesse, too."

She laughed. "And here I thought you were going to chastise my workmanship. As close to perfect as it is. Also, I figured you might be upset with all the chatting."

She hadn't said no, yet. That was a good sign. But she hadn't said yes, either.

"Oh, the chatting is nothing new. These guys chat constantly. But I don't mind because they do a damn good job. And you're right, your workmanship is damn near perfect."

She gave him a smug smile.

"Now I'd like a do-over. Would you be interested in a date?"

He watched every trace of nervous energy evaporate from June's being. "I would love to go on a date with you."

Happiness buzzed all over his body, little bubbles popping against his skin. *She would love to go on a date.*

"Great. I was hoping you'd say that."

"When would you like to go?"

"How about tonight?" He kicked himself. *Tonight?* That seemed too desperate.

Fortunately, she said, "I was hoping you'd say that. Want to meet in the hotel lobby?"

He loved the way her eyes sparkled with humor. She found this conversation amusing. "Yes. Can we tentatively plan for seven? I'd like to see how we finish up here, and make a plan or two for the evening."

"Yep. Sounds good. Can I get back to work now, boss?"

Certain his expression looked as amused as hers, he shook his head. "Of course. Don't let me keep you."

She sauntered off, hips swaying in those jeans, inviting him to run his hands over her curves. He only stopped watching her when he felt eyes on him and looked up to see Riggs, smiling like he'd discovered a secret.

He lifted a chin at his friend. "Shut up, man."

Riggs shrugged. "I didn't say anything, bro. But sounds like you might be taking my advice. I'm proud of you."

"Shut up."

For the rest of the day, Sterling went through the motions, helping build the support for the stage, calling out instructions, making mental notes about supplies they needed. But mostly, he looked forward to that evening, considered how he could make his date with June extra special. If he only had a limited time with her, he had to make it count.

* * *

There were lots of things Sterling loved about summer: the early sunrises in ice-cream pastels, the monsoon storms that quenched and refreshed the dry desert landscape, and the way everything went bright green and vibrant and alive. But the best thing about summer was how the evenings stretched long and luxurious into night, fading slowly, slowly, so you could squeeze out every last drop.

That's what he wanted to show June on their date. He wanted to squeeze every last drop out of the day, with her.

Five minutes before seven he waited in the lobby, his back to the window, watching the elevator. Three minutes later she came down the stairs. Sterling inhaled. She was so beautiful. She'd changed into dark jeans and a flowy white top that showed off the rise of her breasts. And she'd done something to her hair—it cascaded down over her shoulders and collarbone, curling at the ends.

At once casual and dressed up, it was obvious June put effort into preparing for their time together. *For me.* His jeans felt a bit tighter, and he did multiplication tables in his head to keep himself from getting too aroused before they'd even said their hellos. His body moved toward her of its own accord, and he reached out for her as she came down the last step.

"Hey," he said.

She slipped her hand into his. "Hey."

The contact sent a pleasant buzzing up his arm and into his chest where it settled, thrumming. He couldn't quite think of what to say to her, how to sum up his reaction to her. *You look like an angel. I've never seen anything more beautiful. I can't believe you're here to see me.*

He settled for, "You look nice," but immediately wished he'd been able to come up with something more accurate.

"Thanks," she said. "You look nice, too."

Sterling felt like an eternity passed in that moment while they stood there holding hands, looking into each other's eyes. He could see a future for them, one where she smiled at him like that every day. While they stood side by side at the kitchen counter, chopping vegetables and sipping wine. While they walked along the sidewalk on warm afternoons, ice cream cones in hand. While they sat next to each other in bed, backs against the headboard, about to watch their favorite TV show.

That freaked him out. "Shall we?" He offered his arm and she took it, and they walked to his car in companionable silence.

Twenty minutes later they turned into Sweet Springs Ranch.

"Did you forget something at the job site?" June asked.

Sterling grinned at her across the cab. "Nope. I have a surprise for you."

Driving past the stage-in-progress, the old arena and barn, and the big house, he found his grip tightening on the steering wheel. Nerves clawed at his stomach. He couldn't remember the last time he'd worried so much over whether a woman would enjoy a date. As if June could sense his uncertainty, she ran a hand from his shoulder to his wrist, easing his hand off the steering wheel, sliding her palm against his and intertwining their fingers. "I'm intrigued."

When risking a glance at her, Sterling found she did look intrigued, and realized June was exactly the right woman for this date. He felt his nerves evaporate, and that fizzy feeling in his veins. Once again he dared to let in a little confidence. A little hope. He pulled up in front of Travis's barn and put the car in park. "Well, let's get to it."

June raised her eyebrows at him, game for any challenge.

"Have you ever been horseback riding?" Sterling asked as they came around the hood of the truck and he gestured at the barn.

June gasped, and words tumbled out of her mouth. "Is that what we're doing? I went once when I was ten. After that I begged my parents for horses but, as you can imagine, it was always, 'June, we live in a hotel! We can't have horses!' That was probably one of my favorite experiences of all time! Is that what we're doing?"

She grabbed his hand and rushed forward. Charmed by her excitement, Sterling allowed her to pull him along. She opened the barn door, launched herself in, and stopped short when she saw the two saddled horses standing just inside.

"Oh my gosh," she breathed, her movements stilling. "They're so beautiful." She looked back at him like she couldn't quite believe what was happening and then returned her attention to the horses. "What are their names?"

Sterling stepped forward and put his hand on Chewy's neck. "This is Chewy, and this is Leia. They're Travis's horses, but I asked if we could borrow them for a couple of hours."

Although her movements were slow and careful, her energy almost knocked him off his feet when she came up behind him and wrapped her arms around his waist, laying her head on his shoulder. "Thank you. Thank you so much. This definitely goes down as the most special first date ever."

First date. That implied there would be subsequent dates. Sterling leaned back against her. "You're welcome."

She released his waist and stepped back. "Shall we?"

Although his body sorely missed the presence of hers against it, he laughed. "Yes. I'll give you a little refresher, just in case. And then we'll go."

She listened attentively while he went over how to mount, how to use the reins, and how to speed the horses up or slow them down. When it finally came time, she pulled herself up onto Leia's back in one fluid motion.

"You're a pro. You got on this horse like you've been doing it your whole life."

Inclining her head she said, "Thank you. I *have* been doing it my whole life. At least, in my imagination."

Sterling put on the cooler backpack he'd brought and mounted Chewy. They rode out of the barn and he noticed the shade of the sky was already starting to shift.

"There's a certain spot I want to reach before dark," he told June, "but we're going to have to ride at a pretty good clip. Are you okay with that?"

He could feel the giddiness coming off of her when she nodded. "Are you kidding? Of course I'm okay with that."

He'd been away from the place for five years. The ranch should be consuming all of his attention. But Sterling found he couldn't help but watch June. He found himself taking in every detail. The way the setting sun set her skin aglow, the way the color of the sky—a blend of flaming orange and pink—lit up her eyes. The way she smiled at him, an almost childlike joy radiating from her. He didn't think he would ever get enough of this woman.

The trail he'd chosen ran along the edge of the Wilder property for two miles, and then up a gently sloping hill to Prickly Pear Point, which overlooked a wide sweep of the valley below.

It took about thirty minutes for them to reach the overlook. When they did, June gasped. "What a view!"

He was looking at her when he said, "It really is."

The sun, a shimmering disc of fire, kissed the horizon.

June reached out and Sterling took her hand. They sat together, watching the sun sink lower and the sky grow brighter.

"The sunsets out here are really spectacular. Nothing like the ones in Great Falls."

Sterling squeezed her hand. "I told myself sunsets were the one thing I missed about Arizona."

"Are you saying you now realize you missed other things?"

For the first time in what felt like ages, Sterling felt as though he could be completely honest. With June and with himself. "Yeah. I didn't let myself think about it, but there are lots of things I've missed. Most of all, I miss my brothers. For so long, I was afraid they were mad at me, but I missed them like hell. I also miss the little things. There's a bird that comes through every spring. I don't know if it's the same bird, but it's the same type of bird. I always hear the same call. It's like a little song. I've never heard it anywhere else in all the places I've been. I used to feel like that bird was talking to me. Every spring, he came back and said hello."

"That's nice," she said. "Maybe it *was* the same bird, and maybe it *was* talking to you."

"Maybe. I also missed the air on winter mornings. When we'd go outside to do the chores, we could always smell the chimney smoke. It doesn't smell the same everywhere. But now that I've been away, that scent is like home. I miss the way, in springtime, we always get that one late frost. It clings to the brand-new leaves on the trees, and the ice sparkles when the sun comes up. There's nothing else like it."

Sterling noticed that while he spoke, the heaviness he'd carried for the past five years started to lift away. He loved this place. Yes, he'd been telling himself he hated it, that it was an albatross, that he never wanted to see it again.

But maybe that was because he was so afraid of losing it. If he told himself it meant nothing to him, maybe it wouldn't hurt so bad to let it go, to know another family was living there.

Suddenly, a sense of certainty overtook Sterling. Then and there, his childhood home, his family property behind him, a woman beside him who inspired him to let down his walls, he decided he would do absolutely anything it took to save the Sweet Springs Ranch.

Chapter Fifteen

June figured Sterling had to be the most romantic man she'd ever met. First, he surprised her with horseback riding, then a glorious sunset—almost as if he'd had hand in painting the vivid masterpiece—and then he said, "I brought a picnic, but I figure we should head back and eat at the ranch. I don't want to rush our ride, but I don't want to be riding back in the dark, either."

June actually felt herself melting, a phenomenon she'd read about in many a romance novel but never experienced firsthand. "You brought a picnic?"

He tilted his head. "What did you think I had in this cooler?"

"I don't know. First aid supplies or something?"

"It's food. They say feeding a man is the fastest way to his heart, but I swear it works on women."

She could see he was only joking. His eyes crinkled at the corners, his mouth barely managed to restrain itself from smiling. Still, she couldn't help but say, "You trying to get to my heart, Sterling?"

He held her gaze, the humor fading from his expression. "Maybe I am."

With that, he nudged his horse into motion, and hers fell into step.

"This trail makes a big loop, kind of does a tour of the property. But I think we'd better go out the way we came in."

June nodded and gave her horse its head. She figured it probably knew the way back to the barn.

Meanwhile, she admired Sterling on horseback. Just like when he stepped into his role as owner of a successful restoration company to start preparing for the fundraiser, in the saddle he possessed a confident, relaxed air. She saw none of the tension she'd observed that first day at the ranch. He sat tall in the saddle, shoulders dropped, chin lifted. The crease between his eyebrows was gone, and he didn't tap his fingers on his leg—a nervous habit she'd noticed over the past several days.

Instead of looking around, jumpy, like a rabbit who could sense a snake's presence but didn't know exactly where it was, he seemed calm and in control. They rode back in near silence and June listened to the quails calling, their soft hoots gentle in the evening light.

At the barn they dismounted and June asked if she could put up her horse. Sterling led her through the process step by step, periodically coming over to help her, his hand on her lower back to guide her, his breath close to her ear when he demonstrated how to remove the bit. He handed June a brush and she ran it over Leia's back and shoulders, down his neck.

Sterling, making the same long slow strokes June was, said, "I've been debating about where to build our little fire for the picnic. If I were in high school, I'd say we should scrap the fire and go straight to the barn loft."

June paused what she was doing and straightened up to look over the back of her horse at Sterling, who winked. "Don't worry. I'm not a teenager anymore. And besides, I'm not sure the barn loft is in good enough shape for two adults to go up there and make out."

"Are you planning on making out?"

Another flash of humor, this one edged with fire. "Might be."

"Huh." June should be scandalized. There she was, alone on a ranch with a strong, callous-handed man who'd just admitted he planned on making out with her on their first date. Or was it their second date? Either way.

But more than anything, she was aroused. She continued brushing the horse. Not only had she experienced his touch for herself, but for the past few minutes she'd paid careful attention to the way his hands moved over the horse's body. Sterling's sure, gentle caress would feel so, so good on her skin. She had to stop this line of thinking or she'd jump him right there in the barn with the horses watching.

"Where else could we go?"

"Adult Sterling is going to have to think about that for a minute."

June's horse shook her head, tossing her glossy mane and surprising June, who yelped.

"Ah." Sterling held up a pointer finger. "I know just the place. We'll have to dig up a couple of chairs."

It *was* the perfect place. As the sun descended, shooting its rays into the sky, Sterling led June to a spot in the big house's backyard. He found some chairs and a little folding table in the shed and they set those up next to the giant oak tree whose limbs stretched as tall as the house itself. The two of them collected rocks to make a fire ring and wood to make a fire, and Sterling lit it, the flames jumping and dancing.

"Wow," June said as the flames flickered silently, growing larger with every passing second. "You did that in about three seconds."

His cocky grin set her heart aflutter.

On the table, Sterling laid out a masterpiece of meats and cheeses, fruits and nuts, crackers and tiny slices of bread.

"You're an artist," June said. "I didn't realize you're such a multi-talented guy."

With a flourish, he pulled out a bottle of white wine and two plastic wine glasses. "I wanted to impress you."

"It worked."

June picked up a slice of meat and a slice of cheese and rolled them together. "Have you gotten to spend as much time with your brothers as you wanted to since you've been here?"

"As you know, I didn't want to spend *any* time with them." He smirked. "But that changed once I got here and we had a couple of beers."

After popping a roll of meat and cheese into his mouth, he said, "We've seen each other every day, but I'd love to just hang out with them a little more. We've been so busy with all this fundraiser stuff. So maybe when that's over, I'll stay for a few days, lurk around, get in their hair."

"Cash has some nice hair."

Sterling laughed. "He's always kept it long. I can't tell you how many times my parents harped on him to get haircuts. At least right now it doesn't look as shaggy as it did when we were in high school. It was always in his eyes."

"Well, staying for a few days sounds really nice." The weight of melancholy seeped into June's limbs as she realized those few days would happen after the fundraiser was over ... after she left town. And that was only a handful of days away. Suddenly she was anxious to change the subject and focus on the present moment. "I love watching cooking shows. I once saw this guy who spread soft cheese onto a piece of bread like this and then put berries on it. Have you ever tried that?"

Mouth full, Sterling shook his head.

"Let me make one for you." She felt his eyes on her as she picked up a slice and the little cheese knife he'd thought to bring. She spread the cheese and then carefully arranged a handful of berries on top of that. She held out the creation and Sterling's fingers brushed hers when he took it, sending chills up her arm.

"Looks delicious." He held her gaze as he took a bite. Once he started chewing, he nodded, then groaned in appreciation and pleasure. If June hadn't been sitting down that sound would have made her weak in the knees. As it was, the groan conjured up an image of her straddling him, taking him into her body.

"That's really good," he said, mouth full.

"Glad you like it."

A minute later, after June made herself the same treat, Sterling said, "My turn."

He filled the wine glasses and then stacked crackers, cheese, and meat into a miniature sandwich. He put a green olive on top and held it out to her. "You have to eat this in one bite. And then right after you swallow, you have to take a sip of the wine."

She nodded, obeyed. The little sandwich was divine. Creamy cheese, salty meat, and the tangy olive sang in her mouth. This time, she groaned in pleasure, and she saw his eyes light up.

Who knew eating could be such an erotic experience?

June swallowed and lifted her wine glass at the same time Sterling motioned for her to do so. The cold burst of fresh fruit made her groan again. They spent the next thirty minutes repeating the process—offering one another delectable combinations of the charcuterie, watching one another eat them, taking pleasure in the sensual but platonic activity.

"That was delicious. And fun. And even though I could keep eating, I probably shouldn't. I don't want to be too full."

"Same," Sterling said. "But I'm pretty sure that's going down in the books as the funnest first dinner date ever."

June pursed her lips. "I'm not sure funnest is a word."

He smirked. "In my book it is."

They worked together to clean up the remaining supplies and stow everything back in Sterling's cooler.

"Want to lay by the fire and stargaze?"

The sight of the firelight playing on his features made her want to swoon. "Aw, there he is."

"Who?"

"Teenaged Sterling. Earlier, you said you were thinking about making out. And now you want to lay down and stargaze by the fire. I'm pretty sure I know where this is going."

He shrugged, the gesture exaggerated. "You got me." His gaze turned intense when he said, "I mean, we could just stargaze. But I wouldn't be disappointed if that stargazing turned into something else."

"That sounds nice." After a beat, she added, "Especially the part about the stargazing turning into something else."

Her whole body vibrated with anticipation when he grinned at her before grabbing another blanket out of his truck bed spreading it next to the fire. All that anticipation ended up between her legs as he refilled their wine glasses and handed her one.

"I'll put that little table over here, too, so we can set our wine on it."

A few minutes later, they lay side by side on their backs, looking up at the sky. He surprised her by reaching down to link his fingers with hers. Again, the simple gesture sent chills up her arm and neck and over her scalp.

"Our skies are rarely this dark in Great Falls." She made circles on his hand with her thumb. "Seeing the stars like this is really something."

Sterling inhaled, held his breath, and then exhaled long and slow. "It is. Another thing I forgot to appreciate as I traveled the country. I've seen so many versions of the sky, but none quite like this one."

They didn't speak for a few moments, but the night wasn't silent —or even quiet, really. Crickets sang, bullfrogs croaked, and an owl hooted.

"I love it here." Her voice came out in a whisper.

Sterling rolled onto his side, facing her, and cupped her face with one hand. "Could you stay?"

Her heart thudded inside her chest as his fingertips traced her jawline and made their way down her neck to her collarbone. "I don't know," she managed. "I don't think so. My parents would just die if I didn't go home. They act like they *need* me, like the hotel needs me."

Resting his hand on her chest, Sterling said, "But what about you? Do you want to stay at the Hotel Cartwright forever?"

"I mean, I grew up there. It's the only home I've ever known. And I do love it. Who wouldn't? It's one of the top hotels in the nation. Just ask *Hospitality Magazine*."

Sterling chuckled.

"But seriously. I'd love to explore a bit so I could make an informed decision about whether I wanted to stay there. And I'd really love to work on events that aren't related to Cartwright Hospitality. For clients I get on my own merit—not just because they know the hotel."

Wow. She'd never taken the time to clarify these feelings ... and she'd certainly never spoken them out loud. It was as if her whole being opened up. To the possibility of doing something that belonged to her, to the idea of stepping out of what she'd known her whole life, to the excitement of paving her own way.

"Maybe you should. Explore, I mean."

"Maybe I should."

"We can talk more about this later. But for now, how about we kiss?"

June, too, rolled onto her side, and found she couldn't keep from smiling. "How about we do?"

She brought her mouth to his and he slid his hand down to her hip and kissed her back. There were no fireworks or explosions, but a warmth spread through June's body, making her pliable and relaxed as he used his tongue to part her lips. And then her hand was in his hair and their bodies moved together and his hand was on her breast.

The wood in the fire cracked and popped, and the crickets sang, and June wondered why they couldn't stay in this moment forever.

Only hours later, after she and Sterling had talked and kissed and talked some more, and he'd driven her back to the hotel and kissed her until she had not a coherent thought in her head, did June come down off her high.

And that was only because when she picked up her phone to set her alarm for the next day, she saw a message from her mom: *Just got back from Paris. We need to talk.*

Chapter Sixteen

The morning after the trail ride, picnic dinner, and stargazing with June, Sterling woke energized and almost giddy. He wasn't surprised an image of June was the first to come into his mind. June, bathed in firelight, smiling at something he said. Smiling because of him. Smiling like there was nowhere she'd rather be.

Maybe if he hurried, he could run down to the lobby's coffee shop and get her something before she left her room. It wouldn't hurt if he caught a glimpse of her in her pajamas. His body, still warm from sleep, responded to that image by becoming totally aroused. He cursed himself. He should have waited to think about June in her pajamas until she was lying next to him and he could do something about it.

He flung back the covers—grateful for solitude at the moment— and went to grab a quick shower. Downstairs, he ordered a regular latte for himself and a tea latte for June and then had to stop himself from jogging up the stairs to her room. Balancing both cups in one hand, he knocked on her door. Maybe because he'd been envisioning her in bed, he was surprised when she answered almost right away. Even more so that she had her wet hair up in a towel and was wearing a hotel robe. And more disappointed than surprised that she didn't smile when she saw him. He told himself maybe she was just tired, and held up her tea with what he hoped was a devilish grin.

That, at least, prompted a smile.

"Sorry," she said. "I forgot I've been through about a million emotions since you left me last night, and you don't know about any of them."

Something like worry took shape at the back of his mind, an annoying, gnat-like buzzing. "Tea latte?" He held out her cup.

"Thank you." Reverence in her voice, she took it from him and pulled it toward herself like it was a long lost treasure. "I didn't sleep much last night."

Finally, Sterling found his voice. "What happened? Is everything okay? We don't have to—"

She held up a hand to stop him and took a long drink of the latte, her eyes closed. As she took one step into the room and then another, gesturing for him to come in, the tension lines relaxed around her eyes and mouth.

"That's better." She opened her eyes. "What happened is that my parents got home from Paris."

"They were expecting you to be there, weren't they?"

June grimaced. "No. They also weren't expecting the head of security to show them footage of you and I making out outside that suite."

Sterling felt his jaw go slack. "Security footage?"

"Yes. I don't know why I didn't think of it that night. I'm sorry. I'm an idiot. I got caught up in the moment and completely forgot there are security cameras in every single hallway."

"You forgot about the security cameras?"

She looked at the floor, her mouth drawn into a frown. "I can't believe it. I'm so sorry."

A bark of laughter erupted from Serling's mouth. Then, because she still looked so forlorn, he wrapped his free arm around her and nuzzled her face. "You know what? That is the best thing anyone's ever said to me."

"You're not mad?"

He stepped away from her and threw his head back, laughing again. "Are you kidding me? Here you are, this gorgeous, smart, driven woman. That first night we spent together? The best ever. And you're telling me it was for you, too. You were so caught up in the moment, forgot about the security cameras."

A small, reluctant smile tugged at the corners of her mouth. "Well, when you put it that way."

"Please tell me you're not in trouble over this. You're a grown woman."

Finally, making eye contact with him again, June huffed out a sigh. "I'm *so* in trouble. Not because I was making out with someone, but because I was doing it in a common area. On the property. It's kind of an unspoken rule that if I'm going to make out with someone, I'd better do it in private."

"How many someones have you made out with?"

She shot him daggers and he held up his free hand. "I'm kidding. Is this the kind of thing where I can promise it'll all blow over?"

She shook her head and her gaze returned to the floor. "No, and especially not if I don't go home."

His stomach clenched at that. "Are you going to?"

This time when she looked at him, she had fire in her eyes. "The hell I am. I'm going to stay here. Which means I'm going to stay in trouble. But at least I'll have fun while I'm doing it."

"That's the spirit." He held up his paper coffee cup and she tapped hers against it. He said, "Cheers to troublemaking—and having fun doing it."

After they drank, he said, "I daresay you might want to get dressed before you have your fun today. I mean, I love seeing you in that robe, but now that there's footage of you making out with some scoundrel in the hotel hallway, it wouldn't hurt to put on a professional front."

"Thanks for that sound advice." Still smiling, she rolled her eyes. "Why don't you get out of here so I can get ready for the day? But first, tell me what you've got on your agenda."

"Not much. I'll just be at the job site, supervising. What about you?"

Tea still in hand, June walked over to the closet and moved her clothes along the rack. Her back was to him, and the robe barely covered her ass. "I have some phone calls to make and planning to do."

Shamelessly, he let his gaze roam over her legs, from ankle to calf to thigh. God, what he wouldn't give to take her from behind.

She spun around. "Did you hear what I said?"

Dragging his gaze upward to her face, he said, "No. I was staring."

She rushed to the bed, grabbed a pillow, and threw it at him. "Sterling Wilder. I was talking business."

He caught the pillow with one hand, then shrugged, amused. "I guess you shouldn't talk business when you're wearing nothing but a hotel robe and a towel on your head."

"I asked if I could come by today, help out at the site. After I'm done with what I need to do here." Despite her grumpy tone, her eyes twinkled.

"You like that I was staring at you."

She shook her head, rolled her eyes, and Sterling remembered his own parents before his mom had left. His dad was always teasing his mom, and she was constantly pretending to be exasperated.

"Not the point," she said. "So?"

He set down the pillow and his coffee and moved toward her, predatory. Her eyes widened and so did her smile.

"You can. But I require your entrance deposit up front."

"Yeah?" She set down her cup, too. "And what's the fee?"

Wrapping his arms around her waist, he backed her up to the bed. They fell onto the mattress together, and he slid his hands under her shirt to palm her breasts. Her nipples stiffened and he covered her mouth with his.

"Let me see," he said between kisses as he removed the towel from her head, letting her hair fall loose on the duvet. "How much is it worth to you?"

With deft movements, she unbuckled his belt and unbuttoned

and unzipped his jeans. He moaned when she released his cock from his underwear and wrapped her hand around it.

"I don't know," she said. "Maybe a little of this?" She pushed against his chest so he rolled onto his back and slid down to put her mouth on him.

He gasped. "That might do it."

Running her tongue around the head, she continued to stroke the shaft. Then she took him all the way into her mouth, moving up and down slowly, making him ache for her. He buried his hands in her damp hair and clung to her for a few more seconds before urging her upward.

"I'm about a half-second from coming in your mouth," he said, kissing her again. "Let me have a turn."

She tasted like Heaven and moved against his tongue like she'd been waiting for it her whole life. Taking hold of his head, she murmured, "*I'm* supposed to be paying *you*."

He laughed, the sound vibrating against her body as he used his tongue to pleasure her. "Trust me. This counts."

Moans overtook her laughter, and she rode him to the edge, crying out as she released, bucking against him. When the aftershocks subsided, he kissed his way up her stomach and to her neck, finding her mouth with his as she grasped his cock again.

"Let me finish you," she whispered. "Then we can call it even."

As she stroked him, he gave himself over to her strong, sure movements. It wasn't long before he, too, released, the feeling like fireworks that lit up his entire being. June gave him one more slow, lazy kiss, and then peeled herself away from him and stood up, her robe hanging open, reminding Sterling what she tasted like ... what she felt like.

"I'll get a towel," she said. As she walked into the bathroom, she threw over her shoulder, "Have I sufficiently paid my entrance fee?"

Zipping, buttoning, and buckling, he chuckled, totally charmed. "You bet your ass you have."

* * *

Sterling walked on clouds for the rest of the day. He couldn't stop envisioning June's mouth on him, his mouth on her. He couldn't stop hearing the tone of her voice when she was aroused, the sound she made when she released, her hands in his hair. By lunchtime, he couldn't even remember what he'd done that morning ... which items he'd checked off the punch list, which supplies he'd written down to order, which workers he'd assigned to which tasks.

Fortunately, he had Riggs.

"Boss!" Riggs called from the opposite end of the site.

Tearing himself out of his latest fantasy—one where June's legs wrapped around his waist while he thrust himself into her, their gazes locked—was difficult, but Sterling managed. He looked up at Riggs, who motioned for him to come over. He jogged away from where most of the guys worked on the stage, grateful the movement would tamp down his arousal.

"What's up?" Sterling looked over the progress on the temporary office Riggs had suggested. Designed to look like a tiny house, it would serve as the entrance to the fundraiser. People would buy raffle tickets, get bidder numbers and drink tickets, and ask questions there.

"Oh, nothing," Riggs said. "Just wondering what's up with *you*."

"This is looking good." Sterling gestured at the framed-in walls. "Genius idea. It'll really give people a feel for the event right when they walk in."

"Yeah, I think so, too. You know what, though? It wasn't my idea."

"No?" Sterling detected a hint of snark in Riggs's expression—it was the way he held his mouth.

"No," Riggs said. "It was June's."

At the mention of her name, Sterling's pants felt tighter and his chest felt all tingly. What was this sorcery? He shook his head to clear it and said, "Well, it was a good idea. And you've accomplished a lot in just a short time."

Riggs nodded. "I know. So? What's up with you? You've been walking around in a trance all day."

Another image of June looking up at him, her lips wrapped around his cock.

"You're blushing, bro. What is happening?"

Sterling cleared his throat. "Nothing."

"Wait. Is this about *June?*"

"What?" Sterling casually strolled over to examine the framing Riggs had done.

"You tell me."

"I tell you what?"

"Oh, my *God*, bro. You guys hooked up, didn't you?" Riggs's face was the picture of glee. "You told yourself you could keep things professional with her, but you aren't doing that. You can't do that. I can see it, plain as day. You *like* her."

Sterling could blame the summer heat for the temperature of his cheeks, but he knew better. He decided the best course of action was to play it cool. He shrugged. "I mean, who wouldn't?"

Riggs moved fast, punching him on the shoulder, hard. Sterling winced and Riggs said, "Come on, man. 'Who wouldn't?' Give me a break. This is going to be fun. Oh, and speak of the devil."

Gaze on the parking area, he lifted his chin, and Sterling followed his attention to the very woman they were talking about— who was coming toward them with the precision of a laser-guided missile.

"Oh, yeah," Riggs said, as under his breath as he was capable of. "I see it now. She's got a thing for you, too. You guys did hook up. She's wearing it on her face."

She is. Because of me. Because of us.

She was beaming, luminescent in the summer sun as she walked toward them in long strides. Her jeans fit her like a damn glove and Sterling wanted to peel them off her body then and there.

"Hey," she said.

"Hey," he said back.

"Thanks for letting me come."

"Thanks for coming."

The air between them was charged. Crackling with sexual energy.

"You're welcome. Anytime."

Riggs, whose head had swung back and forth during the exchange, whistled long and low and gave a single nod. "I'll leave you two to it."

They were alone (relatively), and Sterling didn't know whether to shake her hand, hug her, kiss her, or lean her up against the tiny-house-office building and have his way with her. When he finally got out of his own head enough to really look at her, he saw that she was grinning broadly.

"It's no secret what you guys were talking about."

"What do you mean?" he tried.

"Were you talking about this morning?"

Panic flooded his veins, replacing the warmth he'd just felt with ice. "No," he said. "Absolutely not." When he saw that her eyes were still laughing, he softened his response. "I never kiss and tell."

"Why was Riggs so awkward, then?" Her lips twitched.

"He was asking if we hooked up," Sterling admitted. "But I didn't confirm or deny. Your timely arrival saved me."

"I guess I shouldn't kiss you 'hello' at this point."

His dick—the jerk—responded that she should, but he ignored it. "Probably not. The hotel's already got footage of us making out in the hallway. The last thing we need is for someone to take video with their phone and post it online." Just as he finished saying the words, he regretted them. "Too soon?" he said.

"Nah," she said. "It's fine. Maybe we should give them some-thing to take a video of, though." She caught her lower lip between her teeth and looked at him through her lashes and he fell for her a little more in that moment.

"Let's give them a shot of you getting to work," he said, and she smiled. "Fine."

They spent the next few hours working together, building panels for the stage floor. Although several women had worked on his crew, Sterling had never invited someone in whom he was inter-ested to come to a job site, much less help out. But he found he liked it with June. They worked seamlessly together, falling into an easy rhythm as they measured and cut and drilled. Meanwhile, they talked. About the stage, the fundraiser, the town, the weather, their favorite foods, and their least favorite foods.

When Riggs hollered, "Quittin' time, everybody!" Sterling felt an odd pang of disappointment. Another one. How was it possible for him to feel like that every time he had to leave her?

Did he have to?

She'd just finished stowing her tools in the trailer and he grabbed her hand. "I'll walk you to your car."

She nodded, and again, he marveled at how easy things felt between them. But was that only because they knew they'd be together only until the fundraiser? He didn't want to think about that at the moment.

"Got dinner plans?" he asked as they reached her car.

She leaned against the driver's door and her gaze raked his body from head to toe and back again. "I don't know. Do I?"

Not for the first time, he laughed out loud. "I'd like you to. With me."

"Then I guess I do. I'm in the mood for salad."

He wrinkled his nose. "Salad? What about a nice, juicy burger?"

"Let's go somewhere that has both. How about that diner down-town? The one on the square? I hear they have salad, burgers, and beer. And we can walk there from our hotel."

"Deal."

Chapter Seventeen

June woke up the next morning and decided it was the last morning she'd wake up alone. Yes, it was her idea for the two of them to go their separate ways after dinner the night before, but it was only because she had lots of prep work to do for the next day.

But here she was, wishing more than anything that Sterling was there in bed with her, that she could run her hand over the stubble she knew covered his chin, that they could get ready together while talking about their plans for the day.

Her phone dinged and she smiled before she even confirmed it was Sterling. She smiled even bigger when she read his text: *I'm tired of waking up alone.*

She wrote back: *I'm still in bed, in the process of waking up. If you want to come over.*

It seemed like forever before he responded. *I wish I could. I have to go to the job site to sign for a delivery.*

She sent back a sad emoji and typed, *Can't Riggs do it?*

He could, but his family's coming today.

June wanted to pout, but she admired Sterling for making it possible for Riggs to be with his family.

That's really sweet of you, she typed. *How long will you be there? You could come with me today, after the delivery.*

It was a long shot. They'd discussed it at dinner. She planned to make the rounds with local business owners, asking for donations for the silent auction and raffle. Sterling had made it clear he worried entrepreneurs wouldn't want anything to do with the fundraiser, with the Wilder family, or with him.

To her surprise, he responded, *Actually, that sounds like fun. Especially if you'll let me take you to lunch.*

She wrote back, *Deal. Just text me when you're done, and we'll meet up.*

Sitting down at her hotel room desk, she pulled up a map of Prescott on her computer and a list of local businesses on her tablet. For the next hour, she mapped out a route. If she was smart about it, she should be able to hit downtown businesses one day, those at the mall another day, and outliers on a third. Once she'd done that, she used highlighters to color code business types. Ideally, she'd get silent auction items and raffle prizes from a variety: salons, restaurants, landscaping companies, hotels, car washes, gyms, florists.

Picturing all the items they could list on their social media posts and advertisements gave June a fluttery feeling in her chest. They could bring in so much money for Sweet Springs Ranch. All she had to do was what she did: plan a kick-ass event that *worked.*

Sterling texted that he was ready to meet up and would be at the hotel in fifteen minutes. They agreed to meet in the parking lot behind the building and when she walked out there, she found herself breathless at the sight of him.

He leaned against her car in his worn boots and perfectly fitted jeans and light blue button-up shirt, the sun shining on his hair and his eyelashes casting shadows on his cheeks. His face lit up when he saw her, and she felt like the only person in the world. Rushing up to wrap her arms around his waist seemed like the most natural thing in the world. He enveloped her and kissed her on the top of the head.

"Good morning," he said, not letting go of her.

"Good morning to you."

"This is a nice greeting."

"I thought so, too," she said.

After a few beats, they stepped back to look at each other. June's heart ached and her throat tightened at the idea that this (whatever it was) could last only for a couple of weeks until she went back to Great Falls. But she couldn't dwell on that now. The fundraiser was her priority.

"Ready to go?" She infused her voice with cheer.

He squeezed her hands. "Ready."

Once they were in the car, she handed him her list. "I figured we'd start with the downtown businesses today, and then move on from there."

She backed out of the parking spot and drove through the lot.

"What do the highlights mean?"

"Different business types. So we can ask for a variety of raffle prizes and auction items."

He whistled, and she glanced over at him as she pulled onto the main road. "I'm impressed. I mean, I already knew you were more than just a pretty face, but this is next-level thinking."

Her eyebrows drew downward, and the corners of her mouth, too.

He laughed out loud. "I'm only half-joking. I mean, you *are* more than just a pretty face and this *is* next-level thinking. But I'm not surprised. Callie said you were good, and I trust her. I'm just saying I'm impressed." She raised an eyebrow and he laughed. "I'm making a mess of it, but I'm saying it."

"Well." She made her voice as prim as she could. "You should be."

Again, he laughed. "I am."

"Good." A few beats of silence passed. "I wanted to start at the other end of town and work our way back, which makes our first stop A Cold One." She shot him a look. "I know you're familiar with it because that's where your brothers said you ran off to the other day."

"I'm familiar with it."

"I figured it'd be a good first stop for you, too. Seems like you get along with the owner."

"How did you gather so much intel, so quickly?"

She spotted A Cold One up ahead and started looking for a parking spot along the curb in front of the bar. She pulled in, put the car in park, and turned to wink at him. "It's what I do."

"Sheesh."

With that, they both got out of the car. As they approached the door, Sterling's chest rose and fell with a big sigh. June grabbed his hand and squeezed. "It'll be fine. You'll see."

"You're right." He opened the door for her.

She gave him a little curtsy before walking in and he grabbed her butt, making her yelp.

The bell rang over the door and Jerry called out, "Sterling Wilder! Second time in a week I've seen you! Are you going to become a regular again?"

He was already pouring a Budweiser. Sterling started to refuse, but June put a hand on his arm to lower it and whispered, "Let's have a beer. We've got to schmooze."

"What'll you have, young lady?"

"I'll take a Hefeweizen."

They sat on stools at the bar and Sterling blurted out, "You should know we're here on business, Jerry."

June's heart warmed when Jerry winked at him. She sent him grateful vibes for showing Sterling kindness. "I figured. Ms. June's got a folder and a clipboard. But it doesn't hurt to have a beer with an old friend, does it?"

Sterling grinned and tipped back his beer. "Maybe, considering it's not even noon."

Jerry made a dismissive gesture. "It's just one beer. You know, I think I'll have one, too. And while I do, you can tell me why you're here."

After pulling a glass from the freezer and pouring himself a Budweiser, Jerry came around the bar and sat next to Sterling. "How can I help you, son?"

June watched Sterling steel himself. He squared his shoulders and straightened his spine and turned toward his old friend. A rush of emotion ran through her—a need to protect him.

"As you know, my dad is a gambling bastard and chose to spend his money on bets and at the casino rather than on his mortgage payments."

June gasped and tried to cover the sound by taking a drink of her beer. Was that what had happened?

"Yes, I'm aware," Jerry said, his voice gentle.

"My brothers and I are putting on a fundraiser to bring the mortgage up to date. We're looking for donations we can use for a silent auction or a raffle. Or donations of drinks for the event. Would you be willing to help?"

"Of course, Sterling. I told you that the first day you came back here."

Sterling's shoulders slumped and June wondered whether it was a sign of relief or mental exhaustion.

"Thank you, Jerry." He reached out to shake Jerry's hand.

"You're welcome, son. I can supply kegs for the event, and I'll come up with a package for the auction. I'm not sure what it'll be, yet, but it'll be good. I'm honored to help you boys out."

Sterling's Adam's apple bobbed, and June felt her own eyes prickle.

"That's wonderful," June said. "Thank you, Jerry."

"Anything for the Wilder boys," Jerry said. "Bottoms up, you two. I assume you have more businesses to hit up."

"We do," they both said. They drained their beers and stood.

"Feel better?" June asked when they got in the car.

"Much."

"Does it make the next place any easier?"

"Depends," he said, one side of his mouth lifting in a half-smile. "Where is it?"

"Sherri's Cupcakes."

"I like cupcakes," Sterling said. "Is it new?"

"That's a question for Callie or one of your brothers," June said. "I have no idea."

It turned out, the proprietress of Sherri's Cupcakes was none other than Sherrilyn Ashford, formerly Bruner, Cash's date to junior prom—and her fondness for Sterling's brother hadn't waned.

"I heard about the ranch," she said when June told her why they were there. "I remember those summer nights in the cornfield like yesterday. I have a stake in this, too, you know. That place plays a huge role in my childhood memories. We can't have it going to foreclosure. Who knows who'll buy it?"

She offered to donate three dozen of her high-end, high-dollar cupcakes to the cause, and to supply mini cupcakes for the dinner.

"Two for two," June said when they got back in the car. She and Sterling high-fived across the console and they were off to their next stop.

They secured donations from Main Street Florist, The Sixth Street Pub, and Warm Loaves Bakery before Sterling said, "Can we get lunch? This emotional roller coaster has me famished."

They agreed on Su's Ramen and over noodles Sterling said, "I can't believe people are supporting us like this."

"Why not?"

He shook his head and June was torn between asking about the gambling comment and letting it lie. Sterling said it to Jerry, not her, and scratching the scabs off old wounds might be counterproductive.

"I figured, even if no one knows what my dad did—the gambling, which I don't know if my brothers even know about—"

"Wait." June held up a hand. "Your brothers don't know that's why he was behind on the mortgage?"

Sterling froze. It was almost as if he hadn't meant to tell her that. He licked his lips and looked away, his gaze straying to the window that overlooked the parking lot. "No. At least, they didn't know five years ago. I found out. I caught my dad and confronted him and then I left."

Although her jaw wanted to drop open and her eyes wanted to widen in surprise, June kept her expression as neutral as possible. She had so many questions: What did his dad say when he confronted him? Did he continue gambling after that? Was it possible there was another cause of him being behind on the payments?

"I know," Sterling said before she could come up with a coherent response. "Leaving without telling my brothers was about the lowest thing I could do. I left them with a huge problem they didn't even know about. Now they're in danger of losing the ranch, and it's my fault."

"Sterling." She reached across the table and took his hand. "It's not your fault."

He shook his head. "Agree to disagree. What if I'd said something? If I'd told them, maybe we could have stopped Dad somehow."

"It wasn't your responsibility."

He waved her off, as if he couldn't see the situation any other way. "Agree to disagree. And anyway, even if it wasn't gambling, letting your mortgage go is unforgivable. It's not like the ranch wasn't producing. Everyone knows that. He had the money. He pissed it away. And yet, everyone is still willing to support us."

June remained quiet, leaving space for him, twirling noodles on her chopsticks.

"I imagined people were going to turn us down cold."

His tone was thoughtful. June kept eating.

"I figured they would laugh in my face. You know, for the life of me, I couldn't figure out why my brothers wanted me to take the lead on this project. They're busy. Trace is trying to get the ranch up and running, Hayes is still helping out at Cool Pines Ranch, and who knows what Cash is doing? But me? I run my own company. I have flexibility. But I'm also the one who left."

"But you came back."

"Reluctantly." He dug into his ramen then, winding a massive amount of noodles onto his chopsticks. He smiled before putting the oversized bite in his mouth.

"Still. You did. And you agreed to help."

"Ha. Primarily because you're involved."

Was she *blushing*? The conversation had nothing to do with her.

"I'm sure that was icing on the cake, but you stuck around because you care. About your brothers and about Sweet Springs."

"I do," he said. "But not enough to tell them the truth, apparently."

June stilled, a bite halfway to her mouth. "You mean, they don't know about the gambling, at *all*?"

"Nope. And now five years have passed. The whole situation has gotten so big and ugly in my mind. It's like when you're five years old and there's that monster under your bed or in your closet, you know? It's giant and hairy and has three eyes and sharp fangs and long claws. The more you think about it, the worse it gets. Now, my monster has radioactive saliva and it breathes fire."

"And you're afraid it's going to come out before you're ready."

He nodded. "And it's going to kill the one thing that's really important to me: my family. June, if they knew..."

"If they knew, they'd still love you."

He gave her a rueful smile. "They would, but they'd also hate me. They'd be pissed."

Couldn't he see how much they loved him? When he'd left that first day in Prescott, they'd known exactly where he'd go—and they'd followed him. "They'd come around. I'm sure of it."

"I'm glad you're sure of it. Because I'm not. Anyway." He made a circular motion with his chopsticks. "Let's wrap this up. We have more donations to ask for."

At least he'd grown a little more enthusiastic about asking for donations. He paid their bill and they headed back out.

They got their first "no" an hour later.

"This is cute," June said when they stopped outside of Sprinkles, an Ice Cream Shop.

"Adorable," Sterling said, his voice playful and over-exaggerated.

She smacked his arm and he opened the door for her. As soon as they stepped inside though, he stopped short. Glancing at him, June saw he was looking at the guy behind the counter like he wanted to light him on fire with his eyes.

"Let's go," he said.

June's mouth worked and she was unable to come up with a coherent response before he turned around.

He hadn't made it to the door when the man behind the counter said, "Sterling Wilder."

To June, the guy speaking sounded like he held something bitter in his mouth.

Sterling's "Mason Rickett" was as monotone as it could be.

Her senses went on high alert. *What is going on here?*

"It's been a while." Mason pressed his lips together while he waited for Sterling to reply.

"It has. Since you screwed over my family."

"You can't blame me for your dad's bad habits, Wilder."

Sterling's nostrils flared. "I can blame you for helping propagate them."

Mason put down the rag he was using to clean the counter, then wiped his hands on a dry towel. "I hear the two of you are stopping by to ask for donations for your *fundraiser*."

"Don't worry," Sterling said. "I wouldn't accept one from you, anyway. We'll be on our way."

Compelled to fix the situation, June opened her mouth although she didn't know what she planned to say. Sterling took her upper arm, turned her around, and steered her out the door.

"What happened in there?" she hissed once they were outside.

"That guy's always been an asshole," Sterling said.

"What was that about screwing over your family?"

Sterling jerked his head at the car.

Inside, he said, "When I found out my dad was gambling, Mason was one of the guys involved. More specifically, he was the ringleader. I asked him to stop lending to my dad, to kick him out of their group. But he wouldn't. Basically told me it was none of my business. Implied I was a dumb kid and had no place butting in."

Ouch. June put the key in the ignition but didn't start the car. "I'm sorry. If I'd known—"

"You couldn't have. I couldn't have, either. An ice cream shop? Awful cutesy for such an asshole. Anyway. It's not on you. Let's let that one go and move on to our next one."

His jaw clenched and his hands were in fists and June had an overwhelming urge to comfort him. The best she could do at the moment was to run a hand up his arm and rest her fingertips on the back of his neck.

"I'm sorry," she said again.

He reached up, wrapped a hand around her wrist, and turned his head to look at her. "Thank you."

"You're welcome. Want to call it a day?"

"Let me see your list."

She grabbed the clipboard out of the backseat and handed it to him.

"We have a few more here. Let's just finish it off."

"All right," June said. "Let's do it."

Her phone rang just as she finished backing out of the parking spot and put the car in drive. The car's screen showed the call was from her mom, and she saw Sterling focus on the screen at the same time she did. They looked at each other, and Sterling's exaggerated grimace made June laugh.

"I'm not going to pick up. Let's just keep driving."

Eventually, as they picked up speed, the phone stopped ringing and June heaved a sigh of relief. Then it rang again.

"I think you might have to pick up," Sterling said.

She didn't know why she did it, but June pressed the button to answer the call over the car's Bluetooth system. She grabbed Sterling's hand when her mom said, "June Cartwright, why haven't I received any travel plans from you?"

"I'm not coming home just yet, Mom," she said. "Remember? I have to be here for the fundraiser."

Silence. Sterling reached across the console and took her hand. They stopped at a red light.

"June Myrtle Cartwright."

The middle name. June blushed furiously not only was her mom chastising her like a child in front of the man she was seeing, but also her middle name was ... well, Myrtle. She caught Sterling quirking an eyebrow at her. How many times had she been teased mercilessly when kids at school heard her middle name? Too many to count. Afraid to make eye contact with Sterling, she stared hard out the windshield.

"Mom."

"You have to come home. I just won't have this."

"I will, Mom."

Her mom's sigh of relief was audible over the car's speakers.

Then June added, "In a couple of weeks."

The beginning of an actual growl came through next, and her mom must have pressed the mute button because the sound cut out for a few seconds before, sounding very composed, her mom said, "That won't work. Do I have to come to Arizona to get you?"

June's head snapped to the right and she looked at Sterling. His eyes were round with surprise. Another driver honked and June realized the light had turned green. She pressed on the gas and said, "No. Absolutely not. Mom, I'm an adult. Which means I don't have to come home when you say so. I've made a decision to help with this fundraiser and that's what I'm going to do."

Before her mom could respond, she punched the end button on the car's screen. Her entire body trembled with adrenaline. Her palm felt sweaty against Sterling's, so she let go and wiped hers on her leg.

"Did that feel good?" Sterling wanted to know.

June's reply came out in a squeal. "I don't know." The next words were rapid-fire. "It felt good and also terrifying. I hate knowing I'm upsetting her. But also I can't just keep doing what she wants, every time, at the expense of what I want. And, shit. I was so caught up in that conversation that I passed our stop."

Sterling gave her thigh a reassuring squeeze. "I agree with you. And I'm proud of you. Sometimes going against our parents feels like the worst thing and the best thing all at the same time. And don't worry about our next stop. We can get it tomorrow, June Myrtle."

Chapter Eighteen

As he'd promised himself—and June—the morning before, Sterling woke up the next day with June curled against his body like a kitten. The sight and feel of her stirred up so much affection and tenderness and also fear. But he tamped down the fear as he made circles on her hip with his fingertips.

She made an "Mmm" sound as she woke and stretched, her body long and lean against his, and his arousal leaping to attention.

"What time is it?" she asked, turning to face him and bury her face in his chest.

"Seven."

She groaned. "I wish you'd woken me earlier. We have to leave in half an hour."

Glad she had her back to him and couldn't see how much that delighted him, Sterling let himself smile a big, goofy grin. "I'm sorry. I only just woke up, myself. I guess we were both tired."

And I slept better with you by my side than I have since we both came to Prescott.

"I guess so." She turned her face to give him a perfunctory kiss on the lips. "Still."

When she got out of bed, his body responded to her absence like she was part of him. He felt her—and missed her—like a phantom limb. He ordered coffee and tea while she was in the shower, and didn't miss the fact that he delighted in doctoring hers up and presenting it to her when she emerged from the bathroom, hair still wet.

She had to leave but he didn't, so he sat on the bed and watched her get ready. There was something about the process, the way she brushed on powder, carefully applied mascara, and combed out her hair that made him believe in magic.

And then she was gone and he didn't know quite what to do with himself. He'd planned to go over to the job site, and figured he'd better get there sooner rather than later. If he sat around the hotel pining after June, he'd fall even deeper for her. And that was something he couldn't risk.

Sterling was working on the stage backdrop when he heard the Wilder family whistle coming from the direction of the big house. He straightened up and looked over to see Travis hauling ass in his direction.

Sterling couldn't think of a reason Travis would have a burr in his saddle, but his elongated, purposeful stride reminded Sterling of the time he'd walked right up to him and punched him in the mouth. Granted, Sterling knew what he'd done that time. He'd flattened all four of Travis's tires so he couldn't leave on time for his date with Jeanette Gomez. Travis thought he was going to get to second base that night and they were all so sick of hearing about it, they couldn't wait to pull a prank on him. He was so mad. Steam-coming-out-of-his-ears furious.

Even bleeding in pain after Travis punched him, Sterling had laughed his ass off when he said, "Why are you wasting time punching me, bro? Fill up those tires and go pick up Jeanette."

Even all these years later, that memory brought a smile to Sterling's face. He promptly erased it though, just in case Travis really was mad at him. He set down his hammer and jumped off the stage, jogging over to meet his brother.

"You should see this," Travis said, shoving a file folder at him. Sterling felt a spike of adrenaline. What if it was proof Sterling had known about their dad's gambling, and Travis was here to confront him?

"What—"

"Just open it."

Vision going blurry at the edges, fingertips tingling, Sterling took a deep breath as he obeyed, laying the folder open on one palm so he could look through its contents. He heard his own sharp intake of breath when he recognized the first item right away. It was the torn-off cover of an architectural magazine. His ugly mug smiled up from the glossy paper. *Making Old Things New Again: Traveling restoration expert specializes in breathing life into historic buildings.* It was paper-clipped to a couple other pages: the entire spread of the full article, pictures and everything.

Sterling looked up at Travis, who nodded. "I found it in Dad's office. I don't know what beef the two of you had, but I do know he was proud of you."

A tiny flicker of joy leapt to life in Sterling's heart. His dad was proud of him. But then his cynical side piped up. *Or, he was watching your success in case he ever needed you to bail him out.* He returned his attention to the folder, flipping the first article over and looking at the next item. It was a newspaper clipping from the *St. Louis American*: *Out-of-Town Contractor Awarded Major Contract to Restore Government Buildings.* Sterling remembered that project. It helped put him on the map. At first, some of the locals were pissed that he—a wanderer and most definitely not a local—won the contract. They wanted their money to stay in town. Sterling got that. He didn't take it personally. And, he figured they would come around when they saw his work. He was right. Over the course of the handful of months he spent there, people stopped by to check out his progress and, ultimately, compliment him.

"I guess you're a pretty big deal, man." His brother's eyes sparkled with pride.

Sterling grunted, not used to hearing accolades from his family members. The next item in the folder was another magazine article about a cliffside hotel Sterling and his crew renovated in California. Not a front-pager, but a nice spread with lots of photos.

"I had no idea Dad was keeping track of my projects."

"He wasn't keeping track of your projects, dummy," Travis said. "He was keeping track of you."

He was keeping track of me.

Guilt swamped Sterling then, cold sludge washing over his skin. After all the horrible things Sterling said to him five years ago, his dad was still interested in what he was doing, still cared about his success. After their final conversation, Sterling left and never looked back. But maybe he should have. Not that he would unsay what he'd said—he'd only spoken the truth. But he might try to patch things up, have some sort of relationship, express appreciation for the life his dad gave him and his brothers.

Sighing, he closed the folder, did his best impression of a smile, and handed it back to Travis. "Thanks for showing me this."

"You okay?"

"Yeah. Just not what I was expecting."

Thinking about his dad brought the memories of his discovery—and the ensuing conversation—back in a rush as if he'd gone back in time and was experiencing them again. One night in the dead of winter he and the guys were at A Cold One. Looking out the windows, he could see the snow falling, illuminated by the strings of Christmas lights on the eaves.

Jerry cut the music mid-song. Sterling remembered it was "Sweet Caroline" and everyone in the bar was singing along with the chorus until the music went silent.

After all the disappointed groans died down, Jerry made an announcement from his spot behind the bar. "Hey, guys! The snow is coming down pretty good. If you're ready to go, now is the time to head home. If you plan on staying, you should probably hunker down. You're going to be stuck here a while."

A few pairs and groups packed it up and headed for the door while others hollered at them for wimping out. Sterling and his brothers decided to stay and when Jerry saw they were among a rather large group to decide the same, he said, "Shit. My beer supplier has been caught in storms for the past two days. We're going to need more beer."

Sterling volunteered to run to the liquor store two doors down. The shortest route was out the bar's back door and into the storage room of the liquor store—where he skidded to a halt when he saw a group of men sitting around a table, a huge pile of poker chips in the center.

That wouldn't have been a huge deal. People played poker all the time. What made it a huge deal was how all those men reacted when Sterling blew in the door, bringing snowflakes with him.

Every single one of them looked guilty: wide, shifty eyes, mouths open in shock. Every head at the table except one swung toward a fixed point. That fixed point was Levi Wilder, whose head didn't move as he stared at Sterling. His expression said, "Caught."

Someone else at the table (Sterling couldn't remember who, because all he could do was stare at his dad and his guilty expression) tried to play it off. "Sterling! How are you, my boy? So nice to see you!"

Another player looked down at the wad of cash he clutched in his fist and said, "You dealing in, boy? You're gonna need more than that!"

The table erupted in laughter and Sterling's heart beat so hard, he could see the blood pumping through the veins in his eyes. "Uh, no," he said once he finally found his voice. "I'm here for beer." While most of the men cracked up again, he jerked a thumb in the direction of A Cold One and said, "Jerry's out, and a group of us have hunkered down there."

The liquor store's owner, Mel Jackson, emerged from the front of the store when he heard that, and helped Sterling haul two cases of beer over to Jerry's. The funny thing about a snow storm, Sterling realized as they huffed and puffed their way through the cold, was that it made the air absolutely quiet.

If that night had brought a thunderstorm or even just a rainstorm, Sterling might not have noticed Mel's uncomfortable silence. The man didn't say a word to him. He just handed Jerry the case of beer and headed back to his store. Sterling spent the remainder of that evening pensive while his brothers and the rest of the bar patrons got rowdy playing darts and singing karaoke.

The next day, he walked into his dad's home office and shut the door behind him with a click.

Levi looked up from his desk and didn't smile. "Sterling."

"Dad." He nodded in greeting. "What was that last night?"

He didn't pretend not to know what Sterling was talking about. "Just a friendly poker game."

"You know," Sterling said, "I'd almost believe you if you all hadn't looked so guilty when I walked in the back door of Mel's."

Levi shut the notebook he had in front of him and folded his hands on top of it. "It was just a friendly poker game. Nothing more."

"Right," Sterling said. "You said. What's the buy-in?"

Levi waved him off. "You wouldn't be interested?"

So this is how it's going to be. Sterling widened his stance and crossed his arms. "I'm asking, aren't I?"

"It's a private club, Sterling. I'm not at liberty to share with you—"

"Whatever." Sterling turned on his heel, took two strides to the office door, and walked out. But he wasn't done. Later that night, he returned to his dad's office only to find it locked. Which he considered suspicious. Like a burglar in his own home, he found a flashlight, used it to find a small screwdriver, and picked the lock.

At first, he found only what he would have expected: invoices for hay and alfalfa, bills for tractor repair and horse shoeing, documentation on oil changes and tire replacements. But something told him to dig for more, and he did.

After a few minutes, he found what he'd suspected: ledgers related to gambling. Not just poker games, but horse racing, UFC fights, pro football and baseball. The breath literally left Sterling's lungs when he saw the numbers on those ledgers. They were *huge*. Levi Wilder had gambled away tens of thousands of dollars in the past six months alone. And he'd borrowed even more—against the ranch. He was so, so far in debt, Sterling figured he'd never recover.

He couldn't let his brothers find out.

They idolized their dad and Sterling wouldn't be the one to ruin that.

The only option was for Sterling to confront him, try to get him to stop, somehow pay off some of what he owed.

The next morning, clutching the sheaf of papers in his hand, he returned to his dad's office. "We need to talk."

Again, Levi made a dismissive gesture and said, "We absolutely do not."

That set Sterling's blood boiling. He thrust the sheaf of papers, now crumpled in his fist, toward his dad. "These numbers say otherwise. You're going to lose the ranch, Dad."

At least his dad had the decency to look chagrined. "I can win this back."

"You mean, you can *gamble* more money in *hopes* of winning it back?" He cringed at the vitriol in his own voice, but plowed ahead. "Based on what I'm seeing on these ledgers, your gambling hasn't been very successful. In fact, it's just gotten you deeper and deeper into debt."

When his dad didn't respond, he said, "Does anyone else know about this?"

His expression made it plain the answer was no.

Rage boiled up inside of Sterling's body like a volcano erupting. He had the presence of mind not to yell. Instead he hissed, "You'd better tell them."

He didn't bother waiting for his dad to answer. He threw the papers onto the desk and stormed out, then left the house for the rest of the day. When after two weeks his dad still hadn't told his brothers what was happening, Sterling left for good.

"Earth to Sterling." Travis's voice pulled him out of his memories, but that white-hot anger still bubbled in his veins.

"Sorry." He shook his head as if doing so would shake out those visions.

"Where'd you go, man?"

If Travis was digging around in their dad's office, he'd discover the gambling for himself soon enough. Sterling had barely spoken to his brothers for the past five years, much less asked them if Levi, the old bastard, had ever told them about all the money he'd lost.

What did they know about the reason he was behind on payments?

"Do you guys have any idea why Dad was behind on his payments?"

Travis shook his head, swore. "No. That's part of what I'm working on today. Going through his paperwork and stuff. I want to see if I can tell where things went wrong in case it's something we need to change going forward. Or, shit, maybe he was just senile and stopped paying the mortgage."

Sterling warred with himself. Telling Travis now wouldn't hurt Levi. He and the others already knew their dad wasn't totally on top of things. But it would hurt Travis. Not only because of Levi's addiction, but also because Sterling had kept it a secret all this time.

"All right," he said, wishing he had the courage to come clean. "Anyway, man, thanks for sharing these with me." He held up the folder. "I had no idea he gave a shit."

Saying the words—with his knew knowledge that his dad did, in fact, give a shit—felt uncomfortable, awkward.

"He did, bro. I know he was terrible at showing it, but he did."

Suddenly unable to speak, Sterling simply nodded.

"I'll let you get back to work," Travis said. "Have a good day."

"Same to you."

Chapter Nineteen

June had been in Prescott only a handful of days and already felt like a local. She was looking forward to the Fourth of July celebration with the kind of excitement she hadn't experienced since she was a child and her parents took her to a real amusement park for the first time.

The Wilder brothers had invited her to join the four of them and Callie, and Sterling swung by her hotel room to pick her up.

"I'm glad we're going to Travis's to have a drink before we go to the festival," Sterling said. "This day is going to require a lot of peopling."

June laughed, delighted. "I'll be a buffer for you. I'm great at peopling."

He wrapped his hand around hers and brought her fingers to his mouth to kiss them. Chills went running up her arm and down her torso, where they ended up as heat pooled between her legs.

"Thank you."

"Tell me more about the festival. I've heard about the food, of course, but what else should I know? What do you want to do?"

They'd reached the edge of town and Sterling turned onto the road that led out to Sweet Springs Ranch. "There's a dunk tank."

June inhaled to speak and as if he could read her mind he said, "Just for the record, I'm not getting in that thing. But I'll bet Cash will. We can try to dunk him."

"Fine," June pouted. "But I wanted to dunk you."

He gave her a side-eye. "The roasted corn is amazing. They put this butter mixture on it. I don't even know what it is. Fairy dust, I'm pretty sure."

"That does sound delicious. Callie was talking about the ribs, too."

"My mouth is watering already! They smoke those things all day until they're literally falling off the bone."

They'd arrived at the ranch and Sterling turned off the car. "Sit tight. Let me get your door."

It seemed like a sweet, romantic gesture until he hauled her out, shut the door, and backed her up to it, pressing his body against hers. "You can't wear an outfit like that and not expect me to want to put my hands on you."

"This old thing?"

Sterling ran a hand up her thigh and under the short denim skirt. His thumb brushed her underwear and she gasped. He smiled a wicked smile and used his other hand to cup her breast.

"Sterling! We're *all* meeting here. Someone's going to see us."

His kiss erased all coherent thoughts. "Ask me if I care." His gaze turned her blood electric.

"I'm guessing you don't." She was breathless.

At the sound of tires on gravel, Sterling winked at her and stood up straight, grabbing her hand and walking toward Travis's front door.

The parking lot was already filling up when they pulled into the festival ninety minutes later and June felt a pressing excitement. Through the fence she could see colorful booths and inflatable slides, balloons and American flags. The smell of meat cooking over charcoal wafted toward her. Country music played and although it had never been her favorite genre, June felt her body desperate to move along with the beat. "This is going to be so much fun!"

Sterling offered his arm. "Even *I'm* excited. I haven't been back in five years. It feels like an eternity, and like I was here yesterday. You're going to love this."

People at the entrance greeted them with patriotic pinwheels and Sterling bought them each a pair of plastic red, white, and blue sunglasses.

"I think the food trucks are over there." He pointed. "And in case you're wondering, the dunk tank is usually over that way."

They headed for the food and both decided on smoked ribs. While they waited for their order, June took in the scene. The place buzzed with activity. Kids zipped this way and that, some of them blowing bubbles, others eating ice cream, and others racing to get in line for the waterslides and bouncy houses. The adults milled around, holding baskets of food and plastic cups of beer, swaying to the music. The proprietor of the smoked meats food truck called Sterling's name. Their order was ready and they found a seat at one of the long tables the organizers had set up. Within a few minutes, the whole crew had squeezed in at the same table and June found herself right in the middle of what Sterling referred to as the Wilder family chaos.

"Hey, Cash," Hayes called, nice and loud so everyone could hear. "You gonna enter the hot dog eating contest later? I hear eating wieners is your specialty."

Cash balled up his already greasy napkin and threw it at Hayes, hitting him right in the face. "You bet I'm going to enter the contest. And when I win, you're going in the dunk tank for that insult."

The balled-up-napkin-turned-weapon sailed back toward Cash.

"Whoops! I guess I'd better be careful. I don't want to get any barbecue sauce in your long, flowing locks."

"Wow," Travis said. "You're just full of it today, Hayes. Better be careful what you're dishing out."

Sterling's brothers continued to sling insults, napkins, and straw wrappers. Even as the energy ratcheted up, June looked across the table to see Sterling watching her. And despite all the excitement swirling around them, the two of them shared a moment. A connection.

I'm falling in love with him.

June would have reached across the table and taken his hand, but by that time his brothers had managed to toss splotches of beans, mac and cheese, and barbecue sauce on the tabletop. And was that a puddle of beer?

As if he could read her mind, Sterling raised an eyebrow and smiled. "Are you numbskulls about done destroying this table? I'd like to go check out the games."

A disorderly cleanup followed, everyone throwing away trash and doing their best to wipe down the table with the tiny napkins the food trucks provided. And then they were off, the group of them strolling along like the little posse June never realized she wanted.

Travis challenged his brothers to a darts tournament, and Callie stage whispered to June, "Brace yourself. This is going to turn into pandemonium, and take about an hour."

Sure enough, after one reasonably calm round, they needed a tiebreaker. June and Callie watched as they as the four grown men bickered over rules and dart placement.

Callie leaned against June and said, "You want to go find something else to do while these monkey-brains act like children?"

Lips twitching with amusement, June nodded. "Did I see a fresh lemonade stand over by the food?"

"You did," Callie said. "Should we hit it up?"

"Absolutely."

Callie put two fingers in her mouth and whistled. "Hayes, Sterling."

The two of them jumped to attention as if they were about to get in trouble. Grinning, Callie said, "June and I are going to get some lemonade. We'll catch up with you."

The guys waved.

The sun beat down on the festival and June pulled her hair into a ponytail as they walked.

"We've both been so busy," Callie said, "I haven't had a chance to ask you how things are going with Sterling."

June wondered whether Callie could see her going all dreamy inside. "I'm happy to say he's actually been a huge help with the fundraiser, despite his early reservations."

Callie scoffed. "That *is* great. It's also not what I was asking about and you know it." She gave June a playful poke on the arm. "I mean, how are things going with the two of you?"

June sighed. "He's pretty dreamy."

"If anyone had told me as a child that a woman would eventually find the adult version of Sterling Wilder *dreamy*, I would have fallen over from shock."

June felt her lips twitch. "I'll admit, if I hadn't met him at the airport before coming here, I probably wouldn't have thought he was dreamy, either. I would have thought he was an irredeemable grump."

"And if we're being honest, if he hadn't seen you at the airport, he probably would have remained in irredeemable grump."

They ordered their lemonade and headed back toward where the guys were waiting.

June was just letting herself bask in the country music, the laughter and conversation, and the tempting smell of fried corndog batter. The sight of Mason Rickett, the owner of the ice cream shop —and the guy who Sterling said screwed over the Wilder family— put ice in June's veins.

"Callie Barrett," he said, voice brusque and unfriendly.

Callie stopped in her tracks and June swore she could feel the nervous energy vibrating off her.

"Mason Rickett."

Mason smiled, the kind of slow, evil smile June had seen on many a cartoon villain. If he rubbed his hands together, anticipating his own dirty deeds, she wouldn't be surprised.

"I hear you and this nice young lady—" his upper lip curled into a sneer and he ran his gaze down to June's feet and back up to her face—"are helping with the so-called fundraiser at the Sweet Springs Ranch."

Callie cleared her throat. "That's right."

"Those Wilder boys might believe they have the whole town fooled. I've seen people handing over money left and right. But mark my words. They *don't* have the whole town fooled. I can see clearly what's going on here, and I won't have one family taking from all the others."

Mason had made the mistake of believing he could intimidate Callie. But June knew he was wrong. Callie didn't let anyone or anything intimidate her.

Sure enough, she lifted her chin and said, "Are you about done? Your bitterness is starting to seep into my lemonade."

Mason may not be able to intimidate Callie, but *she* could certainly surprise *him*. His mouth had dropped open while Callie was talking and he snapped it shut when she finished.

"You have no idea what you're getting into, Ms. Barrett. But I'll give you the courtesy of a fair warning. You might want to un-involve yourself before the fundraiser."

"You know what, Mr. Rickett? I don't think I will."

With that, Mason went on his way, sauntering along like he had nothing in the world to worry about.

Callie, on the other hand, was obviously disturbed by the conversation. She grabbed June's arm and her voice was high and breathy when she said, "What are we going to do, Junie? Even though I know he didn't technically make any threats, I couldn't help but get the sense that he was threatening the fundraiser."

June felt sweat dripped down the center of her back. "Do you think we should say something to the guys?"

Callie shook her head. Her mouth set in a grim line she said, "Not yet. I'd like to do some digging, see what I can find on Mason. Get an explanation for his behavior. Then we can make a plan. And *then* we can tell the guys."

June nodded. "Sounds reasonable."

"For now," Callie said. "I say we enjoy the rest of this holiday. Who knows, this may be the only time you're here for the festival, Junie! We're not going to let old Mason Rickett ruin it for us."

Fighting to undo the sudden wave of tears that threatened, June plastered on her best smile. "You're right." She held up her lemonade cup. "To fun on July Fourth!"

Callie raised hers as well. "To fun!"

During the short walk back to the guys, June was awash in emotions.

This may be the only time you're here for the festival, Junie.

Her traitorous mind went to work as a movie projector, replaying for her all of the magical scenes she'd experienced since meeting Sterling. Dancing in the piano bar. Trail riding at sunset. Stargazing with charcuterie. Joking with the guys while building the framework for the stage. Even today, watching the men bicker like kids.

By the time she and Callie reached the guys, June was feeling downright weepy. Callie bumped her shoulder against June's and said through a bright smile, "Buck up, Junie. Smile. And don't worry about Mason Rickett. We'll take care of him. Put him in a locked box at the back of your mind for now."

Callie was right, June decided. If she had only this single time to enjoy the festival, she should make the most of it. The guys were still arguing over the darts game and Cash had a giant plush octopus stuffed under one arm.

"You may have won, Cash," Travis was saying, "but I still popped more balloons than you."

Callie winked at June. "I don't think they ever grew up."

The group decided to find a shady spot to listen to the music. Just as June settled herself between Sterling's legs on the grass, Sterling announced Riggs and his family were there, along with some of the crew. A minute later, the whole Foster family approached, a rush of energy and a tangle of rough and rowdy arms and legs belonging to Riggs's kids. Sterling and June got to their feet and Sterling opened his arms to hug Riggs's wife. "Sarah!"

Sarah hugged him back, but then playfully pushed him away. "It's this lady I want to meet." She flung her arms around June like they were long-lost friends. "It's so nice to finally meet you."

Charmed, June hugged her back. "It's nice to meet you, too. I'm so glad you were able to come to town for the festival."

"Me too! Riggs says everybody's been talking about it non-stop. And I'm so glad it's outside so these kids can get some of their energy out."

As if to prove how much they needed just that, the kids had run up in front of the stage and were moving with the music, playing air guitar and dancing.

Riggs slipped his arm around Sarah's waist and nuzzled her neck. "Maybe we can sneak away for a quickie while they're occupied."

Her smile proved his comment pleased her, but she acted scandalized. "Riggs Foster. We can't expect Sterling to watch them while we canoodle."

"Why not? It's been so long since we canoodled, it won't take but a couple of minutes."

Still smiling, Sarah said, "It's been so long since we canoodled, I'd love for it to take longer than that."

"Fine," Riggs said. "Let's round 'em up, then, and feed 'em."

June and Sterling watched them go, the littler kids clinging to their parents' hands and the older ones leading the way.

"That's nice," June said.

"It is," Sterling said. He put an arm around her shoulders and kissed her temple. "Really nice."

It was dinnertime when the storm rolled in. From where they sat at a picnic table near the food trucks, June could see the puffy, dark-gray edge of the cloud moving toward the festival.

Travis, his mouth full of carne asada fries, said, "Think we're going to get a monsoon?"

"I think you should stop talking with your mouth full," his brothers said in unison, making June and Callie laugh.

"What's a monsoon?" June asked Callie, who took a sip of her cocktail. "A summer storm. The clouds roll in, we get crazy amounts of rain, thunder, and lightning, and then the clouds roll out. It's nature's way of cooling us off on these hot, humid days."

The idea of all that rain, lightning, and thunder gave June a sense of foreboding, but everyone else seemed unaffected. The band continued playing, the kids continued running around, and the rides kept spinning. June could see Riggs and Sarah standing next to the giant swings, waving to their kids as they went by.

"Want to dance?" Sterling asked her. She glanced up at the sky

—all she could see was gray, now. Then, remembering she was supposed to be getting the absolute most out of the festival she shrugged and said, "Sure."

As if on cue, the band switched from a fast, galloping beat to a slow ballad. Her hand in his, June followed Sterling onto the dance floor where he spun her around once and then brought her into his arms. And then they were swaying, her head on his chest.

"Having fun?" His deep voice rumbled pleasantly against her cheek.

June nodded as she relaxed even more deeply into his embrace. "I can see why you guys all said this is the highlight of the year."

"I had almost forgotten how much fun it is. But it's even more so with you here."

"That's sweet."

"It's true." They swayed for a few more bars.

Then June felt the first raindrop. "Are we about to get soaked?"

Sterling shrugged. "Hard to tell. Sometimes the sky looks so foreboding—you just *know* you're going to get it. And then all you get are a few drops. Other times, the sky looks so dark but nothing's happening. And then it just opens up. Unleashes. And you almost can't believe that much water could come from the sky. It's a toss-up. So I say we just keep dancing."

A few minutes later, just as Sterling had described, the sky opened up and the rain *poured*. June shrieked as the first deluge soaked her hair and shirt.

Sterling laughed out loud. "Well, I guess we know what kind of monsoon we're getting today."

Running for cover, people scattered from the dance floor and parents herded their children under the shade structures while the band rushed to cover their equipment with tarps, which flapped and fluttered in the gusty wind. Meanwhile, Sterling grabbed June's hand and pulled her around the back of a little building she assumed was a shed. They claimed a tiny square of shelter under the door's awning. Pressed as close to the door as they could be, they looked at each other, gasping for breath.

"I forgot what a thrill that is," Sterling said. "And how quickly a good storm can turn you into a drowned rat." Then he was laughing, holding June so close to his body, hers vibrated with it, too. Before she knew it, they were both doubled over, arms wrapped around each other, practically weeping with laughter.

Again, just as he'd described, the rain stopped and the sky cleared. All the festival goers reemerged from their hiding places and the band members shook out the tarps. The lead singer hollered into his microphone, "Should we get back to it?"

A cheer went up and June found herself hooting and hollering along with the crowd. June looked over at Sterling and just like earlier, he was watching her, tenderness in his eyes. When their gazes locked, he let out a cheer, too, before kissing her long and slow. "I guess we'd better finish our dance."

An hour later, dark fell. Slightly sunburned, bellies full, the whole group found a spot on the grass to watch the fireworks. As they started, the first red, white, and blue bursting into the sky, Sterling said, "This has been a pretty great day."

She could see the reflections of the fireworks in his eyes. Again, she thought, *I'm falling in love with him.*

She did the only thing she could think of doing: she took his face in her hands and kissed him. If she was going to leave after the fundraiser, she decided, she would have to kiss Sterling every chance she got.

* * *

After the magical day they spent together—and the realization that she was falling in love with Sterling—June couldn't wait to be with him. Back in the hotel lobby, she asked, "Are you coming to my place?"

She was sure to infuse her invitation with as much coy seduction as she could. Sterling picked up on it, raising an eyebrow. "I was hoping you'd ask."

The tension crackled between them as they walked up the stairs and June couldn't help but wonder if they'd brought some magical, sparkling residue from the fireworks. Sterling ran his fingertips along

June's spine as they walked down the hall to her room. The movement left a trail of heat, which spread throughout her body. By the time they reached her door, she could feel her pulse between her legs, her desire deepening.

As soon as the door closed behind them, June lifted her hair off her neck and said to Sterling, "Will you untie this?"

Desire flashing in his eyes, he turned her around and pulled to loosen the fabric bow. Hands on her shoulders, he bent to kiss the back of her neck, then the curve where her neck met her shoulder, and then the tip of her shoulder. His hands came to her waist and he slid them up under her shirt so he could remove it. Still standing behind her, he looked over her shoulder. "Now this is quite a view," he said, tracing the cups of her strapless bra with his fingertips. He unhooked the bra and when her breasts were free, he cupped them with his hands and started massaging. She leaned back against him, her body feeling at once energized and completely relaxed by his touch. His thumbs teased her nipples and when she let out a little moan in response, he wrapped one arm around her waist and pulled her toward him so she could feel his arousal. "I've been waiting to get you like this all day."

"I've been imagining this all day."

His mouth was close to her ear. "Have you?"

She turned around in his arms and pulled his t-shirt over his head. "As a matter of fact, I have." With one hand wrapped around the back of his neck and the other pressed against his chiseled abs, she kissed him. It was true—she'd spent the whole day thinking about how she loved him, how she wanted to show him that, and how she wouldn't waste another minute of their time together.

Unbuckling his belt she said, "I've also been thinking about getting you out of these."

He chuckled, his lips still on hers, and he unbuttoned her skirt.

When it fell to the floor and he realized her ass was bare, he groaned. "You're lucky I didn't know you were wearing these underwear today. Let me look at you."

He took a step back to admire her, and for the first time in her life, she felt powerfully feminine as she watched him react, looking her over like she was the antidote to anything and everything that ever ailed him. He pulled his jeans and underwear over his hips and stepped out of them, giving June a look at him in all his glory. In one quick stride he was in front of her again, his thumbs hooked in the waistband of her thong, his dick pressing against her belly.

"I want you to make love to me," she told him.

"Well then you're in luck, because I want to make love to you."

He backed her up to the bed. "But first, I want to spend some time with you in this sexy and very patriotic underwear."

She smiled as he eased her down onto the mattress. He grabbed her ankles and placed her heels on the edge of the bed, then kissed his way from the inside of one ankle up to the knee and the thigh and then, finally, when she could barely stand it any longer, he pulled aside the thin swatch of fabric and put his mouth on her.

She gasped and he groaned. "You taste so good," he told her between strokes.

All she could do was moan in response, her body already gathering energy for an orgasm. He kissed his way up her torso, his unshaven face scraping her skin, the pleasure-pain almost making her come undone. He stopped to spend a little time on each breast, kissing and suckling until she arched against him.

"Sterling Wilder! I didn't wait this long for us to make love just to come before you're even inside me."

He stroked her clit with a butterfly's touch while he continued to explore her breasts with his mouth. "Who says you can't come now and again when I'm inside you?" His fingers plunged inside her.

At that, she exploded, her walls clamping down around his fingers, her entire body shuddering. She cried out, felt her nails digging into his back, and rode his hand until the waves subsided. When she lay limp on the duvet, he kissed her sternum and collarbone and then lifted himself so he they were eye to eye.

He grinned down at her. "Ready to do that again?"

"So ready." The words came out demanding and in a groan and he sank into her, holding that eye contact and shattering her world. She saw her own pleasure echoed back in his eyes, and something else, too. She saw their whole future unfolding. This, right here. Fourth of July festivals and Christmas light tours in this quaint but modern city. Babies. Sleepless nights. School plays and soccer games. Sunset trail riding, just the two of them. Somewhere, down the road, a quiet cottage next to a river where they could sit on the porch and reminisce about the life they made together. *If only.* She felt a tear escape the corner of her eye and roll down into her hairline. Then another, from the other eye. How was it possible to be so full of joy and so full of sorrow at the same time?

Sterling stilled, concern etched on his features.

"June! Are you all right?"

She smiled and took the opportunity to wipe her tears dry. "I'm great. It's just—I've never felt this way about anyone else. Believe it or not, they're tears of joy. Let's keep doing what we're doing."

She saw surprise and then tenderness, and then the trademark Wilder cocky grin. "Must've been a really good orgasm."

He kissed the tip of her nose, and then her mouth, and then he started moving inside her again in long, slow strokes.

"Can I tell you something?" His voice was barely a whisper.

"Of course."

Still moving, he closed his eyes and rested his forehead on hers. "I've never felt this way about anyone, either." She sighed, and the two of them moved together, faster, taking each other higher, until they both went over the edge.

He collapsed on top of her and then rolled them both to the side so they were face to face. "Are you sure you're okay?"

She kissed him. "I'm fine. A momentary flood of emotions. But I've closed the floodgates."

"All right. I'll get us a towel. Just let me know if you need to open the floodgates again, and I'll get another."

God, who wouldn't love this man? He returned and they cleaned themselves up and climbed under the covers, backs against the headboard.

"One thing we haven't talked about, Ms. Cartwright," he said, "is what we like to watch on TV."

"I like a good murder mystery," she said. "Those true crime shows are my favorite."

"That's dark."

She giggled. "Does the fact that I like eating popcorn while watching them lighten it up at all?"

"I don't know. Maybe. I know it's getting late but now I feel energized. Want to see if we can find any true crime on TV?"

June sat up straighter. "First, what do you like to watch?"

"I was going to say Hallmark movies, but now I'm embarrassed."

"Liar."

Smirking, he picked up the remote and navigated to the guide. It scrolled for a few minutes and then Sterling pointed at the screen and said, "There! Channel thirty-six."

A spooky forest scene appeared and an even spookier voiceover explained that police found the victim's body deep within the woods.

"If you like this stuff, that probably means you don't need to cuddle up with me out of fear, right?"

June looked over at him, and then scooted closer so their hips and shoulders were touching. "I'll cuddle up with you, anyway."

She was so engrossed in the show that she jumped and yelped when a knock sounded at the door. Unfazed, Sterling got up to answer it and came back with a package of microwave popcorn.

"Where'd you get that?" June asked.

"Oh, just a little place I like to call grocery delivery."

The warm, tingly feeling that had been with June all day intensified. "You ordered that because I said I like watching the shows with popcorn."

Standing there in his underwear while opening the box, Sterling said, "I did."

"That's just about the sweetest thing anyone's ever done for me."

He tore open the package and walked over to the microwave. "Fortunately for me, that's setting the bar pretty low."

The scent of popcorn butter filled the hotel room as the corn popped. When it was done, Sterling brought the bag back to the bed. Between mouthfuls, he said, "You think it was the husband?"

"It's always the husband," June said. "But I think this time may be the exception. I think it was a random hit. Wrong place, wrong time."

"You're the expert," Sterling said.

They grinned at each other and June almost cried again. She wished they could have this forever.

Chapter Twenty

"I call this meeting to order." Sterling cursed under his breath when his brothers ignored him.

June, who sat to his left at the round table in the back room of Smoke, Sterling's favorite steakhouse, leaned close. "Maybe you should try tapping your spoon on your glass."

He smirked. "That's far too refined for this group." He put two fingers in his mouth and whistled, the sound loud and shrill enough to interrupt the Wilder boys' conversation, and that throughout the rest of the restaurant—at least, briefly.

"Like I said, I'd like to call this meeting to order."

Across the table, Hayes said to Cash, "Who put a bee in his bonnet?"

Sterling felt a growl starting in his throat. "Hey, you ladies put me in charge of this fundraiser, which means you have to listen when I call a meeting about it."

"He has a point," Travis said.

Eyes twinkling with mischief, Cash leaned back in his chair and crossed his arms. "Fine. Lay it on us."

Sterling sighed. "Thanks. A lot. Now that I have your attention, I'm giving June the floor."

She picked up the folder from the table in front of her and

pulled out a small stack of papers. Her hand shook, just a little, when she handed the stack to Callie, who sat on her left. "Here. Take one and pass it on."

Travis rubbed his hands together. "Oh, goody. Handouts. I feel like I'm in school again."

Sterling rolled his eyes and waited while his brothers passed the papers. Of course, Cash called out, "I didn't get one," and they all had to check to see who had taken two. It was Travis, who grimaced as he sent the extra down the line.

His own crew would never act like this. But, these were his brothers. He should have expected it.

June cleared her throat. "As you know, Sterling and I have been soliciting donations. The first section on the first page here is a list of everything we have in hand."

Finally, his numbskull brothers seemed interested. The table went silent while they read over the list. At long last, Sterling could focus. First, he looked over the left column, which contained a nice variety of items. Then, he looked over the right column, which contained dollar amounts. Nice dollar amounts. His mouth dropped open when he saw the total value.

He couldn't believe June hadn't shown him this list before the meeting.

When they'd gone around asking for donations, he'd never even imagined the value of those donations would total that much.

Saving the ranch might actually be possible.

Tears stung Sterling's eyes, and he blinked them back, not wanting his brothers to see how emotional he was. Until that moment, he hadn't realized how much it meant to him. The task of raising all that money had seemed impossible, and he'd told himself he didn't care. But he'd lied. He did care, and relief rushed in.

Hayes whistled. "This is a lot, you guys."

Beside Sterling, June relaxed. He could see the tension leave her shoulders and feel her energy change. She elbowed him and winked when he looked over. He winked back. The exchange gave him butterflies. Like a damn teenager.

"Below that," June said, "you'll see a list of the items people have committed to. The thing is, we don't actually have these items yet. Sterling and I plan to do another run around town to pick up everything. But obviously, there are no guarantees."

Hayes whistled again. "With the items on the first list, which we already have, even if we get only half the items on the second list and have a decent turnout at the fundraiser, we'll have damn near enough to get current on the mortgage."

June nodded. "I know."

"Well," Travis said. "I'm impressed. Not that I didn't think you could pull it off, but altogether, this stuff is worth a ton of money."

"I *told* you June was good," Callie said, her voice singsongy.

Pride overcame Sterling as he looked at June, who blushed and said, "Thanks, Cal. But I couldn't have done it without Sterling's help."

"It was all you," Sterling said. "Your expertise somehow managed to counteract my lack of enthusiasm."

"Now, now," Cash said. "I love a good lovefest as much as the next guy. But I think the question on everyone's mind is, can we eat now?"

Travis punched him in the arm. "Dude. The question we should be asking is, what's next? What can we do to help?"

"Oh," Cash said. "Right. What's next? What can we do to help?"

"Glad you asked," Sterling said. "June, do you want to take this one?"

June nodded, cleared her throat, stood up. "You'll be happy to know I have another handout."

Travis pumped his fist. "Yes."

Sterling shook his head and rolled his eyes. "This is a list of what we still need to do. You'll see it's broken into tasks that need to happen ASAP, in the next week, and the day of the fundraiser. I figured we could use my copy as a master, and everyone could sign up for what they're willing to do. So take a minute, look over the list, and then I'll pass mine around."

"I don't see a line item for taste testing," Cash said, and Travis said, "Smartass."

"What? That seems like an important job."

"This looks great, Junie," Callie said. "I'll go first."

She extended her arm for June to hand her the sign-up sheet, but Travis snatched it out of June's hand first.

"No way! I know how this works. Ladies first, then oldest to youngest. I always have to go last and I get the shit jobs."

"And what do you consider the shit jobs on this list?" Sterling asked, a challenge in his raised eyebrow.

Holding up the list, Travis gestured at one of the items. "Like this. 'Mow the area we're using for parking.' Nobody's going to want to do that."

"Fine," Callie said. "You sign up first."

"No way." Hayes grabbed the paper from Travis. "That's not fair."

"I'll tell you what," Cash said, joining in. "I'll sign up first."

Fed up with their antics, Sterling whistled again. They all froze, Travis and Cash both reaching for the paper Hayes now held, and looked up at Sterling.

"I'll tell you what. June and I will go last. You guys go ahead and sign up for the most tolerable tasks on the list. Bring the list to the job site later. I don't have time for this nonsense." Then he turned to June. "Do you want to stick around while these morons figure this out? Or should we go grab a coffee and tea and head to the job site?"

He could tell from the set of her lips and the crinkles around her eyes that she found the whole exchange humorous. But she managed to keep a straight face. "I'll take the second option."

The moment they reached the parking lot, he swept her into his arms and spun her around.

Her laughter filled his ears. "What's this for?"

Setting her down and taking both her hands in his he said, "I can't believe you didn't tell me how much stuff you'd gotten. It's amazing!"

"It's what I do." She shrugged. "I figured you trusted me to get the job done."

He dropped her hands and grabbed her shoulders. "I did! I just didn't know how well you'd get it done."

Her smile seemed shy. "Well, there you go."

"Thank you, June. Thank you so much. When I saw those numbers, I had an epiphany. I've been acting indifferent about saving the ranch, but that's only because I was afraid of losing it. Now that I know it's possible to save it, I'm beyond excited. All thanks to you."

"You're welcome," she said. "It's been my pleasure."

He laughed at the double entendre and leaned down to kiss her. "Mine, too."

Chapter Twenty-One

Still riding the high from the meeting, June sang along to the music playing over Sterling's Bluetooth speaker as they erected the stage's backdrop. White, puffy clouds floated overhead, providing some protection from the hot July sun, and a nice breeze helped with the heat, too. The leaves fluttered on the trees and the birds sang.

She and Sterling hadn't spoken for a few minutes, and yet she still felt unbelievably connected to him as they worked together. Running through her mental checklist reminded her that she should probably wrap up early at the job site and go out to pick up donations. Sterling's whistling along with the music took June into their future again. She imagined him whistling while they worked on house projects, painting bedrooms or planting flowers. On hot days like this, they'd sit on the deck to enjoy cold beers after their projects were done.

"Are you hearing your phone?" Sterling's voice jarred her out of her pleasant daydream. "Or just ignoring it?"

"Oh! I didn't hear it. Why?"

"It's gone off a bunch of times."

June's heart rate picked up. Her phone going off a bunch of

times usually signaled an emergency. "I was just listening to the music, I guess. Enjoying the moment."

She walked over to where she'd stowed her phone on the workstation. Her stomach churned when she saw the many text and missed call notification bubbles stacked atop one another on the screen. She opened her text app first. On top, the most recent text from her mom: *June, this is getting ridiculous.* Just below that, one from Callie: *Call me right away. This is an emergency!!!!!*

She opened Callie's text string. The first one was from immediately after the meeting: *Great meeting, Junie! I'm so proud of you.* And then, just minutes later: *June, call me right away.* Followed by a frenzy of messages: *Have you heard from your mom? Answer your phone! June, are you okay? I'm coming to you.*

What could possibly be wrong?

"Everything okay?" Sterling came to stand beside her.

"I don't know." She groaned and switched over to the text string with her mom.

The first text had come in right after Callie's first text—after her meeting with the Wilder boys: *Surprise! Your dad and I are on our way to Prescott.*

June gasped and Sterling said, "June?"

"Oh, my God." Her free hand, shaking, covered her mouth while she continued to read. *We'd love to meet up with you. Will you send us the address? June, are you alive? Cartwright Family Empire Cardinal Rule Number Two: Answer your phone. Always.*

The missed call log, of course, showed that both her mom and Callie had called several times since the initial text messages.

A new text came in from Callie: *I gave your parents the ranch's address. I didn't know what else to do. I'm sorry, Cal. You're right. Your mom can be very convincing. I'm still on my way.*

She gasped again when Sterling's hand wrapped around her phone and he took it from her to read the screen, himself. His eyes were wide when he looked at her. "Your parents are in Prescott?"

Before she could respond, her phone rang. He looked at the screen, cursed, and handed it to her. He surprised her by grabbing it back and punching the answer button. "June Cartwright's phone. This is Sterling."

Silence came from the earpiece—June could imagine her mom spluttering, the wind taken out of her sails when Sterling answered and not June. Somehow, that made her smile despite what she was certain was about to unravel into a messy, messy situation. Her parents weren't just coming to visit her. They were coming to take her home.

Chapter Twenty-Two

Sterling could see June's fear in her wide eyes after he answered her phone. He was certain she could hear the lack of sound coming from the earpiece. Her eyes got even wider.

Finally, June's mom said, "Hello?"

"Hello!" He forced confidence into his voice and grabbed June's hand. She gave his a squeeze and tried for a smile.

"Did you say this is Sterling?"

"I did," he said. "And although I read the name *Mom* on June's Caller ID, I haven't had the pleasure. Do you mind telling me your first name?"

Another beat of silence. June's mom finally said, "Um, this is Clara Cartwright. Pleased to meet you."

The woman had impeccable manners—he'd give her that. June's lips twitched. Sterling raised his eyebrows as if to mime, *See? It's going well.*

"Pleased to meet you," Sterling said.

"May I speak to June, please?" Syrupy sweet.

"You see, Ms. Cartwright, the thing is, June is indisposed at the moment." He panicked. What could he possibly say she was doing?

"And what, may I ask, is she doing?"

Shit.

The way June pressed her lips together, he could tell she was trying to keep from laughing—and as cheering her up was his intention, he committed to coming up with something. He pantomimed grabbing her hips and taking her from behind. She covered her mouth and walked away.

Barely able to contain his own laughter, Sterling managed, "She's putting up the backdrop on the stage we're building just now. Her hands are full. I would love to relay a message to her, and I'm sure she'll call you back at her earliest convenience."

Another long pause. "Are you June's ... secretary?" Clara asked.

"Quite so," Sterling said. He hoped he wasn't adding fuel to the fire, but he was having too much fun to stop.

She cleared her throat. "Yes, I'd like to leave a message, please. June's friend Callie was kind enough to give June's dad and I the address of ... the ranch. We're heading there now from the Phoenix airport. We should be there in ... Oh, Jim, what does the map say?" Sterling heard June's dad speak in the background, and Clara finished, "in about an hour."

Sterling closed his eyes. June was not going to be happy about that. He had the distinct impression that June's parents—although quite courteous on the phone—weren't coming to Prescott to mess around. They'd expect June to go back with them to Great Falls.

That was like all the clichés rolled into one: a punch in the gut, a knife to the heart, a bullet to the brain.

He realized then and there that he needed her. Not for the fundraiser, although she was kicking ass and taking names, but for himself. He didn't want to be in Prescott without her. He didn't want to be without her at all.

"Of course I'll pass that message on."

"And ... Sterling, isn't it? Could you also remind June of the Cartwright Family Empire's Cardinal Rule Number Two? It's answer your phone. Always. Thank you so very much, dear."

"Absolutely. I do look forward to meeting you. Travel safely, now." He disconnected and even though he'd never met Clara Cartwright, he pictured her on the other end of the line spluttering a goodbye.

As wrapped up as he was in the conversation, he didn't notice June had come up behind him. He held out her phone and she took it, offering him a genuine smile.

"That was amazing. No one controls a conversation with Clara Cartwright, but you just did."

He leaned forward and kissed her. "You're welcome. But that was just the front line. She asked me to deliver a message that she's on her way, and will be here in an hour. It's time to prepare."

Chapter Twenty-Three

June's entire body trembled with nerves and anticipation for the next hour until she finally heard tires on gravel and saw a shiny sedan she assumed was her parents' rental car coming up the drive.

"I can't believe I'm considering running away from my own parents," she muttered. Sterling put his arm around her shoulders and squeezed before dropping it again.

"Can't say I blame you."

As the car rolled to a stop next to her rental car, June felt a tiny flicker of hope. Maybe when her parents saw what she was doing and how involved she was, they would acquiesce. Say something like, "Go ahead and stay, Junie. We'll see you when you're good and ready."

The smile her mom flashed when she opened the driver's door—of course she was driving—snuffed out that flame immediately. June knew that smile. Her mom was preparing for battle.

Sterling put a hand on her lower back. "Oh, boy."

Under any other circumstance, June would have laughed at that. But all she could do was steel herself as she watched her dad get out of the passenger side, his brow furrowed with worry.

Feeling an awful lot like a jointed wooden puppet, June raised her arm to wave, tilting her head awkwardly. "Hi, Mom! Hi, Dad! I'm so glad you're here. I can't wait to show you what I've been working on."

A strangled sound came from Sterling and it was all June could do to keep her mouth stretched into a smile. Clara Cartwright didn't walk—she strode. And at the moment, she strode right up to June.

"Junie!" She wrapped her arms around June's upper body and crushed her in a suffocating embrace. Holding onto June's shoulders, she stepped back and gave her a once-over. "A tool belt? I like this look."

A little more timid, June's dad came forward, arms extended. "Hey, Junebug."

His hug was actually comforting and she let herself sink into it for a second.

"It's good to see you," she whispered.

"And you must be Sterling," June's mom said, her impeccable manners forcing her to make introductions even while she showed her disapproval with the arch of one eyebrow and the way she looked down her nose at him.

Sterling, completely unintimidated, smiled his easy, handsome smile and held out his hand. "Sterling Wilder, quarter-owner of Sweet Springs Ranch. Pleased to meet you."

"Likewise," June's mom said, sounding like she didn't mean it at all.

June's dad shook Sterling's hand with genuine friendliness. "Jim."

"So what is this you're working on?" June's mom asked, her words more of a challenge than a question.

June decided she would proceed as if the only reason her parents came to Prescott was to see what she was up to. She showed them the stage, the dance floor, and the little front office they built. She explained where the tables and DJ would set up and how the silent auction and raffle would work.

Her parents *oohed* and *ahhed* as if they were genuinely interested, but she knew her mom was simply biding her time. Sure enough, after she'd described the entire fundraising event in detail, her mom brushed her hands together and said, "This is all wonderful, Junie. I would like to discuss it further over dinner. Sterling, can you recommend a good place?"

Sterling opened his mouth and for a second no sound came out. He seemed to gather his wits. "Ah, of course. What do you like to eat?"

"Oh, anything!" June's mom laughed, high-pitched and insincere. "Oh, anything! We're easy."

"Then I'd recommend Stover's. They have a great variety."

June's mom gave a curt nod. "That's settled. Come along, June. Your dad's getting hungry."

"Um," June stammered, "can Sterling join us?"

June's mom turned around and gave June a withering stare. "I'm afraid not. This is family business."

On the inside, June groaned. Outwardly, she grinned brightly. "Great. Maybe next time."

She offered Sterling an apologetic smile as she followed her parents to their rental car.

Once the three of them were alone, June dropped the act. "Why are you guys really here?"

Her mom made fleeting eye contact with her in the rearview mirror. "We're here to see you, Junie."

June's insides boiled. Space closed in on her as they drove to the restaurant in near silence. Her mom asked the hostess for a *private* table for three. June felt her jaw clenching so tightly, she didn't know if she'd ever be able to open it again. She kicked herself for not standing up to her parents and insisting Sterling join them.

Looking over the menu, her mom made little sounds of approval. After a few seconds she said, "Is he your secretary, June?"

When June gave her a blank look, her mom clarified, "Sterling. The nice young man who answered your phone."

The humor in that—at least, from June's perspective—made her feel like she could breathe again.

"No, Mom. He was just joking when he told you that. Didn't you hear him say he's one of the owners of the Sweet Springs Ranch?"

Her mom lifted one shoulder. "I heard all that, but young people nowadays, they hold down so many jobs. *Gigs*, I believe they call it, don't they, Jim? You just never know."

"Anyway, what were you going to say?" June asked.

Her mom laughed. Again. "That's right. I was just going to say Sterling made a great recommendation. There are so many dishes to choose from. Have you been here? What do you usually get?"

June could scream. She didn't want to talk about Sterling's restaurant recommendation, the menu, or her favorite dishes. "Mom, can we just cut the crap?"

Out of the corner of her eye, June saw her dad sit up straight, his eyes round.

"What do you mean, June?"

The server's arrival postponed June's response. After he left, June said, "I know you're not here to check out the ranch or the event I'm planning. You're here because your plan is to convince me to go home with you."

In an unexpected turn of events, June's mom actually blushed. *Well, at least she has the decency to be embarrassed.* She glanced at June's dad who looked away and feigned an interest in the vase of flowers at the center of the table.

"We really need you home." All the fake friendliness was gone, replaced by an icy front. June's body responded by going all fluttery. God, how could her mom still have this effect on her?

"You have Maya," June said, her confidence as fake as her mom's friendliness.

"June." Her mom's hand closed around her wrist. "I don't think you understand."

I don't think you understand.

"All I'm asking for is one more week," June said. "The project I'm working on here is going so well. I'm invested. I really want to see how it turns out."

The server was back with their food. June could see her mom's wheels turning. But before she could speak again, June turned to her dad. "What do you think, Dad?"

He actually jumped, obviously shocked someone was asking his opinion. If he'd been a character in a movie, the shock would be comical. But he wasn't. He was her dad and as accustomed as she was to being steamrolled by her mom.

"Well, I—" he cleared his throat, glanced at June's mom—"I think if you're enjoying the event you're working on here—"

"She doesn't know what she's enjoying, Jim," June's mom cut in. "Her senses are all jumbled up." She raised both hands and wiggled her fingers to illustrate. "That young man? Sterling?"

"Nice fellow," June's dad said.

"Yeah? Well, he was the young man our daughter was kissing in the hall on our floor."

His eyes sparked with interest. "Is that so?"

June's mom growled. "Jim. That is not the point. I'm just saying, she's not thinking clearly."

Suddenly exhausted, June started to eat and was disappointed to realize the conversation had stressed her to the point where her favorite dish, sun-dried tomato and artichoke pasta, didn't even taste good. Still, the food distracted her from the conversation. After being shut down by her mom, her dad, too, tucked into his food.

Feeling once again in control, June's mom exclaimed over how good her food was and after chewing and swallowing her bite, she said, "Now. As you know, Timmy's wedding is in just two days. Maya has done a fantastic job thus far, but you will be there on the day of to run the show. Just like always."

"Timmy? Is that what we're calling him now?" June's stomach now roiled with anger. How could this woman, her own mother, completely negate her feelings? Still, she tried to reason. "You just said Maya has done a great job. I'm confident she can manage the wedding. I'll be available by phone." She could hear the desperation in her own voice.

"I don't think you understand, June. You're going to be there."

"I *do* understand. It's just that this event, here, is something of my own. I plan to stay for it."

"June, if you don't come, do you think you're going to get a good referral from your current employers?"

Anger filled June's veins like lava. *"You're* my current employer."

"That's right," her mom said.

"I can get referrals from anyone who has had an event at the Hotel Cartwright."

"I wouldn't be so sure about that."

June could swear her heart stopped. But no, she was still alive, staring across the table at her mom who apparently had turned into some kind of villain while she was in Paris.

"You would do that?" Disbelief made her voice squeaky.

"Let's just say you won't have to worry about that since you'll be coming home with us."

June pushed away her plate. Stood up. Closed her mouth and shook her head. She couldn't believe this was happening, and she said as much to her parents.

Her mom looked at her watch. "We leave first thing tomorrow morning to head back to Phoenix and catch a flight to Great Falls. I expect you to be in our car."

Unable to think of a single coherent response—the potential words including "No," "I can't believe this," "This is a nightmare," jumbled together in her mind—June rotated on the spot and walked out of the restaurant.

When she reached the parking lot, she realized her error: she didn't have her own car. Her mom's offer to drive wasn't born of kindness; it was born of control.

She considered her options: Callie was tied up in court, and June didn't feel comfortable calling any of the Wilder brothers other than Sterling. So, she could call a ride share to get back to her car at the ranch, or she could call Sterling.

The choice was easy. Sterling picked up on the first ring. "I was wondering when I'd hear from you."

Despite what she'd just been through, June smiled. "Here I am."

"So?"

June sighed. Then she realized she didn't want her parents to come out of the restaurant and see her in the parking lot. She started walking. "My mom basically gave me an ultimatum." She described the conversation (as one-sided as it was), and she heard his sigh come through the earpiece.

"I'm sorry, June," he told her. "What are you going to do?"

The summer sun was hot on her scalp and shoulders even as late in the day as it was. Sweat trickled down her back. "I don't know. I feel so foolish, letting her bully me like this. But at the same time, I'm afraid she does have the power to do what she's saying—she could easily stop my independent business in its tracks before I even get it off the ground."

"Where are your parents, anyway?"

"I left them in the restaurant."

"And now you're walking down the street," he said. "I can hear the traffic going by."

"Right."

"I'm on my way. Which direction did you go?"

"East. Away from the sweltering sun. I'm just passing by the smoothie shop. Actually, there's a nice shade tree outside it. I'll wait here for you."

"I'll be there in ten," he said, and she said, "Okay. And, Sterling? Thank you."

"You're welcome. Any time I can come to your rescue."

"You're sweet."

True to his word, he pulled up ten minutes later. The gratitude and relief June experienced felt like twin rushes of sweet relief.

He rolled down his window and lowered his sunglasses. "The Sterling Express has arrived."

Sinking down into the passenger seat, she breathed, "Thank you," and buried her face in her hands. "I can't believe this is happening. It feels like something you'd see in a movie. But it's my life."

He reached out and rested a hand on her leg as he pulled away from the curb. "I'm really sorry, June. If anyone understands how parents can screw up our lives, it's me. Now. Where to?"

"I suppose we should go back to the hotel," June said. "I don't know what else to do."

"May I suggest a different idea?"

"Sure," she said, forlorn. She figured any idea was better than ruminating over whether to go home with her parents the next day.

"Let's go out and have some fun."

Dubious, June looked over at him. "What do you have in mind?"

"I'll show you."

He drove them downtown, turned onto the historic Whiskey Row, and found a parking spot in front of Wild West Saloon.

"We're going to the saloon?" She felt her nose wrinkling and quickly smoothed her features.

"We are," he said. "Not just for a drink, though. We're going dancing."

Momentarily, the idea seemed ridiculous. How could she possibly enjoy herself with her mom's threat hanging over her head? But when they walked into the bar and she could feel the pulse of the music in her limbs and see people moving their bodies in time to that pulse, her mood lifted. If she had just one more evening here with Sterling, she wasn't going to waste it. She was going to *dance*. With him.

While she'd been contemplating, he'd paid their entrance fees.

"Wrist," the bouncer said, his voice gruff.

June jumped and stuck out her arm, and the bouncer wrapped a bracelet around her wrist. Then Sterling's hand was in hers and they were walking into the dark saloon and into oblivion—at least, temporarily.

"Want a drink?" he asked, pointing at the bar.

She leaned close so he could hear her response. "A vodka cranberry. And make it a double."

He was grinning as he walked toward the bar. She stayed close, hooking a finger in his belt loop so they wouldn't get separated in the fray. While he leaned up against the bar to order, she took in the scene. The band played from a loft stage at the back of the space and colored lights flashed from structures on the ceiling. American flags and deer mounts hung on the walls and beer advertisements, showing off bikini-clad women, promised a good time.

This bar wasn't a place June would typically frequent but when

Sterling turned around and offered her a drink, then a long, deep kiss, she figured it wouldn't hurt to give it a night.

"Let's find a spot to watch the dancing while we drink our drinks, so we don't spill on the dance floor," he said, his breath on her ear sending shivers over her skin.

She nodded and he led her through the throng to the edge of the dance floor, where he put his arm around her waist and pulled her up to his body, her back against her front. While she watched the dance floor, he pulled her hair away from her neck and kissed her there.

She leaned against him and let herself pretend, just for this one night, that this could be her life—hanging out at a western bar with a beyond-handsome rancher who had the hots for her ... who cared enough to pick her up after she had a disagreement with her parents —one that might send her packing.

As soon as he saw she'd finished her drink, he took her plastic cup and tossed it, along with his, into a nearby trash. Then he grabbed her hand and pulled her onto the dance floor.

Why did their bodies being together feel so natural, like they'd done this a million times? June clung to Sterling, let him hold onto her hips and move her along with the music. He brought his forehead to hers and looked into her eyes, the intensity in his far greater than that of the upbeat song.

I don't want to leave him.

The thought struck her like a lightning bolt and she clung to him, wishing with all her might that things didn't have to be the way they were, that they'd met under different circumstances, after she set out on her own and could do whatever she wanted.

But they hadn't.

She shouldn't be near tears while they were dancing together, the bass throbbing in their veins, the lights illuminating their bodies, the song reminding them that true love was real. But she was. The situation felt so unfair. She was so angry at her parents ... but they were her parents.

Although she wanted nothing more than to defy them and stay

in Prescott until the Sweet Springs Ranch fundraiser, working at the Hotel Cartwright, the family business, was a duty.

As if he wanted to erase her thoughts, Sterling grabbed her hand and twirled her once, twice, and a third time, making her dizzy and giddy. Then he pulled her in for a kiss—one that lit her soul on fire and made her cling to him like he was a lifeline.

The saloon created a time warp. June had no idea how long they spent there, but when the band took a break and Sterling looked at his watch and whistled, she figured it was late. She was right.

"It's past midnight," Sterling said. "I guess we should get going, considering it's a weeknight."

Close to tears again, June nodded and gulped. "I guess you're right."

Outside, the air was less muggy but just as hot. The cicadas screeched in the trees, a song of mourning for the decision June had to make. Her ears rang from being in the bar for so long. She barely heard Sterling when he said, "Want to come to my room tonight?"

"I'd love nothing more," she said.

They didn't speak as he drove the handful of blocks back to the hotel and parked in the garage, nor as they walked through the lobby and up the stairs. They didn't speak as they walked down the hall to Sterling's room, or as he unlocked the door and they went inside.

Only once the door closed with a quiet click behind them did Sterling say, "Why don't you get undressed?"

Those five words drove June wild and all the could think about was showing Sterling how much he meant to her, how grateful she was to have had this time with him, how much she wished she didn't have to do what she did.

And then they were both naked and moving toward the bed. They tumbled onto the mattress, their hands skimming over each other's bodies, their breath coming in quick gasps. Sterling's rough palm smoothed along June's torso and she relished in the feel of his callouses on her skin.

She knew she would never be the same after this. After Sterling, no man could ever compare. She'd be wanting for the rest of her life, no matter what.

But she had this moment, and she'd be damned if she wasn't going to take advantage of it. She gripped his cock in one hand and stroked it, gently at first and then with greater speed and intensity until he was moving against her, sliding one of his hands back down to find her center, which he teased gently until she was moving against him, too.

And then he plunged into her and the shock of it made her cry out. They were moving together, in perfect sync. As one, they carried each other upward, faster and faster, until they both reached the peak and went over the edge.

Shuddering in his arms, June came down from the high, her heart rate returning to normal, her vision clearing.

"You know what I'm thinking?" His voice was husky, and sent molten lava through her veins.

"What?"

"I'm thinking you've ruined me for anyone else, June." She laughed and his eyebrows furrowed. "Is that funny?"

"No," she said, kissing him on the nose. "It's just that I was thinking the same thing. Although, I wasn't going to say it during our post-coital bliss. I hate the idea of thinking of you with anyone else."

"Oh, I don't think you have to worry about that," Sterling said.

The words carried a certain weight. June figured he really believed what he was saying—at the moment. That might change later when she went back to Great Falls. Not that she wanted to think about leaving him.

"Whoa," he said, his voice gentle. "Where'd you go?"

"Sorry." She dragged her mind away from her dire situation and focused her attention on the man before her. "I was just thinking about reality. Let's stay in dreamland for a while longer."

"Let's."

With that, he tucked her under his body and began to ravish her again, working his way from her earlobes to her collarbone, her sternum and breasts to her ribcage and belly button, her hips to her thighs and her warm center.

They made love again, slow and luxurious. She drank him in,

memorizing every detail: the thickness of his lashes, the color of his eyes, the scent of his skin, the feel of him inside her.

Then, while he slept, she quietly slipped out of bed. She didn't bother with a note. How could she possibly put her feelings into words? Instead, she returned to her own room, where she packed her belongings into the suitcase he'd bought her. Then, without having slept a wink, she wheeled her suitcase to the elevator, rode down to the first floor, and waited for her parents in the lobby.

Regret made her limbs heavy and her stomach sick, but when her parents pulled up in their shiny rental car, she managed to fold herself into the backseat.

She didn't manage not to cry though, and spent the ride to the airport bawling silently, feeling more alone and lonely than she ever had.

Chapter Twenty-Four

Almost before he woke up, Sterling sensed June was gone. Even though he'd expected her to go—her mom had threatened her biggest dream in life and actually had the power to snuff it—bitter disappointment set in when he opened his eyes and confirmed what his body already knew.

Anger rose in his chest and he hissed through his teeth and punched the pillow where she'd lain her head the night before. Parents were supposed to do their absolute best by their children. That both he and June were cursed with selfish parents seemed beyond unfair. A lump formed in his throat and he swallowed it down. He wouldn't cry over their situation.

"It is what it is, Wilder." His voice echoed in the empty room.

In the shower, he considered his options. He was half-tempted to go after her, to chase her parents' car down the mountain to the Phoenix airport and stop her from going with them. He scrubbed his hair and rinsed it, turning the water down, as cold as he could stand. However, with her being gone, the Sweet Springs Ranch fundraiser was one body short. It was all hands on deck to ensure the day went off without a hitch. Even if he did show up in Phoenix, she'd send him back to Prescott to handle things—the fundraiser was as important to her as it was to him. Wasn't that one of the reasons he loved her?

He loved her.

And there it was: the fact of the matter was that he loved her. He would do anything to get her back there, to explore this thing the two of them had going. Rushing through the rest of his shower, he soaped up his body and rinsed, then dried off and brushed his teeth so hard his gums hurt.

For years, he told himself he didn't want a relationship and that, shit, even if he did, he wouldn't be able to have one. Not just because of his job, but because of the Wilder Family Curse. He threw on jeans and a t-shirt and laced up his boots. Then he texted his brothers and Callie to call an emergency meeting.

Everyone showed up in the hotel conference room an hour later.

"I smell trouble," Cash said as he eyed the coffees Sterling brought. "And by that I mean I smell Sterling's stench and not June's floral scent."

Sterling punched him in the shoulder. Travis, Hayes, and Callie came in as Cash was saying, "I'm just joking, bro. You smell great. But where the hell is June?"

"She went back to Great Falls."

All movement ceased. Sterling sensed a collective inhale.

Callie was the first to regain her voice. "I was afraid of that."

"She went back to Great Falls?" Hayes said. "Why the hell would she do that when the fundraiser is only two days away?"

"She felt like she had to," Callie and Sterling said at the same time and Sterling was so grateful Callie understood.

"What does that even *mean?*" Travis wanted to know.

"You'd have to know her parents," Callie said.

"They showed up here and her mom threatened to sabotage her future event-planning business if she didn't go back with them," Sterling said, practically growling by the time he finished the sentence.

"That's bullshit, man," Travis said. "Would her mom really do that?"

"If you met Clara Cartwright, you wouldn't even be asking."

Callie pursed her lips. "Let's just say—have you seen that show where the evil mother hides her daughter in a tower?"

"Rapunzel?" Travis asked, drawing looks from the other three brothers.

"That's it!" Callie touched her pointer finger to her nose. "Rapunzel. Well, June's mom makes Rapunzel's mom look like a sweet, grandmotherly angel."

"Huh," Cash said. He sipped his coffee. "That stinks."

"It does more than that," Callie said.

"It does." Sterling held up the list June had handed out the day before. "But we have this list and fortunately, we know what we need to do. Let's divvy up June's tasks and get to work."

This time, the Wilder boys kept the bickering to a minimum as they decided who would do what. In fact, they discussed assignments with a surprising maturity, doling them out based on what made sense rather than how appealing each assignment seemed. They walked out of the conference room in a pyramid formation that reminded Sterling of a group in a superhero or heist movie ... a group on a mission. He could practically hear the music playing.

Being busy should be a good distraction, but it wasn't.

Driving around town running errands, he saw June everywhere. He could see her out of the corner of his eye while he drove. He could smell her perfume when he got back in the car. He could taste her lips when he closed his eyes.

At the job site, he worked with his crew to assemble the stage and backdrop. The physical work—swinging the hammer, pushing the saw, lifting sticks of wood—alleviated the tension that had been building since he woke to find June gone.

Even so, he imagined her there, too. Making his guys laugh, her muscles flexing while she moved lumber to measure it, quietly looking over the blueprints between tasks.

Sometimes he'd go a few minutes without thinking about her and would feel absolutely crushed when he remembered what transpired. His heart ached for missing her, even though only hours had passed.

He wasn't sure he could stand not texting her or talking to her or seeing her. Touching her. But he kept his phone tucked into his tool belt so he wouldn't be tempted—he didn't want to be the reason she strayed from her dream.

Sterling's phone rang and he was surprised to see Travis's name on the screen. Since Sterling had come back to Prescott, his brothers found him at the ranch whenever they needed to talk to him. And anyway, Travis was due at the ranch any time to help with construction.

When he picked up, Travis said, "We need to have a conversation."

Sterling froze, his whole body on alert, tingling. "Okay. What's up?"

After a long pause, Travis said, "I'd rather have this conversation in person."

"Want to give me a hint as to what it's about?"

"I ran into Mason Rickett today while I was downtown."

Reality hit fast and hard. Rickett told Travis about their dad's gambling. And not just that, Sterling figured as a sick feeling swirled in his stomach, but also about the fact that Sterling knew five years before the other Wilder brothers. Sterling squeezed the bridge of his nose. "Where do you want to meet?"

"I'll be at my place in fifteen minutes."

While Sterling waited, he paced Travis's driveway, trying to come up with a suitable apology. Nothing he could say would suffice. He'd messed up, plain and simple. Travis was going to be pissed and Sterling deserved that. Maybe if he stood there and let each one of his brothers take a swing at him, they'd forgive him. No, even that wasn't enough. He checked his watch for what had to be the seventh time. He wished Travis would hurry up and get there and put him out of his misery.

Finally, Travis's truck rumbled up the driveway. Then his brother was getting out, unfolding his long legs, shutting the driver's door, and walking toward Sterling. Without any warning whatsoever, he did what Sterling had just envisioned: his fist hit Sterling right in the jaw and he stumbled back a few steps.

"I deserved that."

"Damn right you did."

One hand on his bruised jaw, Sterling said, "You really perfected your right hook."

Mouth in a straight line, Travis shook his head. "Why didn't you tell us?"

Sterling threw up his hands and paced the driveway, walking a line next to Travis's neatly planted flowers. "There were a few reasons. First of all, we all idolized Dad. Did you think I wanted to be the one to take that away from the three of you? Me hating him was one thing. But me causing you guys to hate him? That was taking things to a whole nother level."

He stopped in front of Travis, who nodded, hands on his hips, and looked off into the distance like he couldn't quite bear to look at his traitorous brother. "You said there were several reasons."

"I confronted him about it." Sterling continued pacing. "Told him it had to stop or we could lose the ranch. He shrugged it off, told me to go to hell. It was obvious then he'd been gambling for a while. I didn't figure the three of you guys talking to him would have any more impact than me talking to him."

"Probably true."

"I anticipated my leaving would make a bigger impression. That he'd actually care. He'd see I was serious."

Again, Travis nodded. "I get that. But the ranch belongs to all of us. Did you ever stop to think that maybe you should tell us?"

"Oh, yeah." Sterling planted his feet wide and crossed his arms. "More times than I can count. And then, as time passed, I felt more and more guilty for not having told you. I was carrying this big secret, and for every day, week, and month that passed, it got even bigger. Finally, it got to the point where I didn't know if you guys would ever forgive me. I figured it was safer to stay gone than to risk facing you and potentially losing you forever."

"You're an idiot, man."

With a chuckle, Sterling said, "Don't you think I've figured that out by now?"

"So Hayes and Cash don't know?"

His stomach churning anew, Sterling closed his eyes. "No. Neither of them know."

"When I ran into that asshole Mason Rickett downtown, he said he knew I was running errands for the fundraiser and he couldn't wait to tell me that you knew all along. He was practically gleeful about it. I'm sure you can imagine how pissed off that made me."

"That guy definitely has a knack for pissing people off."

"Boy, howdy. And just for the record, I'm still pissed off."

Sterling shrugged. "Fair enough."

"And I expect you're going to have to tell Cash and Hayes."

"I expect that's true."

"And we both know they're going to be pissed, too." Travis took off his hat, ran his fingers through his hair, and put his hat back on.

"You know you've been doing that since you were a little kid."

Travis did it again. "I know."

Despite the fact that he still had to have this conversation with his other two brothers, Sterling felt a lightness he hadn't felt in ages. Holding on to that secret, keeping it from the people he loved most in the world, had been like carrying around a giant boulder on his shoulders. He should have known they would forgive him.

"I guess you're redeeming yourself by working so hard on this fundraiser," Travis said.

"I'm not doing it to redeem myself, you know."

"I know. Which is part of the reason I know I'll be able to forgive you. Someday." He punched Sterling hard on the arm, but he did it with a smile. "I'll leave it to you talk to Hayes and Cash."

"Will do."

"And, Sterling? Don't ever keep a secret like that again, okay?"

"Deal."

Telling Travis was one thing, but Cash and Hayes? That was a whole different animal. A dangerous mystical creature with spikes and fangs. He knew he wouldn't be able to breathe properly until he cleared the air though, so he sent out a text calling for a meetup at A Cold One.

He spent the rest of the afternoon agonizing over how he would tell them, the words he would use, whether to start with his reasons or start with the secret. He rehearsed the different options and discarded them one by one, thinking he couldn't avoid sounding like he was making excuses and had abandoned them out of selfishness.

When they arrived at A Cold One, all of Sterling's coherent thoughts flew out the window, replaced by straight-up fear. They'd be angry, but would they be angry *forever*? They might hate him, but how long would that last? What if they disowned him completely? What if they banned him from the Sweet Springs Ranch, just as he was falling back in love with it?

"I might be sick." He'd spoken aloud, but hadn't really meant for anyone to hear him.

"Need me to get you a trashcan?" Jerry materialized across the bar from him.

"You said you had something to take care of in the back."

"I did." He shrugged. "It's done. I'd offer you another beer, only, I don't want you tossing your cookies on my bar."

Sterling shook his head. "I won't."

By then, Hayes and Cash had reached Sterling.

"Why don't you guys grab a beer, and we'll get a table?"

His brothers looked at each other. Cash raised an eyebrow, Hayes shrugged, and Jerry handed them each a bottle. The dread becoming almost unbearable, Sterling swiveled off his stool and followed them to a booth.

"So what's this emergency meeting?" Cash was never one to beat around the bush.

Sterling wanted to stall, procrastinate, avoid losing his brothers —he'd already lost. the only other person he loved— but he knew he couldn't. "Look. There's something I've got to tell you."

Acting totally out of character, the two of them waited without saying a word.

Sterling took a deep breath. *Might as well just come out and say it.* "Five years ago, the reason I left is because I found out Dad was gambling."

Hayes and Cash continued to look at him, waiting.

"Not just forty bucks or even a hundred at a monthly poker

night. But tens of thousands." He took a swig of his beer, another deep breath. "It started out as monthly poker night. Progressed into horse racing and NFL. Tens of thousands of dollars."

Cash's eyes had gotten really big. Hayes still hadn't moved.

"I confronted him. He told me it was none of my business. So I left. I didn't tell you guys because I didn't want to ruin your relationships with him. And I hoped that when I left, he'd realize what a mistake he was making. But he didn't. And that's why he got behind on the mortgage. That's why we're now in danger of losing the ranch. I should have told you back then and I'm sorry."

For a moment, neither of them responded. For that tiny flicker of time, Sterling thought maybe they wouldn't be pissed. Maybe he was in the clear.

He should have known better.

Hayes spoke first. "So let me get this straight." His voice was deadly calm. He forced his mouth into an unnatural smile. Fire burned in his eyes. All of Sterling's fears rushed back to the surface. "You found out about a huge problem. One that could potentially affect all of us. And instead of manning up, telling us, letting us figure out a solution together, you took off."

His heart thudding, punctuating Hayes's words, Sterling nodded. "I'm sorry—"

Hayes held up a hand. "In all that time, did you bother checking in with our dear old dad to see if he'd stopped gambling?"

That would have been smart. "No." He swallowed.

"And in all that time, did you even consider that you should give us some sort of heads up?"

Sterling could tell Hayes was engaged to a lawyer. "No."

"And when we called to let you know Dad was on his deathbed, did it even occur to you that maybe you should mention his multiple-five-figure problem?"

He knew the situation was of his own making, but somehow Sterling felt railroaded by the line of questioning. "Yes, I—"

Again, Hayes held up a hand. "Then why didn't you?"

"Because you—we—were all grieving. It didn't seem like an appropriate time. What would I have said? 'Hey, guys, by the way, five years ago, I found out Dad was gambling away all of his life savings. I never told you, and now that he's on his deathbed, this seemed like the right time to bring it up."

Cash elbowed Hayes and said in a stage whisper, "Well, there is that."

Exasperated, Hayes closed his eyes, likely praying for patience. He opened them and pinned Sterling with his gaze. "You know, the three of us, we always figured you had your own reasons for leaving. We figured it had something to do with Dad. We hoped that eventually, you'd come around. But this? I don't think any of us would have guessed that you'd betray us like this."

Then Cash spoke. "No wonder you wanted to throw money at this, man. Make it go away. Maybe we should have let you. Taken your money and sent you back to wherever it is you're from. Nowhere, right? You can't settle down, even with yourself. To tell you the truth, I don't blame you. You probably find yourself pretty unbearable."

His words caused Sterling actual pain in his chest. He couldn't remember the last time in his adult life that he might actually cry. In public. Cash's words hurt because they rang true. Sterling cleared his throat. "That may be true. But I'm here because I wanted to help make things right. I'm so, so sorry for keeping that secret. And I just hope you can forgive me one day."

"Me too, brother," Hayes said. "Let's go."

They both slid out of the booth and headed for the door. Sterling watched them go, the similarities in their stride making it obvious they were brothers. His vision blurred.

He didn't bother finishing his beer, just tossed the mostly full bottle in the trash on his way out the door. He should go back to the ranch, oversee the final phases of construction. But he couldn't bring himself to face anyone, not even his crew.

On the drive back to the hotel, he tried to come up with ways he could make things right with his brothers, but nothing, from formal apology letters to ignoring their wishes and paying off the debts, to leaving town immediately, seemed quite right.

He remained in a haze until he got to his room. Then clarity hit him: he'd officially lost everything that was important to him. He'd lost his dad, he'd lost June, and now he'd lost his brothers.

Yes, he still had his company, but what good was that if he was alone? Unable to bear thinking about the situation, he flung himself face down on the bed and gave himself over to the oblivion of sleep.

Chapter Twenty-Five

June told herself she didn't want her mom to see her cry, but she failed at fighting back her tears on the long drive down to Phoenix. The farther they got from Prescott, Sterling, Callie, and all the Wilder brothers, the worse June felt. Her anger at her parents paled in comparison to her anger at herself. Why did she let them railroad her into going home with them, when what she really wanted was to stay in Prescott with her new friends and the man she loved and pull off a successful event that would ultimately launch her dream business?

Because you are a coward. I will never forgive you.

She couldn't decide what was worse—kissing goodbye that fundraiser and the start of her dream business, or leaving Sterling behind. Why she had agreed to go home was beyond her.

Oh, right. Because your controlling mother threatened you.

Her threat had seemed legitimate at first. But as time passed and June sat behind her mom—unable to look into her eyes and fall victim to her mystical superpowers—she realized Clara Cartwright couldn't possibly stop her from going out on her own. Sure, she could refuse to give her references. And she could *try* to stop other clients from doing so. But most of the Hotel Cartwright clients loved June, and would likely be willing to say so publicly. Even if they weren't, she was perfectly capable of building her business from the ground up. She could find new clients who wouldn't be under her mom's thumb at all.

By the time they reached the airport, her throat felt tight, her eyes burned, and the tension in her shoulders was giving her a headache. When her dad offered to get her suitcase out of the trunk she gave him a terse, "I've got it."

And when her mom offered to buy them breakfast while they waited for their flight, she said, "I don't have an appetite."

Her parents went to eat without her and when they came to sit with her at the gate, her mom tried to pretend everything was normal. "They're predicting afternoon storms here, so I'm glad we got an early flight."

June stared out the window. She watched people arriving and departing and wondered how many of them were going where they wanted to, and how many felt like they had to

"Did you hear me, Junie?"

She shook her head.

"I said that when we get back, you should probably meet with Maya and have her bring you up to date on Timmy's wedding."

She didn't bother acknowledging that.

Being in the airport reminded June of Sterling. Although they'd met less than two weeks before, she couldn't believe how well they'd come to know each other. During that first interaction, he'd been a handsome, charming stranger. When she saw him at Sweet Springs Ranch, he'd been the surly opposite. Her lips quirked. He was still handsome. But way less charming. And then she'd gone and fallen for him.

An airline employee announced it was time to board. June didn't bother waiting for her parents to gather their things. She buckled herself into her first-class seat and put on her earbuds.

The plane ride back to Great Falls reminded her of her flight to Phoenix. The one Sterling insisted she take so she could start her mini-vacation. She'd missed him then too, in the way someone misses an idea. But now, leaving their shared destination, she missed him like a woman misses a man. She sat first class, then, too. A flight attendant handed her a glass of champagne, which she downed and handed back before he even had time to give her parents their glasses.

"Care for another?"

"Don't mind if I do."

Gulping down two flutes of champagne was probably unwise, she realized as her world started to spin. But, if she played it right, it might help her fall asleep and pretend none of this was happening.

"Junie." Her dad woke her, his hand gentle on her forearm. "We're about to land. I didn't want you to get spooked when we touched down."

She covered his hand with hers. "Thanks, Dad."

As they breezed down the jet bridge to the terminal, June's mom was all business again. "Maya is going to meet us at the airport, June. She'll take us back to the hotel. And then the two of you can have a little meeting in the office."

Naturally, Clara Cartwright had every last detail planned. At that point, responding seemed pointless, so June quickened her stride and headed for the baggage claim. She was fairly certain she looked foolish, wrestling her giant suitcase off the conveyor belt, but she refused help from her dad anyway. Her refusal probably hurt his feelings and June felt some guilt over that. But he'd stood by while her mom acted like a maniac. And anyway (she could hear the little devil on her shoulder), wasn't the Cartwright Family Empire's Cardinal Rule Number Three to be self-sufficient?

June hightailed it out to the curb, leaving her parents behind once again.

Sure enough, because Maya was totally competent, she was already there, her car parked with its trunk open. She rushed toward June, her face pinched with regret. "I'm so, so sorry June. I tried. I promise you, I tried."

June threw herself into Maya's arms. "You don't have to apologize. Thank you for trying."

Maya gave June one more squeeze before straightening up, plastering on a bright smile, and waving. "Mrs. Cartwright! Mr. Cartwright! Welcome back. I'm so glad you arrived safely."

Finally, alone with Maya in the office an hour later, June felt like she could let her guard down.

She sat down at her desk and put her head in her hands. "I can't believe my life has come to this."

"I'm so sorry. I wish I could make it better for you."

"You already have, Maya. If you hadn't been willing to take over, I never would have met Sterling." A bitter laugh slipped out of her mouth. "I never would have lost him, either. But you know how the saying goes."

Maya stood up and walked across the room to the locking cabinet. June should have been interested in what she was doing, but she couldn't bring herself to stop thinking about Sterling and her parents, and Timothy Alexander.

At that point, her forehead was flat on the table. She felt something cool against the side of her hand and looked up to see Maya had poured her a drink.

"This won't put you and Sterling back in the same ZIP code, but it might take the edge off being here."

Barely managing a smile, June sat up straight and picked up the glass. "Thank you." The honey-colored liquid warmed her insides immediately and with that warmth came a rush of gratitude for Maya. "I really appreciate everything you've done. The least I can do is stop moping around and help you with this wedding."

"Actually, you'd be surprised." Maya shrugged. "The whole thing has gone more smoothly than I expected. Timothy Alexander —or *Timmy* as your mom is now calling him—loves me. He turned you into such a villain in his mind that he thinks I'm a hero."

June snorted. "I mean, you *are* a hero to me, but don't you think *he's* the villain?"

"I do," Maya said slowly. "But in his mind, he's the protagonist. I just make sure that in everything I do, I make him feel like the main character."

"You're a genius."

Maya winked. "I know."

"Show me what you've got."

Maya grabbed a folder off her desk, took out a sheet of paper, and turned it around so it was right-side up for June.

"Here's the schedule." She pointed at each section. "Week before, day before, day of, day after."

"Wow. Maya, this is impressive."

She winked. "I've been watching you."

June took another sip of her drink. "Gosh, you know how to make a girl blush."

Maya proceeded to show her a detailed list of vendors, what they were providing, and when they would show up at the hotel. She also had a list of everyone in the bridal party, including the bride and groom's family members.

June couldn't believe Maya's efficiency and organization, and she told her so.

"Well, I suppose since I'm here, we may as well do all the setup we can."

Maya nodded. "Let's. I have a feeling with two of us, we can bust it out in a couple of hours."

They started in the reception hall and after carrying in the tables, chairs, linens, and boxes of decorations (including dozens upon dozens of sparkling snowflakes), the two women turned on some music and got to work. While June extended the legs on the tables, arranged the chairs, and spread the tablecloths, she found herself thinking about the Sweet Springs Ranch fundraiser. She'd imagined doing all of these tasks for that event, with the people she'd come to care for. But here she was, halfway across the country, setting up a winter wonderland in the middle of summer.

"Maybe we should turn down the thermostat to forty degrees," Maya called from across the room where she was arranging vases on the buffet table.

June chuckled. "That would be amazing. We could just tell Timmy we wanted the guests to really get the full, authentic experience."

Maya snickered. "I don't think he'd give us rave reviews on Insta, which seems to be very important to your parents now that they're back from France."

Shaking her head, June carried on with the tablecloths.

Maya appeared in front of her. "Are you okay?"

June blinked. "Of course. What do you mean?"

"I've been talking to you and you haven't responded. Are you just off in lala land?"

She used her palms to smooth out the tablecloth she'd just spread. "I shouldn't admit it, but yes. I just keep thinking about how I'm going to miss out on preparing for the fundraiser in Arizona. This is actually my favorite part of an event—" she gestured at the room around them, everything taking shape. "I love the anticipation of it all. The energy of preparing. But I won't get to do that for the Sweet Springs fundraiser."

Maya pressed her lips together and pursed them to the side, which June recognized as her thoughtful expression. "I didn't know that about you."

Shrugging, June said, "Yeah, I know. It's weird. These are the small moments, right? A lot of event planners would probably say they enjoy the moment when the bride walks down the aisle, or when the bride and groom exchange vows or kiss. But me? I like these quiet moments. The behind-the-scenes stuff."

"Tell me more about this Sterling character." On her way back to the buffet table, Maya threw a smile over her shoulder. "Sounds like he's pretty dreamy."

June's body went molten at the images of every version of Sterling she'd met so far. "He *is* pretty dreamy."

She shared with Maya all the high points. When she talked about all his sweet gestures, she didn't skimp on the details. When she talked about what he looked like in jeans and a white t-shirt, she didn't skimp, either. She told Maya how well he got along with his crew and how good he was with a set of tools and of course, she described the way he handled her mom with extraordinary finesse and a twinkle of humor in his eyes.

By the time she was done describing him, June's heart ached. He was undoubtedly the most wonderful man she'd ever had the pleasure of not dating. She hadn't been lying when she told him he'd ruined her for anyone else. No one would ever compare to him.

That's when she went from sappy to devastated and the tears fell freely from her eyes.

Maya looked alarmed and darted around the big room looking for a box of tissues. She finally found one on the guestbook table just inside the door and rushed back to June, pulling out a few tissues and shoving them out her as she approached. "I'm so sorry, June. I didn't mean to upset you. He sounds like a really great guy."

June waved her off. "No need to apologize. It's not you. It's my parents. And me, for not standing up to them. It's the whole situation. I wish I could go back in time and refuse to come back here with them." She threw up her hands. "But then I'd be leaving you to deal with Timmy alone, and that wouldn't be fair, either." She sniffled and dabbed at her cheeks and nose with the tissue.

"I really appreciate you coming back, June. You're the best event planner I know, and I wasn't sure I was ready to pull off such an important wedding by myself. For what it's worth, maybe you can go back to Arizona as soon as the wedding is over."

June wailed. "I don't think they'll have me. Can you imagine? I ditched them right at the peak of the pre-event frenzy. I left them one body short. And one brain. Although I did give them a very detailed list."

"Of course you did." Maya patted her knee. "Where do you think I got my list-making skills? You know what? I say we put on some more upbeat music and finish this up. Then we can cruise through tomorrow."

June nodded. Dabbed at her cheeks and nose again. "Okay. And, Maya? Thank you."

"Anytime, June."

Eight hours later at four a.m. on the dot, a knock on her door jolted June out of a dead sleep. She thought she imagined it, so she closed her eyes. But no, there it was again. A gentle knock. Five little raps. June rolled out of bed and padded to the door. Maya stood on the other side, wearing her pajamas, a bathrobe, and her glasses, and carrying her laptop under her arm.

"Maya. Is everything okay?"

Maya brushed past her and into the room, her movements businesslike and efficient. "Everything's fine."

June's eyes felt sandy. She blinked and rubbed them. "What are you doing here, Maya?"

"Sorry. I haven't slept. And I've consumed way too much caffeine. I'll take it one step at a time. Go shower and put on some decent underwear."

Chapter Twenty-Six

When he woke up the next morning Sterling felt like he'd been run over by a truck. Not physically—he hadn't slept that many hours in as long as he could remember. But psychologically? He'd been pummeled on every plane and surface.

At some point during the night he'd gotten under the covers. Now, with the light blazing through the window (he hadn't closed the drapes), he pushed aside the duvet and stood. That task, in and of itself, felt monumental. Seeing his brothers again was almost more than he could bear. But he had to. He'd spent the last five years avoiding them and he owed it to them to man up and see this fundraiser through.

The morning was already muggy when he set foot on the family property. His crew was there, the guys oblivious to what transpired between him and his brothers. Actually, as he looked over the scene he figured he could probably cut them loose. They milled around, stacking leftover boards, folding the pop-up shades, and picking up loose nails. As far as construction, the site was ready for the fundraiser. He could finish up the painting and trim work. Sending them home was the logical thing to do, but he couldn't stand for them to go.

They hollered out greetings when they noticed him but kept working, for which he was grateful. Although it was unnecessary, Sterling walked over to the makeshift desk and unrolled the blueprints.

"What's bugging you, boss?" Riggs appeared at his side.

Eyes still on the blueprints, Sterling shook his head. "Nothing, man. Just going over this one last time. Why do you ask?"

His foreman hitched a hip onto the desk and crossed his arms. "Oh, you know. Just because you look like shit, bro."

"I showered."

Riggs inclined his head. "I can see that. But your whole, I don't know, bearing. You look ... sad."

Tears threatened again. "June left yesterday. Her parents came into town and basically forced her to go back home and oversee that wedding for that douchebag groom."

Riggs hissed through his teeth. "That's a crappy move."

"Tell me about it. And then there's my crappy move." He explained what had gone down with his brothers. "Talking about it with someone outside the family is kind of a relief," he added, "but it doesn't take away from the fact that two of them aren't talking to me. I know I screwed up and I know I deserve it, but man, it feels terrible."

"*Sounds* terrible. Geez, you've had a rough twenty-four hours."

"That's putting it mildly."

"Anything I can do?"

That Riggs asked, and that he would do anything Sterling needed, gave Sterling some comfort. Maybe he wasn't as alone as he felt. "I wish there were. And I appreciate you offering."

Riggs put a hand on Sterling's shoulder. "I'm real sorry. It's a huge double whammy. I'm sure everything will work itself out in time. They're your brothers. They can't stay mad at you forever. And June? After seeing the two of you together, I have a feeling that will work itself out, too."

"One can only hope."

Riggs walked off, leaving Sterling alone with his thoughts. Which wasn't a good thing. He needed something to keep himself busy. He took his task list out of his pocket. Most of the items had to happen the next day. Some of them were originally assigned to June: *set up tables and chairs, put on tablecloths and chair covers, organize silent auction items, pick up flowers.*

There wasn't much for him to do at the moment and he cursed himself for being so efficient during the days leading up to the fundraiser. Because he needed to be busy, he decided to do the one thing that had always helped him clear his mind: go for a ride.

Travis was quick to let Sterling borrow one of the horses, and as soon as he walked into the barn, the energy there began to smooth out the uncomfortable buzzing he'd carried around in his body since June left. How could he have come to rely so much on someone he'd only just met? Now he didn't know how to live without her.

He inhaled the scents of the barn. Fresh hay, old wood, and the musky smell of horses. The animals perked up when they saw him, pricking their ears and making the chuffing sound he hadn't realized he missed.

He found himself walking over to the stall, scratching their necks, talking to them like they were old friends. He wasn't foolish enough to think horses never got mad at humans, but at least when they did, making things right took only a few minutes, a couple of treats, and a few good neck rubs. If only things were that simple between brothers.

He decided to ride Chewy; Travis had told him the horse loved to gallop and Sterling wanted to go fast. Instead of taking the trail he and June rode together, he opted for a long, easy ride around the property—a big, curving circle that would allow him to break Chewy into a full-on canter and just *run*. Although his movements were calm and certain as he put on the saddle and bridle, it was as if the horse could sense his desire to go fast. He mounted and Chewy danced in place, his energy matching Sterling's.

Getting him to walk as he exited the barn was difficult. Sterling had to pull back on the reins to keep the horse from bolting. Once they were outside, the sun warm and the birds chirping around them, he gave the horse his head—and they were off.

Chewy's hooves thundered and Sterling could feel his muscles contracting and lengthening as they picked up speed. His hat nearly blew off his head and he had to shove it down as the horse followed the trail north.

After a full minute, the two of them fell into a rhythm together, and all conscious brain activity faded. Riding required Sterling's full focus and he almost couldn't believe it when they rounded a corner and came east back to the barn. As if the horse could read his mind, he went right past the barn to head north and do the loop again.

Sterling whooped and Chewy picked up his pace, almost throwing Sterling out of the saddle.

By the time they'd made four full laps, they were both sweaty and breathing hard and worn out. Which was exactly what Sterling was going for. Putting up the tack and brushing the horse was just as meditative as riding, and Sterling found he felt a million times better after forcing his mind blank.

After offering treats to both Chewy and Leia, Sterling headed back to the site, where he sat in a camping chair at the makeshift office and gazed out over the scene, his body feeling like rubber and his mind clear. Tires crunched on gravel and dread made Sterling's skin instantly cold and clammy when he imagined having to face Hayes or Cash. He glanced toward the driveway to see who it was, and relief replaced dread when he realized the vehicle, a shiny sedan, didn't belong to either of them.

"You know who that is?" Sterling asked.

"Nope." Riggs walked toward the parking area.

Sterling remained in place because he wasn't equipped to deal with anyone. He watched as Riggs froze, mid-stride, then broke into a jog while waving. Someone he knew ... a friend and not a foe. Sterling could breathe a little easier. Riggs reached the car as it parked. The driver's window rolled down but Riggs's body obscured Sterling's view of the driver. He went back to his useless examination of the blueprints. The site went quiet. He straightened up to look again.

Was he seeing a ghost? More specifically, *June's* ghost?

There she was, a summer vision in a dress that would fit somewhere between orange and pink on the color wheel. Her smile was the brightest thing about her and his heart went wild. It sang and danced inside his chest as he realized she wasn't a vision, but a living and breathing human. *His* human. And then she was in his arms and he was spinning her around and they were both laughing and his crew was cheering.

"You came back," his words were muffled because his face was in her hair, but she understood him.

"I did. I couldn't stay away."

He set her down and held onto her hands. "I'm really glad you're here, but what changed? Did your mom change her mind about groomzilla?"

A flash of uncertainty—so quick, Sterling could have missed it—flickered in her eyes before she answered. "She didn't change her mind. But I got back and Maya showed me everything she'd done to prepare. I helped her set up. As I suspected, she's handling it like a pro."

"I'm glad to hear that."

"I went to bed last night feeling so defeated." Her voice cracked. "And then Maya knocked on my door at four this morning and when I answered, she bustled in and told me to get in the shower."

Sterling raised his eyebrows.

"Apparently, she couldn't stand me not being here. She said, 'June, I won't stand by and let your parents bully you. I won't stand by and let you lose the man who, let's face it, has the potential to be the love of your life.'"

Sterling's heart may have skipped a few beats at that.

"'I won't stand by and let you miss that fundraiser. So get in the shower, brush your teeth, and get dressed. You have a flight to Prescott in two hours. You've got to be on it.' Or something like that. I'm summarizing, but you get the idea."

"She bought you a ticket to Prescott?"

June nodded. "While I was in the shower, she ordered some sort of witches brew that cleared the cobwebs, laid out this outfit and a sweater—which, let's face it, I couldn't have chosen better, myself—and steered me and the suitcase I never unpacked down to the lobby."

"I think I might love this Maya character. I hope I get to meet her someday, thank her in person."

June laughed. "I love her, too. But wait. I haven't gotten to the best part, yet. When we got down to the lobby, my parents were coming in."

"What were they doing up so early?"

June grimaced. "They go for a walk at four every morning. They were just getting back."

Sterling's stomach lurched. "I can only imagine what your mom said."

Remembering that moment, laughter bubbled up from inside June, and she giggled as she said, "You should have seen her face. They were both as surprised to see us as we were to see them ... and then my mom's expression just morphed into outrage. She asked just where I was going and I stood my ground. Maya and I literally ran to the car, and she drove like a bat out of hell to get us to the airport. My parents tried to follow us, but they couldn't keep up. I suspect they gave up at some point—they probably figured it was more efficient to cut their losses and go plan for the wedding without me."

Sterling laughed out loud. "I can't believe this. I wish I could have been there to see your mom's face."

"It was scary," June said, growing serious again. "But I told myself, they can follow me to the airport if they want, or all the way back here to Arizona. But they aren't going to stop me."

The breeze lifted a few strands of her hair and he tucked one behind her ear. "What gave you this sudden boost of confidence?"

She grinned. "You did. Well, Maya, too. When she was talking about how she wasn't going to stand by while I let go of the man who could very well be the love of my life, I thought, you know what? She's right. I can't let my mom control me anymore. She can't really stop people from providing references and reviews. And even if she could, I could just start from scratch. I like to think I'm capable."

"You are. I've seen it firsthand."

"And then there's the most important thing. We haven't known each other for long, Sterling, but what we have is special. Maybe you don't plan on settling down anywhere anytime soon. And I don't know what my own future is. But what I do know is that since I came to Prescott, since I started spending time with you, I have felt braver and more sure of myself than ever before. You bring that out in me, Sterling. Because you believe in me. And from our first meeting, when you stepped in to help me without really having met me, you've proven that you're willing to support me. I don't care where we go, or how many times we move, or where we end up. All I care about is that we're together. I've never felt this way about anyone else. Ever. And I don't want to let go of that."

While she spoke, she held tightly onto his hands. She continued to look at him, her eyes brimming with tears, her forehead etched with worry like she wasn't sure whether he even wanted her back in Prescott.

Her words awoke the hope he had quashed. It sprung up from its slumber and stretched its arms above his head. "I'm so glad you're saying this, June. Since the first moment I saw you scattering your clothes all over the floor at the airport—"

She gave him a playful swat on the arm.

"Since that moment, I knew you were special. And after we spent that evening together, I knew you'd changed me and I'll never be the same. You being here for the past two weeks only proved me right. You are special. You mean the world to me, June. And I don't care either where we go or how many times we move or where we end up. I just care that we're together."

Then she was hugging him again, her arms tight around his waist, her head on his chest and her heart beating against his.

"When you left, it was like I was deprived of oxygen. I understood—I wasn't angry—but my life force was depleted. I saw you everywhere. At the hotel, the job site." He gestured at the space around them. "I felt your absence in my bed." His own eyes stinging with the threat of tears, he barked out a short laugh. "I realize how foolish that sounds. You were gone for thirty-six hours. But I thought it was forever, June. And I knew I couldn't live without you forever."

"Then I'm glad I came back."

He rested his cheek on the top of her head and she sighed into the embrace.

"I'm glad you came back, too."

She took a step back and made a show of brushing her hands together. "Okay. Now that that's out of the way, what's on the agenda for today? Want to bring me up to speed?"

"I would love to."

He gestured toward the stage and they headed that way.

"You know," he said, "you leaving us one body short added a lot to my plate."

He winked as she shook her head. "I'm really sorry. Leaving was one of the stupidest things I could've done."

"But you're here now. You can help me set up the tables and chairs."

"I guess I'd better change first."

"Don't. I like the way you look in that dress."

The smile she gave him in response made him want to take her behind the barn and have his way with her, but he couldn't do that with his crew hanging around.

The rental company had stacked the tables behind the stage and Sterling and June quickly fell into a rhythm working together to roll them out to the designated seating area.

"Sterling?"

"Yeah?"

"Is everything okay?" June laid down the table she was rolling and went to work setting up its legs. "It's just that when I pulled up I saw you standing there by the table. And you just looked so... sad."

His brothers. June's return had almost made him forget he wasn't on speaking terms with Hayes and Cash.

"I can tell this is big. What's going on?"

While they continued working, rolling tables, straightening legs, and putting the tables upright, Sterling told her everything. He started with the discovery of his dad's gambling, and didn't stop until he got to the part where Hayes and Cash walked out on him at A Cold One. June listened, interjecting appropriate reactions here and there. Having someone to share the story with made his heart feel somewhat lighter. Even so, he dreaded the next two days, which would require he, Hayes, and Cash to work side by side to pull this thing off.

"I'm sure they'll come around, Sterling," June said when he finished.

"Are you?" He immediately regretted the bitterness with which he spoke. "I'm sorry. It's just that this is exactly what I've been worried about for the past five years. I feel like I just got them back, and now I'm in danger of losing them again."

She stopped what she was doing and came over to wrap her arms around him. "I can say with ninety-nine percent certainty that they will come around."

He chuckled. "I'm worried about that other one percent."

"They love you, Sterling. I may not have been able to say that when we first met, but now I have evidence. After spending most of my time with you and your family for the past two weeks, I could see that at first, they were guarded. Maybe your return seemed too good to be true. But as soon as they realized you were here to stay, you all fell back into being brothers so quickly. Yes, they razz you, give you a hard time, throw punches every now and then. Half the time they don't listen when you talk. They drive you crazy. And they'd say the same about you. But when it comes right down to it, the four of you are brothers and nothing can take that away."

"Not even me acting like a great big idiot and keeping a giant secret for five years?"

"Not even that." She touched her lips to his in a way that felt a lot like a promise.

Chapter Twenty-Seven

Armed with her task list and a team of people to command, June stepped seamlessly back into her role as primary event planner for the Sweet Springs Ranch fundraiser.

By late afternoon, her entire body ached from moving furniture and striding across the property countless times.

But her heart was light: not only was the event prep running perfectly, with all cylinders firing and all deadlines met, but things on the home front were going swimmingly. She texted Maya several times throughout the day and each time, Maya gave a thumbs-up and a positive report.

Timmy is in a great mood and even bought me a snowflake charm for my bracelet.

The site is fully prepped. All vendors have arrived. Guests are seating themselves as we speak.

The wedding is starting, and the bride is here (I was half-afraid she'd be a no-show).

It didn't hurt that June had blocked her parents' numbers so they couldn't disturb her.

She was in the middle of hanging string lights when Travis's truck pulled up to the job site and he, Cash, Hayes, and Callie tumbled out, running up to hug her. Cash carried a six-pack of beer and opened the bottles by hand, giving them out to everyone except Sterling.

Hurt passed over his features, but he quickly schooled his expression into neutral and grabbed a beer for himself. June wished she could tuck him safely inside her heart and protect him from the pain of his brothers' anger, but at the same time it was hard not to feel buoyed by their excitement about her return and energized by the cold and refreshing beer.

"To June!" Cash said at one point, lifting his beer while everyone chorused, "To June!"

June's heart actually swelled at that, and she felt more at home than she had in ages.

That night when she and Sterling finally made it to his hotel room, she knew for certain coming back was the right choice. For herself, for her business, and for Sterling.

Just inside the door, they stopped and turned toward each other. He took her face in his hands and kissed her with so much tenderness, she almost melted right there on the spot.

"I'm so glad you're here." His whisper was hoarse and full of emotion.

"Me, too."

He brought his lips to hers again, this time with more urgency, and she found herself gripping his waist and pulling her hips against his. His hands moved from her face to her shoulders to her elbows, and then to the hem of her dress before making their way upwards against her skin. She shivered under his touch, moaned as his hands found her breasts, dropped her head back as his mouth came to her neck.

She unbuttoned his shirt just as she'd been wanting to do since she drove up to the ranch that morning and saw him standing there, his arms gleaming in the summer sun. She groaned with impatience when she found his undershirt and yanked it free from his waistband so her hands could roam over his abs. She unfastened his belt, unbuttoned and unzipped his jeans, and slid her hand inside his underwear to stroke him. This time, he groaned, pulling her dress over her head and taking off his jeans in what seemed like one fluid motion.

And then, somehow, like magic, they were tumbling onto the bed, the mood changing from sweet to urgent as he unhooked her bra, threw it to the side, and feasted on her breasts. She yanked off his shirt, desperate for his skin on hers. When she got it, she made a purring sound, and then giggled.

"What's so funny?"

"Oh, just that I feel like such a sex goddess right now."

"I'll make you feel like a sex goddess."

He lifted himself up and plunged into her, and the pleasure was so great she could barely breathe. Then they were moving together, gazes locked, rising higher and higher until they, shattered, together.

They remained attached while they rode the waves and when their bodies finally stilled, Sterling said, his voice husky, "I love you, June."

Her throat tight because his love for her was palpable, she said, "I love you, Sterling."

"You know what else, June?"

"What?"

"I'm famished."

She laughed again, equally delighted by his candor and the fact that she could laugh in this intimate moment with him.

"What do you say we order room service?"

They did, and put on a true crime show while they ate in bed. After a couple of episodes, she said, "Big day tomorrow. I suppose we should get to bed."

She would have imagined their lovemaking would throw them both into the oblivion of sleep, but she found she couldn't stop thinking about Maya, wondering how the wedding was going. And when she looked over at Sterling, she saw that he too lay awake, blinking at the ceiling.

"What are you thinking?" She ran her fingertips from his belly-button up to his sternum and then smoothed her palm across his chest.

"You first."

Using that same fingertip to trace his collarbone and the profile of his shoulder, she said, "I was thinking about Groomzilla."

He smiled. "I'm not sure that's a good thing, considering we just had sex that would've knocked my socks off if I hadn't already removed them. And there you are, thinking about another man."

"Very funny. I was wondering how everything went. Even though Maya literally dragged me to the airport to come here, I still feel guilty about leaving her."

"Can you text her?"

If she hadn't already fallen in love with Sterling, she would have then.

June got up and carried the room service tray to the table. "I could try. I hope the wedding is over by now. But I could see Timmy wanting to dance until the clock struck midnight and some magical fairy ice pumpkin carriage showed up."

"That sounds terrifying."

"Doesn't it?" She flopped onto her back on the bed.

"I can see why you left." He turned toward her and settled his hand on her stomach. "Go ahead and text her."

"I will. After you tell me what's keeping *you* awake." She interlaced her fingers with his. He nuzzled his chin onto her shoulder. "Hayes and Cash still haven't spoken to me."

"And it's eating you up."

"Pretty much."

Again, June wished she could protect him from pain, erase it, do something to make him feel better.

"You could talk to them."

Sterling shook his head. "I don't think I can. I already apologized, so shouldn't they come to me?"

"I guess this is kind of unprecedented territory. I don't think there are any rules in the books. So I'd say you just do whatever feels right."

He closed his eyes. "Okay. I'll think about it while you text Maya."

She slid out of bed and put on one of the hotel's robes. The thick cotton felt soft and cool against her skin. She found her phone and texted Maya: *How's it going there? It's almost midnight—the witching hour. Has the frozen pumpkin carriage arrived?*

Maya's response came through almost immediately. *LOL. No ice pumpkin carriage. But believe it or not, the wedding has been spectacular. The reception is almost over. Timmy and his beautiful bride are about to go out to the limo. Which is not made of ice. I've got to go hand out the snowflake confetti for the guests to shower them with. But no need to worry. Timmy's thrilled. He'll be giving us a great write up on Insta. Gotta go.*

June responded: *Great work, Maya. I knew you could do this. You're amazing. And thank you again for taking over for me.*

Because she wasn't expecting an immediate response she set her phone face down on the night stand.

"So?" Sterling had turned down the TV volume and lay on his side. She sat on the edge of the bed. "All's well in Great Falls. Timmy and his new bride are heading to the limo and Maya said the wedding was fabulous."

"That's great news."

She kissed him and stretched out alongside his body. "I'm so relieved. And now we need to fix your problem."

Rolling onto his back, he scrubbed his hands over his face. "We can't fix it. I've apologized."

"Sterling Wilder, this is hurting you and you know it. You know what I've learned in the past twenty-four hours?"

"What?" He kept his face covered.

"You can't just sit back and wait for shit to go your way. That's what I was doing and it nearly cost me my dream—and you. I won't let you risk losing your brothers because you're too afraid and too *stubborn* to be vulnerable with them."

He uncovered his face. "Did you just call me stubborn?"

"Damn right I did. Now, are you going to get them together yourself, or do I have to help you? Because I will. I'll call them and arrange a meeting if it means getting the four of you to talk."

"I like you when you're bossy," he said, rubbing her stomach again.

She swatted his hand away and sat up. "Get up. Put on a robe. Text your brothers. Make a plan for tomorrow."

"Fine." He sat up. "Geez."

"Geez, yourself."

After a long, lingering kiss, he put on a robe and got back in bed. He spent a couple of minutes texting, then set down his phone and pulled June into his arms. "Okay, now I can sleep."

"Told you."

"You were right."

"I could get used to hearing that."

Chapter Twenty-Eight

The next evening, Sterling took his time getting dressed; he was preparing for an important occasion and wanted to feel and look like it. Figuring Hayes and Cash might not agree to meet him if he extended a simple invitation, he texted Travis and laid out his plan.

When Travis got in Sterling's car at the ranch shortly thereafter he said, "So let me get this straight. You're going to drive to Hayes's house and I'm going to go in and get him without telling him you're there. And then we're going to do the same thing at Cash's."

"Right." Sterling feigned confidence even though the plan sounded pretty ridiculous when Travis repeated it back to him.

Fortunately, Travis just shrugged and put on his seatbelt.

A few minutes later, they arrived at Hayes's house. Travis went up and knocked on the front door while Sterling waited in the car, windows down, his heart in his throat and his stomach in knots.

A shaft of light illuminated Hayes's silhouette when the door opened. Sterling might throw up. Travis spoke for a minute—Sterling could see his hands moving—and then Hayes peered around Travis to look at Sterling's car. He shook his head and Sterling felt tears threaten. He'd been right—they would never forgive him.

But then the door opened wider and Hayes came out and he

and Travis walked down the walkway. A rush of relief made Sterling's heart beat even faster.

"I've got shotgun," Travis said, and Hayes said, "You can have it, bro. I don't want it."

That hurt because they always fought over shotgun, but Sterling didn't say a word as his brothers shut their doors. They went on to Cash's house, where Travis must have tried a different lead-in because Cash came right out but stopped halfway down the driveway when he saw Sterling's car.

"What the hell, Trav?"

Maybe I should have left the windows up.

"He just wants to talk to you." Travis sounded resigned. He'd expected this.

"Bullshit. He probably wants to grovel, and I'm not interested."

He *did* want to grovel. Not that his brothers owed it to him to listen, but he hoped they'd hear him out. Sterling shrugged and nodded, even though Cash couldn't see him.

Chuckling came from the backseat. Sterling looked at the rearview mirror but couldn't see Hayes to glean from his expression whether his laughter was a result of amusement or derision. Travis responded to Cash, but he kept his voice too quiet for Sterling to hear him. Whatever he said worked, because before long the two of them were walking toward the car.

Nobody said anything about shotgun.

"My job here is done," Travis said once Sterling put the car in motion. "Now why don't you tell us where you're taking us."

Sterling had carefully considered the location for this conversation, but wasn't sure how it would land.

He cleared his throat. "We're going to the water tower."

Silence.

The water tower was the scene of many high school parties, teenaged shenanigans, and late-night conversations. Most of the activity took place on the ground beneath the giant structure, but the deepest talks happened when the kids climbed the spiral staircase and sat on the platform that encircled the tank, legs swinging and arms slung over the lowest rung of the railing.

He wished he could read his brothers' minds so he'd know how they felt about heading to the water tower now, as adults. He figured that since no one had opened a car door and jumped out though, they weren't going to refuse to spend a little time there.

Just like old times, he backed in just inside the gate so they could make a quick escape if anyone called the cops. As one, his brothers got out, shutting their doors in unison. He wondered how long it would be before he felt like one of them again. Without thinking too hard about that, he got out too, and jogged to catch up to them at the bottom of the staircase.

Hayes was the first to set a foot on one of the metal stairs, which creaked, protesting. Cash, of course, laughed, and stepped aside, gesturing for Travis to go next. The staircase moaned when Travis added his weight, and Cash stepped away from the bottom stair.

"I'm gonna let them get all the way to the top before I test this thing."

"Good thinking," Sterling said, thrilled that Cash had spoken a full sentence to him and also tempering his reaction so Cash wouldn't know he was thrilled.

The rusty metal continued to groan and creak as the first two brothers made their way up. At one point, Travis jumped to the next step, making the whole structure shake—and Hayes yelp and grab the railing.

"Idiots," Cash muttered.

Even though it was a one-word sentence, it was still a full sentence and the second one Cash had spoken.

"I was thinking the same."

Hayes and Travis had reached the top and Travis walked onto the platform that encircled the tank. He leaned against the railing and lifted both arms in triumph. He whooped. "We made it, boys. Who's next?"

Suddenly the mood felt just a little lighter.

Cash gestured for Sterling to head up and Sterling figured that was in case the staircase broke on this run. Normally, he'd punch Cash in the arm on his way by, or say something about how Cash was sacrificing him, but the mood wasn't *that* light.

Sterling tested each step before placing his full weight on it, but he could swear the thing was sagging and swaying as he ascended. Normally, one of his brothers would crack a joke or let out a whistle or make a loud noise to scare him, but they remained silent as he took one step after another.

The journey felt interminable, but he did eventually reach the top and Hayes and Travis scooted down to make room for him on the platform. They all looked down to where Cash stood.

He placed a tentative foot on the bottom step and it let out the longest creak yet. Hayes bellowed, "Easy there, Cash. I think your burger habit is catching up with you."

"I could still beat the shit out of you." Cash's voice lacked the bravado his words suggested he should have.

He broke into a run on about the fourth step and Sterling held his breath until he'd made it safely to the top, chest heaving. "Sterling's stupid-ass plan would be a really lame way to die."

That stung but Sterling didn't let on. He didn't even call his brother any of the seven or so names that jumped to the forefront of his mind. Instead, he started saying what he'd brought them there to hear. "I screwed up. And I'm sorry. I've already explained my reasoning, as flawed as it was. I don't have anything new to say, just that I hope, with time, you can forgive me."

The temptation was strong to keep talking, to re-explain his thought process, to try to convince them to treat him normally again. So he pressed his lips together and waited, even though he was afraid one of them might say something cruel about how stupid he'd been or how selfish he was or how they never wanted to see his stupid face again and he should go back to having no home, no significant other, no place to land.

None of those words came out of their mouths. The sounds of crickets chirping and bullfrogs croaking kept the air from being totally still and silent.

"Can I make a confession?" Hayes's voice was gruff and his eyes were on Sterling's.

Sterling nodded.

"When we first found out the ranch was going to foreclosure, I just *knew* there had to be a mistake. Then Trav showed me the mortgage statements and I blamed myself. If only I'd stayed at the ranch instead of ditching it for a different one ... I could have helped more."

"Me, too, man." Cash had finally caught his breath and sat down on the platform to let his legs dangle. "I kicked myself for not knowing about it sooner, not checking in with Dad more, taking his 'I'm doing fine, son' at face value."

Hayes nodded and sat down next to Cash. "Right. Me, too."

Travis sat down, too, and said, "Well, you guys couldn't have blamed yourselves as much as I blamed myself. I was the one who stayed. I should have asked him to see the mortgage statements years ago. But I trusted him. I let him retain his role as the dad, the grand patriarch."

"And then," Hayes said, "I was pissed at Dad. How could he have done that without ever letting on that we could lose the place? I mean, I know gambling is an addiction, a legit mental health issue, but you'd think that at some point he would say to himself, 'Gee, maybe I should let the boys know we're in danger of losing their childhood home.' God, I was pissed."

"Right there with you," Cash said. "Me, too," Travis added.

"And then here you come, Sterling." Hayes gestured at Sterling, the only one who remained standing. "Sit down, will you?"

He did.

"And then here you come, admitting you knew Dad was gambling all along. God, it felt good to be mad at someone other than Dad. Blaming a dead guy isn't very satisfying, is it?"

Travis and Cash mumbled that it wasn't, and Sterling felt the right corner of his mouth pulling upward, just a little.

"So, we got pissed at you," Cash said. "Much more satisfying."

"I *am* sorry," Sterling said.

"It was still a dick move." Hayes shrugged. "But our reactions were probably bigger than necessary. Right, Cash?"

Cash snorted. "Right. But I second that. Dick move, Sterling."

"I acknowledge that and it won't happen again."

"Better not," all three of his brothers said at the same time.

"Did anyone bring beers?" Cash's words sounded easy and casual—normal—and Sterling sighed (carefully, so the others wouldn't see his chest rise and fall).

"You know I did." His grin was audible. "It was my Plan B if this conversation went to shit."

"I think we're all good." Hayes bumped Sterling's shoulder with his. "But Sterling's got to climb down those creaky-ass stairs and bring them back up. All in favor?"

"Aye."

Chapter Twenty-Nine

Everything was going off without a hitch. June stood on the stage at the Sweet Springs Ranch fundraiser, overseeing the final set-up.

She'd wanted bougie Prescott, and she'd gotten it. The dance floor gleamed in the late afternoon sun. High-top cocktail tables with white coverings occupied the area immediately to the west of the parquet. String lights brought those two areas together. Big barrels framed the bar, which was adorned with a white covering and the lightest pink flowers. White shade tents covered the auction and raffle tables, where more flowers sat in fat vases amongst the items. Opposite the cocktail tables, the dining tables, also draped in white, looked elegant with their thick white candlesticks and yet more flowers. The band was still setting up, but calm country music played over the speakers.

Officially, the event didn't start for another hour, but curious Prescott residents were already coming through the gate, perusing the auction table and raffle items and ordering drinks from the bar.

The Wilder men, gloriously reconciled, had spent the morning setting up all the auction and raffle items while June and Callie spread tablecloths and arranged centerpieces.

Goosebumps ran over her skin. It was happening. Her first non-

Hotel-Cartwright event was going to be a success. She could feel it. She decided a celebratory drink was in order—for her—and she approached Jerry, who was tending. Inhaling the spicy scent of the flowers, June experienced another flare of satisfaction.

"Looks like a great turnout so far." He squinted at the gate, where people had lined up.

June's pulse quickened as her gaze followed Jerry's."It does. We should have no trouble making enough money to bring the mortgage current."

When she tore her eyes away from the guest line to look at him again, he handed her a wine glass that was cold against her fingers.

"What's this?"

He grinned. "Peach sangria. Most refreshing drink you'll ever have."

"Jerry! I didn't know you were so bougie."

"Just because I own a run-of-the-mill bar where guys order pitchers of beer and play darts doesn't mean I don't know how to make a fancy drink, Ms. June."

"Well, it's perfect. When we first conceived of this idea, I said I wanted bougie. And you delivered."

"Damn straight."

She sipped the drink and her eyes closed in ecstasy. "Jerry. This. Is. So. Good. I hope you made a lot of it, because it's going to sell out."

"I sure did."

"Good. I'm going to go check on everyone, make sure everything is ready. Thanks for the drink."

"You bet. And June? I can already tell this evening is going to be spectacular. I hope you're proud of yourself."

Her grin was completely involuntary and she could tell it was giant. "Thanks, Jerry. I am."

She walked over to the silent auction table and noted all the items were lined up perfectly, with the clipboards placed beneath them—also lined up perfectly. A pen sat on each clipboard and, as she'd instructed, someone had set a jar of spare pens at the end of the table. On another table, the raffle items were on display, each one set up for maximum "wow" factor. They all looked great, but June straightened a couple of bows and one cellophane bag, anyway.

She turned away from the table, planning to head for the band with cold waters in hand. She wanted to make sure they had everything they needed before the official start time.

Only, something caught her eye.

It wasn't the couple just coming through the gate ... it was the couple behind them. Despite their unusual attire, she recognized them: her parents.

What are they doing *here?*

Frozen in place, she considered their presence here. Would they travel this far just to sabotage her event? No, surely they wouldn't. They couldn't possibly be expecting her to go home with them this time. The Alexander wedding was over, and according to Maya, Timmy had already made a small-but-powerful post on Insta, praising Maya and the hotel and promising more, longer posts to come. Her parents didn't know June knew that, so maybe they were there to gloat.

She didn't want them to see her just yet. She sprang into action. Doing her best to hide—almost the entire setup was wide open, so she slinked over to the silent auction pop-up shade and stood in the back corner—she continued to observe them.

For once in her life, Clara Cartwright looked uncomfortable. Uncertain. Like she didn't know quite what to do in this environment. She seemed to have lots of questions for whoever was manning the gate. June assumed she'd chosen the outfits for both her and June's dad. She'd gone for what she thought was Arizona-appropriate attire. She wore a paisley button-up shirt tucked into brand-spanking-new jeans and even newer cowboy boots. Her hair was in loose pigtails. June's dad wore jeans that looked like he'd taken them off the store display and stepped right into them and a plaid shirt in the same shade of blue as his wife's paisley shirt. Normally, he wouldn't be caught dead in a plaid shirt.

They'd finished paying and came through the gate. June's mom clutched her purse in front of her and looked around, wide-eyed, like she wasn't sure where to go or what to do first. Then June's dad spotted the bar. His gaze rested on it, his eyebrows lifted, and his eyes lit up. He pointed at it and said something to June's mom, who nodded and let her shoulders sag, just for a minute. Still somewhat hidden in her spot, June smiled. Seeing her mom vulnerable was endearing. Not enough to inspire June to forgive her just yet, but a *little.*

When they reached the bar, June watched Jerry peer at her mom like he was trying to figure something out. People did often remark on how much June favored her mother, and she wondered if Jerry was putting together the pieces. He handed her mom a glass of the peach sangria. She took a sip while June's dad accepted a beer. Then she nodded and smiled, the first genuine smile June had seen since she spotted them at the gate, and dropped a bill into the tip jar.

June checked her watch. Ten minutes. She couldn't waste what time she had left hiding from her parents. She caught up with them as they made it to the dining area, where June's mother once again led the way while looking decidedly uncertain.

"Hi, you guys."

June's mom jumped, yelped, and spilled a little sangria on her hand. Again acting totally out of character, she licked it off and then said, "June! There you are! We called. We texted. Did you get—"

June shook her head. Even though the butterflies in her stomach were making their way up her torso and into her throat she feigned calm. "No. I blocked your numbers."

As she expected, her mom's eyes widened in shock while her dad gave a small shrug as if to acknowledge they deserved to be blocked.

"What are you guys doing here?"

"Oh!" June's mom took several gulps of the sangria. "That is quite good, you know. You should really try some, Junie."

June raised her glass and her mom tittered. "Oh! I didn't see that. Isn't it good? Delightful, really!"

"We came here to support you." Her dad's voice was gruff. "Didn't we, Clara?"

"Well, yes! Of course we did! We wouldn't miss it."

As recently as three weeks before that, June would have given her right arm for a compliment about how the space looked. But now? The fact that her mom didn't offer one didn't faze her.

"You did?"

"Of course! Why else would we come all the way to Arizona?"

"I don't know, maybe to drag me back home so I could take care of business at the hotel?"

Another loud and tittering laugh from her mom. "Oh, Junie!" She made a dismissive gesture. "That was a one-time thing. You were right. Maya did a fantastic job with the wedding. Timmy was just thrilled. And he's given us a rave review on Insta. Of course, no one does it quite like you..."

June's dad grabbed June's free hand. "What your mom means to say, June, is that we are sorry. We didn't realize quite how important this was to you."

"He's right, of course, Junie! We *are* sorry." For the first time, her expression was serious and her eyes rested on June's for more than a fraction of a second. "*I'm* sorry. I thought I knew what was best for you and for the hotel, but I'm starting to see those two things might not always be the same."

June nodded. Some of the tension she'd carried in her chest since leaving Great Falls loosened. Looking at her dad and then her mom she said, "Thank you. Both. That means a lot to me. I've got duties to attend to, but I hope you both enjoy the evening."

"We will, Junie," her mom said. "I'm sure of it. This all looks wonderful."

Her dad grunted. "I like the setup. The man at the gate mentioned a silent auction. Should we go see what there is to bid on, Clara?"

"We should."

Erasing all the effects of her parents' actions over the past week might take some time. Still, her heart a bit lighter, June left her parents and went in search of Sterling.

The sun went down, the string lights clicked on, and the band continued to play. People ate and danced and bid on the silent auction items. Music and laughter and friendly conversation once again filled the air at Sweet Springs Ranch. June stood with Sterling at the edge of the dance floor.

"Tell me I'm not the only one who's been checking the bids on the silent auction items." His voice, conspiratorial, was close to her ear.

She chuckled. "No. I've been checking them too, under the guise of straightening the baskets, changing over a full bidding sheet, or putting out a fresh pen. But if my mental math is correct, that silent auction is kicking ass. And that raffle ticket jar is stuffed."

He put an arm around her shoulders and squeezed. She inhaled his now familiar sent and closed her eyes.

"Seems like your parents are enjoying themselves."

Still leaning against him, she opened her eyes and found them on the dance floor. "I can't remember the last time I saw them dance."

"Let's make a pact to make sure our kids can never say that about us."

Her cheeks flushed and her heart leapt. "Are we having kids?"

He kissed the top of her head. Lips still against her hair he said, "I sure as hell plan on it."

"Then I guess it wouldn't hurt to make a habit of dancing." She took his hand and led him onto the dance floor. The song was just ending, and Sterling smiled as soon as the first notes of the next one came through the speakers. "Did you request this, or is it just coincidence?"

She winked at him. "You'll never know. But either way, it's pretty romantic, right?"

"The most."

Then they were dancing, their bodies pressed together as they swayed to the same song they'd danced to on the night they met. For the first time that day, June didn't think about the raffle or the fundraiser or seating arrangements. She closed her eyes and laid her head on Sterling's chest, thanking her lucky stars.

Chapter Thirty

Three months later

Sterling led June across the driveway of Sweet Springs Ranch. "The suspense is killing me. When can I take off this blindfold?"

He chuckled. "Really soon. I promise."

They walked a little farther and Sterling took a moment to sink into his gratitude. For the warm fall sun, the light breeze, the particular chirp of the bird he remembered from his childhood. Most of all, for June. Here she was, real and solid, her ribcage firm against his palm as he guided her toward the surprise he'd been planning.

"Okay." He drew out the word. "I'm going to take it off now, but keep your eyes closed."

He grabbed the knot at the back of her head, but before he could pull off the blindfold she stopped his hand with hers. "Wait."

He froze.

"Is it bad if I admit I was hoping this was also a ploy to take me somewhere and have your way with me while I was blindfolded?"

The blood rushed to Sterling's face and he had to fight back his laughter.

"We'll save that for later. But right now..." He pulled off the blindfold. "Open your eyes."

She did, and then immediately covered her eyes with her hands. "You didn't tell me the whole gang was here."

Cash whistled. "Well, we all know what you guys will be doing tonight, June. No big deal. We're all family now."

"Uncover your eyes. You haven't even seen your surprise yet and you're kind of ruining my moment."

The sound of June's giggle turned Sterling's insides all warm and fuzzy.

"Sorry." She opened her eyes again and gasped. "Is that what I think it is?"

"Yep. It's our home for the next six months to five years, or however long it takes us to renovate the big house."

She squealed and flung her arms around his waist. "I love it! It's perfect."

"You haven't even seen the inside yet, June," Travis said.

She laughed again. "I know, but I can tell I'm going to love it."

"Want a tour?" Sterling offered a hand, palm up, and led June over to the RV steps. He swept her off her feet and carried her across the threshold while his brothers and Callie cheered.

"To be honest, the tour won't take long." He showed her the bedroom and its closets, the extra storage in the kitchen, and the reclining couches in the living area. Then he whistled and his brothers and Callie came inside.

"There's just two more things." Sterling had planned this moment down to the second. "Close your eyes and hold out your hands."

June did, her smile wide. On cue, Callie placed the kitten in her palms and she gasped and opened her eyes. "A kitten?"

"I thought we could name him Hairy."

June's squeal caused another ripple of laughter and she looked at Sterling with tears in her eyes. She pulled him close to her chest and nuzzled his fuzzy head. "I love him. Hi, Harry."

"Okay, just one more thing." Sterling extended his arm and Travis placed a miniature suitcase in his hand.

Again, June gasped. "It looks exactly like my old suitcase!"

Sterling felt a little thrill that he was able to surprise her twice in one day. "The suitcase that brought us together." He unzipped it to reveal a sparkling diamond ring.

Yet another gasp made Sterling's heart soar. He dropped to one knee. "June Cartwright, from the moment I laid eyes on you, experiencing a major suitcase disaster in the Great Falls airport, I knew you were special. From the moment you decided to stay and help with our fundraiser, I knew I was smitten. And from the moment we —" he cleared is throat and everyone laughed—"I've known I'd never love anyone like I love you. Will you do me the honor of being my wife?"

She nodded, her eyes sparkling with tears. "Of course I will."

He slipped the ring onto her finger and stood, and she moved into his arms and put her lips on his. The Wilder boys and Callie cheered, whistling and hollering and clapping, and Sterling knew he'd never been so happy in all his life.

An impromptu celebration broke out, with Travis bringing the grill, burgers, and hot dogs from his house and Cash running out to get beer and wine while Callie and Hayes moved the picnic tables.

Once they all had plates and drinks and were seated, Cash stood. "Listen up! I want to propose a toast to June, who came here as a stranger and is staying as family. Thank you, June, for all you've done for us. And, to Sterling. Thank you for being a suitcase-replacing hero—a handsome one, from what the ladies say—and bringing June into the family. I speak for all of us when I say I'm so glad you're back. We love you, bro."

"Hear, hear," everyone chorused.

June leaned against Sterling and turned her head. "Hear, hear."

"Hear, hear." He kissed her, long and deep. "I love you, June Cartwright."

"I love you, too, Sterling Wilder. So much."

The End

About the Author

Hilary Dartt loves great adventures, whether she's writing, reading, or living them. The author of twelve novels, Hilary lives in Arizona's high desert with her husband, their three children, and her Weimaraner, Leia. She loves camping, exploring in the Jeep, and dance parties with her kids. Learn more and sign up for her newsletter at www.hilarydartt.com.